Introduction

That Special Something by Eileen M. Berger
It seems that Christie's family by marriage have invited themselves to her lakeside home for another Whitley family reunion. She had always enjoyed these—but that was before her husband died in a tragic accident. How can she host a reunion alone? An unexpected phone call may give her hope. Will a long-simmering friendship reignite the flames of love in Christie's heart?

Storm Warning by Colleen Coble
Randi and Brock were inseparable, until he vanished without explanation a month before their wedding. Now their meteorologist friends from Valparaiso University have arranged a storm-chasing reunion. Can Randi risk seeing Brock again? Or, can she go another five years without knowing the truth of his leaving?

Truth or Dare by Denise Hunter
A stupid stunt in high school has left Brianna VanAllen questioning her self-worth for the last five years. She didn't expect to dig up those old painful memories when she returned home for her high school reunion. But, paired with Jake Volez on a project at her parents' ranch, Brianna must face issues of forgiveness and put her heart at risk again.

Too Good to Be True by Janice Pohl
It's a miracle when Daniel Taylor shows up at Minneapolis General Hospital in answer to an Internet plea for a kidney donor. Kathryn Donaldson's cousin Glenn is nearing death, and she has given up hope. She can't trust in Glenn's faith and she doesn't believe in miracles. How long will it take for Kathryn to understand the depths of God's love?

Reunions

Four Inspiring Romance Stories
of Friends Reunited

Eileen M. Berger
Colleen Coble
Denise Hunter
Janice Pohl

BARBOUR
PUBLISHING, INC.
Uhrichsville, Ohio

That Special Something © 2000 by Eileen M. Berger
Storm Warning © 2000 by Colleen Coble
Truth or Dare © 2000 by Denise Hunter
Too Good to Be True © 2000 by Janice Pohl

Illustrations by Mari Goering

ISBN 1-57748-728-1

Scripture taken from the HOLY BIBLE: NEW INTERNATIONAL VERSION®. NIV®. Copyright© 1973, 1978, 1984 by International Bible Society. Used by permission of Zondervan Publishing House.

Published by Barbour Publishing, Inc., P.O. Box 719, Uhrichsville, Ohio 44683 http://www.barbourbooks.com

 Member of the
Evangelical Christian
Publishers Association

Printed in the United States of America.

Reunions

THAT
SPECIAL SOMETHING

by Eileen M. Berger

Chapter 1

Christie ripped open the envelope on the way back from the big metal mailbox at the end of the driveway—and stopped short, her big male German shepherd taking another step before turning. "I can't believe it! How *could* they send out this mailing without checking with me?"

Trevor's head tilted to the side, intelligent brown eyes questioning, perhaps worrying that he'd offended her. Christie reached down to rub behind his ears, where he especially liked it. "It's not you, dear friend, it's my in-laws! You know I like them, but—with things as they are, wouldn't you think they'd ask before sending word to everyone that this year's Whitley reunion will be *here?*"

She'd enjoyed hosting them before, but that was because Jerry so loved planning, organizing, and getting things set up. For that matter, he enjoyed just about everything and everyone—and people loved him.

"That's why it's so hard," she explained needlessly. She'd found herself doing that a lot lately. "It's not fair that my husband, my love, the man who worked so hard and had so much fun and—and loved me. . ."

She bit her lower lip to still its trembling, unbidden moisture in her eyes making the placid Lake Lenore water in front of her seem to shimmer in the afternoon sun. "He was too young to die—we had too much living yet to do. . . !"

Trevor rubbed the side of his head and neck against her thigh, giving that little mewling sound of canine grief—or was it sympathy? She'd never heard him do that until his master died.

Christie knelt there on the mowed grass at the edge of the woods, circling Trevor's strong neck with her arms, cheek against the warm dark hair the color of her own. "It must still be awfully hard for you; after all, I was married to him for a little less than a fourth of my life—not even seven far-too-short, wonderful years— and he was your master, the one you loved above all others for your entire eleven."

She started to cry. Again. And this time she didn't tell herself to stop, that fourteen months was too long to grieve. She'd managed, largely by keeping very busy, to get through the days and the weeks, expecting the months to care for themselves. For the most part, they had—not easily—but she'd survived.

"Thanks, Trevor, for being so patient with me." She tried to smile, at least a little, as she got to her feet and wiped away the final tears with the hem of her cotton T-shirt. "I'll try to do better, I promise."

The phone started ringing as they got to the four steps leading up to the verandah of the large log house, which Jerry's grandparents had built right in the center of their property at this end of the long lake.

She ran up and into the house, lifting the phone on its fourth ring, just before the answering machine would have taken over. The cheerful voice on the other end responded to her greeting with "Hi, Christie; this is Nate."

"Nate?" She hadn't heard Nathanael Mitchell's voice for a long time. "Where *are* you? Still in Hong Kong?"

"No, I've finished there and am told I'll be back in New York for a while."

"How long? Days? Weeks?" She laughed. "Each time Aunt Susan speaks of you, you're in a different country."

"You don't talk to Mom too often, then; this last assignment, supposedly for about six weeks, ran for twelve —which isn't too unusual."

She knew of his work with JTE Electronics, that he was the one usually sent to oversee the installation of new systems throughout America and elsewhere. "Do you *enjoy* being away so much? Not seeing family and friends?"

There appeared to be no hesitation at all. "As you may remember, I always liked challenges, so yes, I do enjoy my work; but no, I *don't* like being away all the time. I miss out on too many things going on with friends and family.

"And, speaking of friends and family, how are *you*?"

"Doing well, thanks. And busy. This was a good year with my second graders, but I'm enjoying my summer vacation as much as I'm sure they are."

"You must look forward to it, especially living there in your beautiful lakeside home."

She wouldn't admit that she sometimes considered moving into town, rather than living here by herself all year round. "Everything's especially lovely this year in north-central Pennsylvania. The laurel's still blooming throughout my woods, and all the property owners around the lake have plantings which are putting on a spectacular show. You should see how nice it looks."

"Great idea, I'm glad you suggested it." There was a smile in his voice. "Would thirty minutes be too soon to take you up on your invitation?"

"Thirty minutes?" She'd assumed he was calling from New York, although he'd never done that.

"I'm here at Mom's," he explained. "How about my coming to see your blooming laurel and everyone's plantings, then taking you for supper?"

She glanced at her watch. "I—didn't realize it was this late."

"Or I could stop at Bernardi's and pick up one of their super-duper, extra-long, with-everything hoagies and some tossed salad or coleslaw."

In spite of that too-familiar clutching sensation in her chest, her mouth watered at the very suggestion of those sandwiches she hadn't so much as tasted since

Jerry died. *Maybe it's time.* . . .

She cleared her throat and hoped her voice wouldn't betray hesitancy. "The Bernardi special sounds good. We can eat it at a picnic table in the shade or down on the sand, near the water. I have melon for dessert and just made iced tea—though I can brew coffee, if you'd prefer."

"The tea sounds perfect."

❧

Nate! She'd always liked him, and they'd dated some during senior high, but when he left for MIT and she went to Bucknell, they saw little of each other. They'd remained friends, so when they met at church the summer they graduated, they stood outside—catching up with one another's activities, plans, and dreams.

His mother had started for her car. "Can you help me carry food over to the pavilion, Nate?"

He glanced from her to the covered area across the rural road. "Sure—in just a minute." Looking back at Christie, the left side of his mouth quirked upward. "Are you staying for the picnic?"

"Not this time." Christie shook her head, almost regretful. "Mom and Dad are going to Williamsport for a fiftieth wedding anniversary celebration, so we didn't bring even one tureen."

"Hey, we both know the terrific cooks in this church! Even without looking, I'm positive there's enough food to stuff twice—*three* times the number of those eating here."

Of course he was right. "But it feels as though I'd be sponging off others."

"Tell you what, Christie. . ."

You sound and look so conspiratorial, like when we were ten or twelve and you wanted me to go along on a hike through the mountains or do some crazy activity.

". . .Let's pretend you're my date—in which case Mom's multiple offerings will cover you as well."

She told herself she should go home, but didn't—and it was there, on that beautiful, hot, mid-August day, that she met and fell in love with his cousin, Jerry.

❧

She'd already taken care of Saturday's sweeping and dusting and had mowed the extensive lawn the evening before. After cutting the cantaloupe into bite-sized chunks, she gathered silverware, cups, paper plates, and napkins and made sure the sports blanket was where she could grab it if Nate chose to eat on the beach.

Trevor's low growl, then barks, alerted her to Nate's having turned into the curving driveway. Tucking a jar of pickles into the picnic basket, she came around the verandah and started down the steps as he pulled to a stop and got out.

"Welcome!" she greeted, extending her right hand.

He accepted it with his left one, his right arm circling her shoulders as he gave her a quick hug and a kiss on the cheek. His eyes were dancing as he released her with "Remember me? I've been away so long, you forget we're kissin' cousins by marriage—you know, the Whitley/Mitchell connection."

Her laugh came easily. This was so like the boy and young man she used to know that it was like stepping back in time. He seemed right at home as they went up the steps together, saying, "We were delighted when Mom brought in the mail this morning and we found you'd volunteered to host the clan again for this year's get-together."

"Well. . ." She wasn't sure she should state that *her* receiving a copy of that letter had been a shock.

Her hesitation gave him the chance to add, "Mom says she heard Jerry say, two years ago, that you'd have it here again this year if someone took the one between —which, of course, Uncle Pete did, in Cleveland."

She had not gone to that one—it was too close to losing Jerry, and she was afraid she couldn't bear up under the sympathy she was sure to receive. "I didn't get there."

"Nor I. I was in Brazil."

She paused at the door. "Where would you prefer eating, on the porch, at the picnic table," indicating the redwood table and benches, "or down on the beach?"

"Where do *you* like to eat, Christie?"

"I—usually end up eating here on the front porch when the weather's this nice, but Jerry liked variety—so you're free to take your pick."

His hand reached to give hers a quick squeeze. "Let's try the beach. I'll bring the sandwiches and salad from the car. Shall I come back up here to help carry?"

"No, thanks." She indicated the wicker basket. "Everything but the blanket is already in there."

She'd spread the blanket on the sand by the time he sauntered down the slope, and they sat there companionably as they began eating. She blotted away flavored olive oil from her lips. "Thanks for bringing the hoagies, Nate. They are, indeed, every bit as good as I remember."

He set his on the paper plate. "I take it you haven't been indulging of late?"

"Jerry and I both loved to cook, so *this,*" raising her sandwich several inches, "was something of a break. Things we do—or don't do—aren't always deliberate decisions, you know; it's often the unthought-of associations with the past which influence us."

He nodded as though he understood. "Jerry was a good man, Christie. *Every*body loved him—including me."

She nodded, focusing almost unseeingly on the sandwich, which had started this particular conversation. Her voice was hardly more than a murmur as she said, "It was a Saturday evening, as beautiful as this one, and we'd been working among the trees, clearing away some of the undergrowth and dragging branches and burning them over there, in the clearing.

"We were tired and filthy! Jerry said he was going in and calling Bernardi's to ask them to make us a couple of hoagies. While I was taking my shower, he'd drive in, just as he was, to get them for us."

"Oh, Christie!" His voice was choked, face empathetic, somehow sensing the significance of her words. "I'm sorry—I'd never have suggested this had I realized!"

Even through the film of moisture in her own eyes she saw the anguish in his warm brown ones. He was reaching for her hoagie, but she pulled back her hand, determined to finish the explanation. *And* the sandwich. "He was killed by a drunk driver on his way back to me. With these. . ."

They'd been sitting perhaps eighteen inches apart, but suddenly he was beside her, arms around her, her head against his shoulder. She wasn't aware of his removing the sandwich from her hand, but then she was clinging to him, needing his strength, his presence.

They got up and walked closer to the water for a while, saying nothing, before returning to the blanket. He called her attention to the boaters down near the lake's far end. She didn't at the time realize it was a distraction to allow him to tuck the hoagies back into the opaque bag in which they'd been brought.

She didn't mention they were missing, just joined in eating the cabbage salad. It wasn't until they were spearing their melon chunks that she admitted her shock at reading the "invitation" to his extended family.

"You don't have to go through with this, Christie."

"Somehow, with all that's happened since, I'd forgotten Jerry's telling them that two years ago."

"I'll get the mailing list from Uncle Bill and send out word immediately that it's," he shrugged, "not convenient for you to have them at this time."

She shook her head. "But I *can* have it. For that matter, it's probably something I should do. I haven't kept in touch with many of them and have done precious little entertaining since Jerry's gone."

"Well, *if* you do it—and I'm not at all sure you should even consider it—don't try what he did, getting all that electric circuitry and water and portable privies so people could move in with campers and tents and everything and stay for—how long *was* it?"

Remembering brought a smile to her lips. "Your cousins from Alaska brought their camper a week early, then day-tripped out of here and visited folks for twelve days. Several others with campers and tents stayed almost a week."

He grinned back at her. "No *wonder* they want to come back! Maybe they had good reason for not checking before sending the letter; they didn't want any possibility of your 'No.' "

They dropped the paper products in the garbage can and took the basket and blanket to the kitchen before going back out to walk through the trees. Not a leaf stirred in the quiet of early evening.

"The tents were set up over *there,* beyond where the six—no, seven travel trailers and campers were parked. See?" She indicated insulators on several trees, where Jerry had left them when removing the wire so they wouldn't be a detraction from the "naturalness" of the surroundings. "He wanted to provide at least some

lighting for any who chose to be around after dark—
and, as he reminded me, there'd undoubtedly be some
who couldn't get along without a curling iron or morning coffee."

"Sounds like he took care of everything."

"He ended up having a lot of help, actually, once
people caught his enthusiasm. He had that wonderful
ability of getting people to think of things for themselves and believe his thoughts were their own ideas—
like deciding beforehand that they'd bring their own
grills and utensils. We let everyone know that there'd be
at least three big group meals, on Friday night, Saturday
noon, and Sunday at two o'clock."

"And it worked out well?"

She laughed, almost surprising herself.

What do I do now? Nate asked himself. Christie had
gone from tears and apparently being upset at the
thought of having his clan gathering to now giving an
almost flippant "Apparently they worked *very* well,
since they're coming again in less than two weeks."

"Christie? You don't have to do this." *Does she realize I just repeated myself?*

"I know, but in telling you about two years ago,
I'm remembering the *good* things, not just the work
we put in. Mike and Kathy have been involved with
scouting for years, so they took over much of the responsibility with the kids, along with Uncle Bill. He's
done a lot with church camping. They're the ones who

made up schedules for monitoring children, not only when swimming but while they played.

"Others led, or at least went with groups on hikes and nature walks. Those with fishing licenses took advantage of the opportunity to do that, while some just rowed around in the boat and canoes. A few just relaxed with reading, loafing, and, of course, catching up with news concerning the many other leaves on the family's branches."

He gave her a grudging smile, which developed into a laugh. "You're really something, Sprout." The old name had slipped out—he hadn't called her that for years. "Let's leave it this way—you think things over and tell me at church tomorrow if you *truly* want to go through with this.

"*If* you do, I want to be involved. I must drive back to the city late tomorrow afternoon. I'll be tied up with things there through Thursday but then am promised at least a couple of weeks off."

"Because of how well you did overseas?"

"Partly, I trust." He allowed himself to shrug. "But mostly it's in acknowledgment of the fact that I've been putting in sixty—eighty—even some *hundred*-hour work weeks while away.

"What I'm driving at is that once I do get back, I'd enjoy helping with whatever it takes to do the setup here." He'd held her in his arms only a few minutes ago, but now just touched the back of her hand with his fingertips. "Remember, though, Christie, even if you do want the reunion here, you can still request that people stay at campgrounds and be here just Saturday; everyone else does that."

"I—feel sure now, Nate, but realize it's good to have escape hatches, especially at a project's beginning. Should I decide by the time church is over tomorrow that this is too much for me, physically *or* emotionally, I promise to tell you."

Chapter 2

Previously predicted clouds did move in over-night, and Christie needed an umbrella when going to her car. The rhythmic swish of the windshield wipers easily kept up with the gentle rain—but also made her rethink the tentative decision made sometime before this morning.

At that time, it seemed a good idea to go along with Nate's suggestion of inviting everyone for just a one-day get-together. However, should it be raining then, *would* they come? Just as bad was the realization that if as many came as before, there'd be no way of handling them on a rainy day, even though her house was fairly large.

She was grateful for having brought her umbrella when she had to park some distance from the old white country church which was so dear to her. She made it inside more quickly than usual, for many of the farmers and their wives—and some town-folks, as well—usually socialized out on the wide courtyard until the very last moment.

She slid her dripping umbrella into the large brass holder and walked up to sit with her mother in the fifth-row-back pew they'd used as long as Christie could remember. She smiled and nodded at people, most of whom were closer to her than some of her relatives. She did not see Nate.

She supposed she shouldn't have been surprised when Mother whispered, "I hear Nate came to see you yesterday."

Christie nodded but was spared answering when the organist began her prelude, followed immediately by the service. This pastor had been here for over fourteen years, and she appreciated his sermons. She'd taken his pastoral skills for granted until Jerry's death.

She shifted uncomfortably on the unpadded wooden seat, wondering again how long it would be before almost everything she thought of did not lead back to Jerry's death. Well, she *would* concentrate on the message, she told herself and sat up even straighter. . . .

◈

Nate arrived only a moment behind her, but Christie had not looked around as she raised her umbrella and briskly started for the church. By the time he parked and was out of his car, she was too near the building for him to call to her.

What has she decided? For her sake, I almost hope she'll settle for a one-day event—but I've been cooped up with computers and people for so long that I'd enjoy just working among her trees and trying to do those things Jerry did two years ago in making things ready for our family.

He tried to hold back the next thought as soon as he realized it was coming. It was far too dangerous to face the fact that he'd also like to be with Christie in other ways Jerry had been. That he would like to marry her.

He almost came to a standstill there at the edge of the parking lot with the warm summer rain's innumerable little plops hitting his big black umbrella and his shoes getting wet. Where had that idea come from, anyway? He'd never consciously thought it before, though now that he had, Nate realized that his deep sorrow, his anguish over his cousin's death had been even more for Christie's grief than his own.

He felt almost guilty for these feelings—yet Jerry had been gone for well over a year. *Oh, God, I really hadn't admitted my love for her until this very minute. Is it wrong for me to love her? Or, Lord, did You disclose it to me now, when I'm about to begin a good long vacation— the first in such a long time?*

He entered through the same door she had, set his furled umbrella to drip beside hers, and glanced around the large, rectangular, white-with-gold-trim sanctuary. He'd been brought here as an infant and had fond memories of Sunday school and youth fellowship, of Children's Day performances and Christmas plays.

It hardly seems possible I've been gone this long. He considered going up and sitting in the fifth row, but did not. In such a close-knit community, sitting with her in church could be construed as staking a claim; although as of this morning he wouldn't mind that in the least, he wouldn't embarrass her like that.

Instead, he started to slide in next to his mother. She smiled up at him and moved closer to the aisle, a silent invitation to sit between her and Dad. This, too, was like old times; but then he had not liked such closeness, interpreting it as their desire for control. He was now mature enough to appreciate her willingness to share him with his father—it was part of the unity which characterized this marriage he used to take for granted.

Prelude. Call to worship and invocation. A welcome given by the pastor, leading into praises and prayer concerns. A junior message on reaching out to one another, followed by the unison reading of a Psalm. Offertory and Doxology followed by a choir anthem, then a Scripture passage leading into the sermon with its printed title of "Taking Time for God."

That made him a bit uncomfortable, but he sat perfectly still. He came to church when he was home, of course, but it wasn't so easy while in San Francisco or outside of Paris or in Argentina or Hong Kong. He had work responsibilities—he was expected to get things done in the shortest possible time and authorized to require that same dedication of those assisting him.

Well, he wasn't going to solve anything by sitting here this morning working on that instead of listening to the sermon—or, for that matter, by sitting here staring at the back of Christie's lovely head. The big, centrally located chandelier brought out highlights in her short, only slightly wavy hair. *What has she decided?*

Christie had to drag her mind back to attention several times but knew it wasn't the fault of the sermon. Yes, she was glad for the reminder to take time for God. *I couldn't have gotten through those first months without Jerry if I hadn't done that, but I'm not so faithful now. Does that mean I'm "healed" enough to think I don't need Him so much? Or am I attempting to live without His constant guidance?* Neither of those possibilities was acceptable, and she had to consciously keep from wriggling.

People still sometimes complimented her on being so strong, so brave—her keeping things going and continuing on so well. What would they think had they seen her fall apart yesterday?

What had Nate thought?

She came back to the present as the final hymn was announced and everyone stood to sing it.

The service was over and those in front, behind, and across the low semi-partition down the middle of the wide center-section were visiting with Christie and her parents. She longed to look around, to make sure Nate was there, but instead made the effort to give full attention to those around her. *If* he wished to speak with her, he'd wait.

It was several minutes before she started toward the Sunday school wing. The wide doors were standing open and she talked with several more friends before going through them. Mother and Dad were detained, but Nate was there—was coming to speak with her. "Have a good night, Christie?"

"Yes, I did. In spite of falling apart yesterday." She was hoping that would reassure him, but it didn't.

"Christie," his voice was soft and low, "I'm sorry about the sandwiches."

"I'm not." Her smile was genuine as she touched his arm. "That still happens to me sometimes, but far less often than it used to. And, as much as I always liked Bernardi's, I'm sure I would have tried them sooner or later. It's better it happened this way—except for your shoulder's getting wet."

There was a slow grin. "Hey, my shoulder's honored to have been of service."

Before she could respond to that, Nate's mother, Jerry's Aunt Sue, came to give her a hug. "I was just talking with your mother, asking her and Sam to join the three of us for brunch over at Herrold House. Lynne said that suited her fine. I hope you're free, too."

Christie glanced at her mother, who nodded. "I would like that. I haven't been there for a while."

Nate looked a bit uneasy as his mother enthused, "I want to tell you how pleased we are about your inviting everyone to your place again this year."

So he's said nothing about his suggestion! Her smile was for both of them. "It may not be quite so big or elaborate as before, but the welcome is as heartfelt."

Aunt Sue gave her another hug, but with classes

starting, there was no time for further conversation. Was it a coincidence that Nate sat beside her? There were two other seats across the circle, but he took the one next to her—perhaps so a couple coming in late might sit together.

There was joking and talking before things settled down into study mode. Everyone was interested in where Nate had been this time and what he'd seen. "I didn't get around much in Hong Kong," he admitted. "I'm kept so busy on these jobs, I have neither time nor energy for sightseeing."

When no one considered that a good reason for missing an escorted tour or something, he raised his eyebrows. "I'll keep your advice in mind for my next trip."

Someone else asked what Christie wanted to know: "Where will that be?"

"I'm not sure yet. There are several possibilities— probably in central Europe."

⌘

It was decided that all six would ride the fifteen miles in her father's car, so it wasn't surprising that Christie found herself in the backseat between Nate and his mother. Aunt Sue monopolized the conversation, as usual. Once they arrived, however, Mother sat beside her, giving Christie opportunity to speak with others.

Uncle John talked about all that had been done two years ago and asked how he might assist with reunion preparations. Nate must have been deliberately waiting for her to state her plans, because when she said she'd like things pretty much as before, he mentioned that it wouldn't be hard to reconnect the electric wires to the insulators still attached to the trees.

"So—you really want to go to all that work to make campsites again?" Uncle John asked.

She nodded. "Everyone cooperated before with keeping things running smoothly. I think we can count on that again."

By the time dinner was over, Dad, Nate, and his father had written lists of contacts to be made, along with suggested responsibilities. Christie shook her head in amazement. "With you three engineering everything, I could leave right now and not come back until that day!"

Nate grabbed her arm as if to keep her from fleeing. "Not so fast, dear lady; there will be *more* than enough for you to attend to."

Time passed too quickly. Since Nate needed to return to the city, the group went back to the church for their cars. Within minutes, they were saying good-byes.

She had not had one moment alone with Nate. *And why do you think you should have?* she scolded herself. *We're cousins, after all, not lovers!* That led to another question: *Why did I even think that word?*

☙☙

Nate had serious thinking to do on his long drive. It was true he'd hoped to see Christie while home this time, but it was the receiving of that invitation which gave him the excuse to call and go out there.

He'd always admired and liked her; he'd even thought

he was in love with her for a while back there in high school. But there'd been college and being with many other people—and then that whirlwind courtship and marriage of Christie and his favorite cousin!

He could honestly say he hadn't been jealous. As their best man he saw the love and the devotion they had for one another. Now, he remembered his spontaneous hope that some day he, too, might experience those emotions.

Until now that had not happened—*until yesterday, that is.* He couldn't explain what took place, or why, for until then Christie was "his cousin's widow." Now this woman he'd dated ten years before was the woman that he, Nathanael Mitchell, at the ripe age of twenty-nine, was in love with.

"It's amazing, Lord." He didn't usually talk out loud as he drove, but this really was a most unusual situation. "I'm not worthy of someone like her, but I do love her— and hope that some day she may come to love me. I suspect that could be difficult for her, though, God, since Jerry and I were such good friends, as well as cousins.

"Please help this to not be a problem for her—help me to move slowly, to not frighten her with my love. She accepted my support yesterday when she needed it; help me to continue helping her, not only with reunion preparations, but with her future." He hastened to add, "Please let her future include me!"

❧

Late in the afternoon, Christie took Trevor for a three-mile-long walk all around the lake. The sun had come out again, and everything was clean and sparkling. It did not bother her that within minutes her sneakers were soaked—she'd change when she got home.

Her house was over forty years old, and all newer ones were required to be set back a minimum of seventy-five feet from the water, and as many of the original trees as possible had been left standing. People were used to other residents walking across their frontage as they circled the lake, so there were many friendly calls of greeting and comments about the surrounding beauty.

A number of children and adults swam or sunbathed along the shore. Canoes and rowboats floated out on the lake. Christie felt grateful that no motorboats were allowed, for the stillness was almost complete except for songs of birds and an occasional croak of a frog.

A narrow two-lane road had been built over the dam at the far end of the lake, so she and Trevor crossed that, then went down close to the water again as they started back toward her beautiful log home. It was the only one which could be seen from anywhere along the shore.

She and Jerry used to make this circle at least once or twice a week, and it had been hard at first to come without him. He was the one who always noticed the little things, from the first arbutus breaking forth in early spring to the silent, immobile fawn behind a clump of laurel or a trout, completely still in this clear, pure water.

He had unlimited patience when out in their canoe or boat, fishing. She'd stated from the beginning that she'd gladly cook fish of any variety—but only if it came to her as fillets. She still missed having them. Having *him*.

Christie whistled, and Trevor came back to the shoreline from visiting with Jeb McFarland's collie. They walked a little more rapidly the rest of the way.

After eating a sandwich and finishing the coleslaw from yesterday, she went out on the porch and sat in one of the folding chairs with rockers. The slope here was such that, although the back of this floor level was raised only one or two feet, the front, where she now sat, was a full story aboveground.

All of the houses built along this much of a slant had safety precautions of one kind or another. Jerry came up with the idea of using wide boards instead of just a rail at the top—making a long, porch-wide table. He then created the lower, matching bench on the house-side of it, so this is where they usually ate during the summer, shoulder to shoulder, looking out at this beautiful scene. It had also proved to be a favorite place to correct papers, shell peas, or do other tasks.

She now propped her feet on the bench and started reading the novel she'd begun a week before. It was fairly good and she'd probably finish it; but unless it improved appreciably, she might not pass it on to friends, as was her custom.

She enjoyed these long summer days, and the sun's setting tonight had an even more brilliant display of color and radiance than usual. She continued reading off-and-on, but it was beginning to get dark when the phone rang.

Nate's cheerful voice responded to hers, telling her he'd had a pleasant, uneventful trip. "Look, Christie, don't you do a lot of extra work there until I come."

"But. . ."

"When I go in tomorrow, I'm telling them that something came up and I *must* be free starting from noon Thursday, at the latest."

"You won't get in trouble with that?"

"Hardly! I got to thinking that, if I don't give a deadline, I could end up with other responsibilities— and this way my debriefing and input will be given priority." There was a small chuckle. "And that's not meant as throwing my weight around—it's just that there are *always* important things on the table. I seldom demand or even suggest that my agenda be taken care of first— but *this* time I'm going to."

"Good for you! But as to work I do here, whatever is done adds to my own appreciation of my home."

"Well, go ahead with some things, but I'm looking forward to stringing those electric wires and rigging up the wash house and things like that."

She smiled there in her kitchen. "I'll make calls tomorrow to reserve the large tent for meals and at least a couple of those portable toilet facilities."

They talked over other aspects of the reunion. She hoped that by Friday or Saturday they'd have some idea of how many to prepare for—especially how many sites to set up among the trees. It was too early now to even think of food and beverages.

Shortly before they hung up, she mentioned her walk with Trevor. Nate said he looked forward to soon doing that with them. It was not just good manners that made her say she'd look forward to it, too. . . .

School had let out late this June because all the ice and snow of the past winter caused them to not only use all scheduled snow-days but a few more. As a result, she'd hardly begun the thorough annual housecleaning she normally planned to have completed before the end of June.

Actually, with only one woman and a dog here most of the time, she didn't let that bother her much—other than the living room and kitchen. Since she did make good use of the big fireplace, she'd have to not only brush down the walls but wash them.

That was her major activity for Monday and Tuesday, and the next day was spent organizing and taking care of things in the basement beneath the large, open kitchen/living room and bath. Two sets of bunk beds stood along one wall of the paneled room to the left, and there was a closet as well as several serviceable chests of drawers.

This small bathroom with its shower stall was a double blessing, serving not only guests beyond the number which could be accommodated in the three upper bedrooms but those coming for picnics and swimming.

The rest of the lower, cemented level was used not

only for the laundry, but to store the two canoes and the rowboat during the winter. It had also been Jerry's shop.

All of his tools were still there—right where he'd left them. Even an elaborate birdhouse sat there, partially painted, but with the roof not yet attached. She used only the dust-brush attachment to go over the workbench surface, but moved nothing.

She could not.

After his death, she'd found the anniversary card Jerry had already purchased, although that date was a full six weeks away. On it was a fancy, Victorian-style birdhouse with two rather cocky-looking bluebirds and the words, "They think THEY'VE got fancy digs, but. . . ," inside was the end of the message, "You, my darling, have made my house a HOME." Beneath that, in his own bold, slightly slanting handwriting were the added words: "And my heart's *your* CASTLE—forever! With all my love, Jerry."

Chapter 3

I *will not cry!* she told herself firmly, and although her sight was a little blurry, she walked over and unlocked the double doors, pushing them open and walking out into the fresh, clean outdoors. The screen doors closed behind her as her dog came running from where he'd been lying in the wooded area, obviously delighted at her being with him.

"We both still miss him an awful lot, don't we, Trevor?" She leaned over to rub his head and neck, then scratched him there between his front legs, like Jerry used to. Over by the trees, she picked up a two-foot-long stick. Trevor's full attention was immediately on this as he nervously danced with excitement, breath coming quickly. He'd already started running toward where it sailed as his mistress threw it with practiced overhand force and was almost immediately back with it, hoping for more fun.

The stick went in various directions as she continued toward the shore, and she finally sent it out over the water. Trevor, an accomplished swimmer, quickly brought even this back. She heard the phone start to ring, but Christie made no effort to answer, knowing from experience that she could seldom get there before callers hung up. She tossed the stick a few more times before disciplining herself to go back inside.

She pushed the answering machine's "play" button and was mildly annoyed that no message had been left, yet it ratified her decision to not run for the phone. Had it been something really important, the caller would have left word.

Christie always had cheese on hand, so she made a sandwich to eat out on the porch. Trevor came trotting up to be with her, hoping for a treat. She realized he was longing for food as an indication of her love or care. How easily she could relate to that—but must not acknowledge it for her dog, nor for herself.

If I'm really that determined, she told herself as she finished the sandwich, *the logical way to prove it is to return to the basement.* It was not a thrilling thought!

Christie put the small plate and her glass in the dishwasher and went back down the wooden steps, her hand sliding easily along the smooth wooden railing. No, she wouldn't demand of herself anything connected with the birdhouse, but she *could* clean the bathroom.

She had just finished that and scrubbed the kitchen floor when she heard a car arrive. *Who can that be?* Going into the master bedroom, she looked through the window toward the parking area, then went running out the door.

Nate had fretted ever since not getting a response to his cell phone call when going through the Pocono Mountains. Maybe Christie was away this afternoon. Of course she wasn't expecting him until tomorrow, but he pulled into the end of her driveway and made the double-jog to where he could see her car. He'd just gotten out when he saw her running toward him down the steps, face alight. "You're back *early*, Nate."

He met her only a couple of feet from the steps, arms wide—and she came into them! "Christie!"

She didn't stay there. After the briefest of hugs, she pulled away. "How did you happen—"

Even though longing to keep her close, he refrained. "It *worked*, my telling them I had things which must be done."

"You'd better stay with a company that regards family outings to be this special!"

He hadn't thought it necessary to share why he needed to be away, but Nate didn't tell Christie that. "It's mighty good to be back!"

He suspected he looked as happy as she did, but then her face took on a look of concern. "Are your folks expecting you for dinner?"

He shook his head. "I didn't know till almost noon that I'd be free to leave. Then I stopped at my apartment just long enough to throw a few things into my suitcase."

"And now you're here!" she finished. They started up the steps, side by side but not touching. "I have steaks in the freezer. I can thaw them in the microwave while you start the grill."

"I have a better idea." He reached for her hand. "Let's go out to eat."

She stopped there with her foot on the top step, head tilted slightly. "On one—no, *two* conditions."

"And they are. . ."

"First, that we don't do this all the time while we work together—that we *will* usually eat here. Secondly, that we choose one of the Chinese restaurants tonight, 'cause I haven't been there for a long time."

"It's a deal!" He thrust out his hand. "On both conditions."

Her shower couldn't have taken more than four minutes, and they were in his car heading for the restaurant not long after that. "You're amazing!"

"Because I didn't take time to curl my hair?"

He grinned. "Because you accept the fact that you're lovely just the way you are. Your short hair is just as beautiful even when you don't do what*ever* others do to theirs! And," he lightly rubbed his knuckles against her jawline, "your coloring's just right without covering it up with stuff."

He loved her all the more for saying just, "Thanks, Nate."

He filled her in on the calls he'd made. The Alaska cousins said they were skipping the reunion this year but might be present for the following one if they learned early enough when and where it would be held. They'd like to bring a couple of the other grandkids next time.

Several of the West Virginians were coming in their travel trailer, as they had two years before. Nate's brother from Albany would be bringing his wife and three kids. They would stay in a scout tent, while his sister preferred staying in town with in-laws. "I'll check with Dad later tonight or tomorrow morning, to see how he made out," Nate promised.

"Great! My father-in-law told me yesterday that he has at least nine stay-overs for sure and probably another five—and suspects some must already be on vacation, since he's been unable to reach several he'd been assigned to contact."

They spent much of the evening getting caught up with one another's activities. He'd said on Sunday that he'd not toured much in Hong Kong, but now spoke about people he'd been associated with there. "They were hardworking and intelligent, and we even got to the point where I could kid around with them, which pleased me. Though I was never invited into any of their homes, we did eat a number of meals together."

"Do you keep up with these contacts after you're home?"

He shook his head. "I hate to admit there are only a few with whom I've kept in touch. When I do, more often than not it's by E-mail."

"That *is* easier, isn't it?"

"Very much so!"

The restaurant they'd chosen had a large buffet, and

both of them returned for another serving of the small shrimp. Neither commented about it, but they did seem to have a lot of food preferences in common.

Christie didn't ask if he'd received word as to where he'd be sent next. She didn't want to even think about that tonight. They dawdled over their food so much that little was above room temperature by the time they ate it. Although the name of each dish had been clearly displayed, she couldn't have told later what she'd eaten.

He walked up the porch steps with her when he brought her home, and she considered leading the way on around the porch to sit with him on the swing out front. It was such a beautiful moonlit night, she didn't want to go inside—but told herself she must. Nate was too comfortable to be with, too enjoyable, too. . .

She stopped at the side doorway and drew in a deep breath. "I've had a wonderful evening, Nate, both the dinner and your company; but I've been up since five this morning, and I need some rest if we're to start work tomorrow."

He seemed to start saying something else, but his words, following the clearing of his throat, were, "That's about the time I got up, too. It's probably best for us to go to—for us to sleep."

He squeezed her forearm, saying, "Good night, Christie. Sleep well," and started back down the steps.

She unlocked and opened the door, then pressed the switch to turn on the powerful parking-area light which she'd neglected to activate before leaving for dinner. She continued standing where he'd left her until his car lights disappeared and she could no longer hear the fading sounds of his engine.

There are times when I almost wish you wouldn't agree with me so readily, Nathanael Mitchell. I would have argued—at least I hope I would have—that it was best for you to leave right away, but I can't deny my wanting you to stay.

For a little while.

Though convinced she'd said and done the right thing, she was annoyed with herself. If they were going to be working together for the next ten days, she must maintain control of her decision making. *And I refuse to examine the reasons for my even thinking that, or my emotions right now!*

❦

Christie woke and looked at her digital alarm: 6:12 on this sunshine-filled day! She got up, slid into a bathrobe, and went to the kitchen to start the coffee. Looking from the window, she saw Nate already there at the edge of her woods. While the percolator did its thing, she went in and brushed her teeth, then slid into jeans, a long-sleeved cotton work shirt, and athletic shoes. It seemed strange not to take a shower, but there was no point in that until later, since their agenda was to drag brush this morning. She went out onto the porch and called, "Good morning, Nate. What an early riser you are!"

He ambled toward her across the dew-wet grass.

"I'm so used to getting up early, it's impossible to break the habit even when on vacation—and it doesn't help that my circadian rhythm hasn't caught up yet with my being back in the States."

"I hadn't thought of that, with your going so many places for extended periods." She again wondered how long he'd be able to stay home. Even though she'd been with him on only a few occasions, Christie already knew she would miss him when he left. "The coffee's ready, and I'm planning on French toast."

"Sounds *very* good." He started toward the steps. "By the way, you're beautiful in the morning."

She laughed, though her cheeks felt noticeably warmer. "You do know how to make a woman feel special, even when she hasn't gotten around to putting on makeup and only ran a comb through her hair."

He was at the foot of the steps, then coming up. "Just callin' things the way I see them." He followed her through the dining area and into the kitchen. "So what can I do here after I wash my hands?"

"Just keep me company. The egg mixture is ready, but it will take a few minutes for this iron skillet to heat sufficiently." Opening the refrigerator, she removed cartons of orange juice and milk, got the bottle of maple syrup from the cupboard, and carried them to the table. Place settings were already positioned so she and Nate could both look out through the sliding doors and the permanent glass panels making up three-fourths of the lakefront view.

"Mom prefers her big frying pan, too. She *has* a griddle but never uses it."

"Same here." The drops of water she sprinkled onto the iron surface sizzled and danced a bit before evaporating so, having established that the metal was sufficiently heated, she greased the surface. Adjusting the temperature a bit, she dipped slices of bread into the mixture, coating both sides, and laid them in to brown.

Nate walked over to the screened door. "It's smooth as a tabletop right now."

She went to stand beside him for a few moments. "That's one of the many things I enjoy about living here —the lake's variability. It can be like this, or choppy, and sometimes even have fairly large wavelets coming ashore. It's frequently as clear and blue as the sky above it, like now, but ranges from that to deep purple and almost-black."

He nodded but added nothing as she returned to the stove to flip the French toast to brown on its other side. There was no need for verbal communication; she felt perfectly comfortable with him.

Like it used to be with Jerry.

Her breath sucked in sharply, like a gasp, but then she asked, "What did you say?"

He turned back toward her. "This has got to be one of the most peaceful, beautiful spots in the world."

"I think so. It was love at first sight when I was brought here the first time. I never dreamed of someday owning it."

"My memories go back to earliest childhood. My—our grandfather built this place, you know, when his sons were still at home, and they love it, too. It rubbed off on the next generation, as you well know."

He took the indicated seat. "Grandma and Grandad generally ran an open house, with us kids spending much of our summer vacation here and other relatives dropping in for an afternoon or a week—however long they wanted to."

She felt a bit awkward. "Was it a problem with any of them when Jerry and I were given the opportunity to buy it?"

"Not that I know of—and I'm sure I'd have heard rumblings had that been the case."

"I hope not, and we *did* try to keep up the—what you called the 'open house.' " She then asked, "But now, with Jerry gone, *could* there be resentment?"

His warm hand covered hers on the table. "No, Christie, there is not now, nor will there be a problem."

"But. . ."

He shook his head as he squeezed her hand. "If, after Jerry's death, you'd decided to sell this place, someone else in the family would undoubtedly have bought it. I probably would have, myself, to keep it from going to strangers. But it *was* your property as well as Jerry's, and we understand that the right-of-survivorship, as well as the mortgage insurance, make it yours alone."

His hand still covered hers. "And the responses we're getting to your invitation for this reunion—honestly,

Christie, you should hear the reactions of those on the phone! Even ones who can't make it appreciate what you've done—what you're doing to continue our family traditions."

Perhaps this is the time to tell him this wasn't my idea, that it was—

He was going on, "And I was delighted to have this time free and your permission to help you prepare for it."

"But you've worked so hard these past months. Aren't there things you look forward to doing when you get back? I feel almost guilty, tying you down like this."

He started laughing as he reached for the maple syrup. "*This* is what I was looking forward to—visiting with family and friends, working out-of-doors, swimming in Lake Lenore—things I haven't had opportunity to do for far too long. Really, Christie, what more *could* I ask for?"

❧

Christie had underestimated by far how many branches had fallen in a year. Some were so large that she and Nate together dragged them to the cleared area they'd established. It was near the water, but a distance from her sanded beach and small dock. She could handle one and sometimes several medium-sized boughs or an armload of smaller ones.

He was coming back from the ever-enlarging pile as she brought more. "You don't need to prove to *me* how strong you are."

"I'm trying no such thing!"

"Just *look* at you, Christie, dragging half-a-tree's worth of branches."

"I want to get this done!" *I'm just warm from my labor. Certainly Nate's comments shouldn't make me uncomfortable.* "I've neglected keeping up with this, even knowing that hard winds bring down more branches."

He stood there, hands on his lean hips, looking around. "It's remarkable what a good job of self-pruning trees do. Look how far up the lowest branches are on the older ones."

"Um-hmm." She pulled her shoulders back and twisted a little from side to side. After a busy year in the confines of her schoolroom, she wasn't used to hours of such strenuous exercise. "We've nearly finished clearing this area where the campers and tents will be set up and down there by the lake, so I'm going to work on the east side of the driveway next."

He veered in that direction, but waited for her to join him. Although they now had to drag brush farther, it was more fun and seemed to go faster as they worked together.

For their break, they sat on the porch with tall glasses of iced tea and chocolate chip cookies from the freezer. Christie liked baking, but had not done it much since being widowed. He returned to the job before her when she decided to prepare potatoes, carrots, and onions to place in the slow cooker with the beef she'd started earlier.

She was especially grateful for having done this when they broke for their noon meal—and they again ate on the porch, sitting on the bench with their bowls on the extensive "table." "Ya know, Christie, one of the things I remembered and dreamed of in Hong Kong and other places was sitting right here, looking out over this lake."

"I would have, too." Her voice went soft. "It's—like it becomes a part of you."

He nodded, still focusing on the water. "It *is* a part of me. Even if I were never able to come here again, I'd remember it and return here in my mind for peace and calm, a sense of stability, and for renewal.

"And inspiration."

Those are my feelings, too, but I wouldn't have said it that well. She was almost relieved when he stated he was ready to begin work on those branches again.

It was after 4:30 when she pulled off her work gloves. "I've had it for today, Nate! I'm going in and taking a couple ibuprofen tablets for the sore muscles I already have—and to hopefully forego discovering I have muscles I don't yet know about!"

"Am I glad to hear you say that!" His little laugh was self-deprecating. "I've been thinking it, but had too much pride to admit to being less tough than you."

She smiled. "Are you up to going for a swim or a boat ride?"

"I've been hoping for that, too. I even have my swim trunks in the car."

"Great! How about bringing them in while I pour us iced tea? Or soda?"

"Tea sounds best right now."

"*And* ibuprofen?" she suggested.

"Not this time."

"Still afraid to let me see how un-tough you are?"

His quick smile showed his recognition of her teasing. "I admit to some muscle soreness, but not enough to bother with. Swimming should take care of it."

Chapter 4

The water felt cool at first, then just right—as everything else had been on this glorious June day. It had been far too long since Nate was here to swim—not even once since Jerry's marriage, since this lovely woman became part of his family. "You probably don't remember, but we came here together when we were in high school."

"Of *course* I remember. You brought me twice for family picnics and swimming. That was before we started college."

He frowned. "Have you any idea why we stopped dating?"

"I'm not sure there was a reason. I still considered you a good friend, but you were in Massachusetts and I stayed in Pennsylvania. I assume you were dating?"

He nodded. "And I assume *you* were dating here?"

"Um-hmm. And then, years later, you introduced me, as your friend, to a favorite cousin—and the rest is history—a very good history. I don't believe I ever thanked you for that, but do now."

"You're more than welcome." *How could I have been so stupid as to let you go? Perhaps it's not too late. . . .*

Could she have realized they were approaching deep water with this conversation when she challenged him to a race out to the platform built just above water-level two hundred feet or more from the beach? He expected to take it easy, but found her to be a very strong swimmer; even exerting all his will and muscle, they reached it at the some moment.

Did you plan for us to get here at the same time? Did you slow down so I wouldn't be embarrassed at losing the race? He pulled himself up and turned to sit with his feet in the water. "You don't ever have to hold yourself back to keep from winning, Christie."

She looked startled, then almost indignant. "I *didn't*. If I had, you'd have won! This is not the Olympics, Nathanael Mitchell. I meant it simply as a fun challenge."

He raised his bent arm horizontally in front of himself, as if warding off a possible blow. "I didn't mean to offend you, Christie. I admit to *trying* to win, and here *you* are—not even winded!"

She laughed. "The water's usually too cold for me to swim until about Memorial Day, but I've had these last weeks to get back into shape; whereas *you,* poor man, were busy with computers and engineers' drawings and —and whatever else you're involved with."

"I'll accept all the sympathy I can get." His voice switched back from being whimsically plaintive. "The thing is, I do like what I'm doing. It's a slave driver, but I willingly do what I'm assigned."

"*Could* you refuse these away-jobs?"

"Probably." His head cocked to the side. "I do an equally good job for them in the office and labs as in the field. I enjoy the challenges of working here as much as working with new people and bringing them up to applicable standards."

"What about languages? I remember your being in my Spanish class, but I haven't even tried using it since then. Have you?"

"I'm not as good a linguist as I wish but do try." He shrugged. "I'm always assured of having a capable translator, so we do surprisingly well."

They swam awhile longer before going up to the house for sandwiches and fruit. Christie had offered the use of the shower, but he said he'd wait until he got home—then was almost sorry that could be understood as indicating that he was leaving right after eating. She did not ask him to stay.

When walking to the car, he did ask if she might want to go somewhere for ice cream, but her response wasn't what he'd hoped for. "Not this evening," she said, and didn't ask if he'd like to come back in and share ice cream from her freezer. He'd seen some there—but why *should* she ask him to stay?

He'd forgotten Mother's mentioning that she and Dad had a dinner meeting this evening. After a leisurely hot shower he stretched out on the couch to read the paper and look through several magazines. He too often stuck to professional journals and news magazines. It was refreshing to peruse a *Pennsylvania Magazine* and *The Biblical Archaeological Review.*

By then he was yawning and found himself rubbing his eyes. Nate glanced at the mantle clock. *Not even 9:30 and I'm ready for bed! It's probably because of all that fresh air and exercise.*

He wasn't thinking of fresh air and the work he'd accomplished today as he dropped off to sleep—it was the one who'd been with him who filled his dreams.

❧

Trevor's low-throated growl and pointed ears alerted Christie to the visitor on the porch, and she went around the table on the wall-side so as not to startle him when she turned on the outside lights. The raccoon was used to this, so hardly even showed surprise as he picked up one of the peanuts she'd left for him.

She enjoyed watching his delicate-looking fingers tear away the shell, put the nut into his mouth, and savor its flavor. Checking the trees off to the right, she saw the telltale reflected light from the eyes of a deer—and yes, there were two smaller ones, probably the same doe and fawns which came frequently, thirst drawing them from the wooded hillside to the lake.

How excited some of the relatives were two years ago at seeing these wonderful creatures! But after all this time, Christie was still thrilled by living with nature and having nature come to her.

I hope you'll continue doing this while my guests are here. I only wish I knew some way to let you know that no harm will ever come to you here. She went to bed less than a half-hour later, planning to read more of that novel. Unable to get interested in it tonight, she folded the cover's flyleaf to mark her place, rolled over, and slept.

She was up and dressed by the time Nate arrived in the morning, bringing still-warm cinnamon rolls from the bakery in town. "I suppose we should get started," he said a little later, after finishing his second roll and coffee. "This morning's weather report predicts rain to move in by early- to mid-afternoon."

"In that case, perhaps we can burn all those branches and brush we've been collecting—*if* there's not much wind," she suggested as they got to their feet.

"There's not supposed to be."

They continued with what they'd done the day before right up to when the gentle rain began. Then, with hoses already connected from the house, buckets down by the lake, and two fire extinguishers at hand, they started the fire.

It burned steadily and safely, flames and smoke rising straight up in the still air. As the temperature remained in the upper seventies, neither of them minded being soaked through while continuing to toss in brush and branches from where they'd been placed when the original pile got too high.

Christie stood beside Nate after the final additions were made. "I'm glad to have this taken care of!"

"There *is* still more."

"I don't even care if that's done before they arrive," she told him. "It's only at the far edges of the property, and that makes it more *rustic*—not so parklike."

"Oh, I almost forgot to tell you that Dad says there are two *more* campers to set up space for—with a total of six additional people."

"Great! It does help to know that before you and your dad and uncle string wire tomorrow."

"We'll prepare several extra sites for tents or campers, just in case."

"I must check something else, too. Jerry borrowed sawhorses from both your dad and his—to put planks on for the tables, you know. And they got benches from somewhere, possibly the firemen. I must ask about that when I see the men tomorrow."

⁂

Nate did ask his father that evening then also called his uncle, getting hoped-for responses from each. However, the call he received from New York wasn't as much to his liking. Not right now, anyhow. There was a problem with a setup in Arizona; could he leave tonight and get things squared away?

"Isn't there someone else free to do it this time?"

"No one we *know* can handle this."

He asked additional questions and even called the crew there to see if he might give input over the phone —but the complications were such that his presence was required.

Sighing, he called back to his chief and asked that their travel agent locate and arrange for the first flight to Phoenix either from Avoca or Harrisburg—or even Newark or Baltimore if absolutely necessary.

As he waited for that report, he went upstairs, packed his suitcase and carry-on, and brought them back down. Nate didn't tie up the phone by calling Christie, though he wanted to explain the situation and promise to do everything in his power to get back to help with the reunion.

By the time he got the information; however, it was nearly ten o'clock, and he had to leave immediately if he was to make that flight from Harrisburg. *Thank goodness I stopped for gas on the way home!* The stations in many towns through which he'd be driving didn't stay open during the night.

Christie had said she was very tired and was going to bed early, so, although he twice picked up his cellular phone, he returned it to the seat beside him.

Christie awoke with a smile on her face. It was Saturday morning—one week from the *big* reunion day, and Nate and the two older men would soon be here to string the electric wire and do other things. Her father-in-law had called the evening before to report that the sawhorses, boards, and benches were taken care of, so she need not worry about them.

Coffee was perking by the time she heard the car coming in her driveway, so she went to meet it—and felt momentary disappointment at seeing only her father-in-law and Uncle John. Nate would, of course, want to drive himself, so he'd be free to come and go. But then, even while getting out of the car, Uncle John called, "I guess that son of mine got in touch with you, right?"

She could only hope the tightening in her chest wasn't reflected in her face or voice. "I haven't seen or heard from him since yesterday."

He turned to Dad Whitley. "These kids! You try to teach them manners, but they just don't pay attention!"

He was obviously trying to make light of something she didn't understand. "Why *should* he have contacted me?"

"He got called out again last night and is probably in Arizona by now."

I must control what I say—how I look! "Oh? What happened?"

"I haven't a clue; well, he *did* say something about some setup being down— something like that. It made no sense to me."

She couldn't have anticipated the disappointment she was now feeling—the personal pain, the sense of loneliness. He'd seemed to treasure her friendship—it even seemed that their friendship was becoming, or had a chance of becoming, more significant.

But he had not called—not to explain or say *goodbye* or anything. She started to clear her throat, which seemed unaccountably thick, but controlled that urge.

These men were smart enough to put two and two together and realize this upset her. "Coffee's ready," she reported with forced brightness, leading the way into the kitchen. "Does either of you want sugar? Milk?"

They accepted the coffee. Black. She offered cereal or toast, but they assured Christie they'd eaten. "Well, I'll leave the coffee on *warm,* so help yourself later—and there are homemade ginger cookies here should you want a snack."

They each took one and pronounced it excellent. The phone rang as Christie was on her way out the side door. The men went on down the steps to check the wire she'd told them was on the concrete slab. "Hello?"

"Hi, Christie! How are you doing this morning?"

Nate sounded just as always. "Fine, thanks. The men just got here. You gave me quite a surprise."

"Me, too! I fully expected to be off for weeks."

"Does this happen all the time?"

His short laugh, contained little humor. "Not all the time, thank goodness—but it does happen. I tried to get out of it, but they do need me here."

As if you weren't needed here! "I'm sorry. Do you have any idea how long you'll be away?"

"Not yet. It's only about six A.M. here, you know. I got one person's rundown on the way from the airport and have asked for an emergency meeting with all supervisors."

"And this is Saturday," she reminded. "Probably no one's too happy about the situation."

"I'm not either, Christie." His voice sounded like that. "I'd much rather be with you, but this is how it is."

"You've already given days of your time here."

"And I'll do everything in my power to get back soon."

How can I resent his making this decision? "I hope you can. I know how important family is to you, and they'll miss seeing you—for the third year in a row, isn't it?"

"Don't remind me!" There was what sounded like a groan. "I'm hoping our problem's not as bad as it sounds. Sometimes just having a new set of eyes and ears makes it possible to get to the root of difficulties."

"I'll hope along with you; for that matter, I'll even *pray* about it and for you."

"Thanks, Christie, I'll be counting on it. And I'll also be praying for you—I promise."

She heard sounds in the background, then his voice, "I've gotta go. Several of the supervisors have arrived."

"And I, too, should be out there with Dad Whitley and your father, pretending I'm *you*."

That got a chuckle, followed by "I'd much rather you remain the wonderful *you* that you are."

"Have a good day, my friend."

"And you have a good day, too, my—Christie."

❧

Her day passed with unbelievable rapidity as she helped string those electric wires. Then the tent arrived. She'd ordered it for the beginning of the following week, but was grateful it was brought now, on Saturday, while the men were still here.

Her father-in-law called to have the portable toilets delivered right away, also. "These are on me—and it's worth a few extra bucks to have them taken care of now." In the same spirit, they set up the "wash station," with hoses bringing water from the house for hand-washing, cooking, and other uses. Showers would be taken in the two bathrooms at the house, but other needs would be met here.

When Nate called that evening, she reported, "Things are progressing *very* well. In bed this morning, I fretted about how we could possibly be ready for the first arrivals on Wednesday; but now, looking toward the lake and to the right, the 'Whitley Campgrounds' appear remarkably complete.

"And your mom brought a big shepherd's pie for lunch, which was sweet of her. She knows how much I like lamb."

He was pleased things were going well at the lake but wasn't yet sure about his Arizona situation. "We did find one discrepancy but aren't positive that's responsible for all the difficulties. I'm sure hoping it is!"

"And then you can come home?"

"Then I will be home!" The almost-repetition of her words was said as solemnly as though giving a vow.

❧

Christie was invited to her parents' home for lunch after church the next day, as were several relatives and friends. She didn't get home until late afternoon, then took

Trevor for another long walk around the lake.

She wasn't surprised when many of the other residents did more than just call greetings, and she mentioned this to Nate when he called that evening. "Everyone was wondering what was going on up at my end of the lake."

"Your neighbors sound like a bunch of busybodies."

"I'd be curious, too, if one of *them* had this much activity on his property and suddenly a huge tent and a couple of smaller ones were erected."

"What did they think of your big reunion celebration?"

"Some were overwhelmed by the scope of it, but I think many were envious."

"I can relate to that!" That was definitely a sigh. "I'm still hoping to get there for at least part of it."

"Especially for *Saturday*," she emphasized. "We're up to at least eighty-five for then and haven't yet heard from some."

"And the first ones come on Wednesday?"

"As of now. . ."

∽

Wednesday came soon—almost *too* soon to do everything she'd hoped to accomplish—a beautiful, clear day after a night of showers. But she was a little depressed. *No, not depressed,* she corrected herself. *Disappointment is not the same as depression.*

Nate had not called yet. She had no reason to think he should, or that he might even want to—and yet he *had* phoned each evening while away. Until last night.

To the best of her knowledge, the first arrivals would be the Smiths from New Hampshire. Carol Whitley Smith was Dad Whitley's sister, whom Christie met for the first time at her own wedding and then again here, two years ago. They'd be coming in their camper and probably wouldn't arrive until middle or late afternoon.

Christie was barefoot and in denim cut-offs, busily scrubbing the lakeside porch floor when she heard the sound of a well-tuned engine coming in her driveway. She wiped her hands on her shorts and finger-combed her short hair as she went around the corner onto the side porch. *I wish I'd at least have brought out sandals.*

The vehicle had parked on the other side of her car, so she was going down the steps before she realized this *wasn't* the Smiths. The door slammed and he was coming around his car and hers. "*Nate,* you're back."

His arms were wide, and it was the most natural thing in the world for her to run into them, to hug him, also. "Christie!" His voice sounded husky as he almost whispered her name. "Oh, Christie, it's good to be home."

Home? "I didn't know. . ."

"Even I didn't know for sure that I'd be able to get away until last night. Then there were travel arrangements to make and getting to the airport. It was too late to call, especially with the time difference!"

She was leaning back against his arms, her smile belying the moisture in her eyes. "It's so *good* to have you here." And then she was clinging to him, head nestled between his cheek and shoulder.

Her hair tickled his cheek as his lips brushed her forehead. He longed for the taste of her lips but, as she was apparently not yet ready for that, he continued holding her as closely as she was holding him. "I missed you so!"

Her head moved a tiny bit, undoubtedly a nod accompanying the muffled, "Me, too."

"And I'm sorry I wasn't here when you needed me."

Her head did tilt upward then, so their gaze could meet, even though their lips had not. "Your dad and Jerry's did so very much. I think we're just about ready for the influx."

He was amused by her use of that word, but before he could respond, she looked startled, then pushed herself away. "The New Hampshire Smiths are planning to get here sometime this afternoon, and I'm in the middle of scrubbing the porch. I thought they'd arrived early and I," looking down at herself, as though horrified, "*I* look a mess. . . ."

His arms felt empty without her. "You look wonderful!"

Her head tilted somewhat saucily. "I know better, but thanks, anyway." She started up the steps. "And now I must finish that porch and go make myself presentable."

"You're far more than just *presentable*," he insisted as he followed her to where she picked up the mop and again started working on the porch floor.

Her grin was gaminelike. "Maybe that works for other girls, my friend, but I know better. However," she rinsed out the mop, "there *is* hope, once I finish here." Then, before he even began a response, she asked, "Did you call your folks? If not, you know where my phone is."

He hesitated for only a moment before going in to the small counter demarcating the kitchen and dining areas. Actually, he *had* used his cellular phone to let his parents know he'd arrived at the Harrisburg airport. He'd almost called Christie, too, but wanted to see her face when she learned he was back, hoping she'd respond with joy.

And she had! She'd run to him, hugging him as tightly as he'd held her. But there was so much they didn't know yet about one another. Would she be offended to learn he'd contacted his parents but didn't call her?

He left shortly after telling her he needed to go home for a little while. He would be bringing his parents' camper back with him, hooking it up to the electricity right away, and would stay there alone tonight and tomorrow night. That would make things simpler for Mom and Dad, since they couldn't come till Friday afternoon.

Chapter 5

*W*ell, Christine Whitley, you sure made an idiot of yourself that time! she scolded. *You ran to him as though you had every right to. Yes, he did take you in his arms, but the poor guy didn't have a choice—you threw yourself at him!*

And the way she was dressed! She was seldom this sloppy, but had been in a hurry and wanted to get this done and. . .and she'd probably really messed things up —no wonder he left right away. *Would* he come back yet today?

I didn't so much as ask how he happened to come this much earlier than expected—though I guess he can't actually "expect" anything with his kind of work.

That was an angle she must not lose sight of if. . .*if what?* She clamped her teeth together as a quick, hard breath forcefully escaped. She didn't want to admit what her mind and emotions were pushing to have accepted. No, she did not want to love this man, this remarkable, loving man who had so recently come back into her life.

*So what does "not wanting to be in love with someone"
have to do with reality? And why did this have to happen
now? Fourteen months without my wonderful husband,
without a date, without a hug or kiss except from my parents.*

Was I too lonely? Too. . . ?

She did not even have the questions, much less
answers!

But let's face it, she told herself, *I've just had a small
sample of what must be extremely difficult for any woman
whose husband can be called away at a moment's notice, for
any amount of time!*

She didn't let herself consider from where that "H"
word had come! She was going to ignore it.

She washed the mop and set it out to dry in the heat
of the sun, then headed for the shower, after which she
put on clothing more appropriate for welcoming the
first of Jerry's—and Nate's—relatives.

The Smiths, Aunt Carol and Uncle Bert, their
daughter, Peggy, with her nine- and eleven-year-old
boys, arrived after four. Christie welcomed them and was
just starting to direct them to their assigned site when
Nate got there and took over. Her father-in-law and
Uncle John had given her instructions, but she was more
than happy to turn this over to Nate, who within minutes had the camper situated and electricity hooked up.

They did have a propane stove and refrigerator but,
used to traveling and camping, had their grill set up
within minutes. In what seemed like no time, they were
cooking hot dogs and insisting that Christie and Nate

join them. They'd also stopped somewhere and bought a three-bean salad and coleslaw and said they wanted everything eaten.

Afterwards, Christie stayed at the house while Nate took the rest of them around the lake in the flat-bottomed boat. There were no phone calls nor arrivals while they were gone.

The guests turned in early, saying they wanted to be fresh and ready for their planned drive over to Steamtown the next day. Nate stayed with Christie on the porch for another half hour. Seeing him try to hide another yawn, she reminded, "You didn't get much sleep last night."

"Not just last night," he admitted. "I put in fourteen-to sixteen-hour days—not counting the drive to and from my motel. It will take more than one good night's sleep to catch up, but it'll be a start."

His arm had rested along the back of the swing, and she'd been quite aware of the warmth of his fingers through the cotton T-shirt covering her shoulder. Not wanting him to think she was waiting for him to draw her into an embrace, she stood up and turned to reach for his hand. "You're entitled to get to bed early tonight."

She wasn't sure if there was a small tug on his part or if it was her own emotional pull but, whatever it was, she resisted it by taking a small step backwards. She stood at the side of the porch as he started along the slanted path. Raising his hand in a small salute, he said softly, "Good night, Christine."

She wondered at the semiformality of his having used her given name, but there was enough light to see that wonderful smile, as warm as ever. "Goodnight, Nathanael." She, too, was smiling as she went inside, locked the doors as she always did, and got ready for bed.

The Smiths were gone by 8:30 the next morning, but three other *branches*, as Nate referred to these parts of his family tree, came during the day. This was the first time that one cousin had been there; Ginger and Steve had been married less than eight weeks and referred to themselves as still on their honeymoon. Nate suggested, "Christie, would you like to take them out in the canoe so they can enjoy the lakeview of this wonderful spot? I'll hold the fort here."

She smiled appreciation. "I'd love that." On the way down to the dock she made sure they were both swimmers, so she just tossed in three flotation cushions. "We have a rule that anyone under twelve and all nonswimmers must wear life jackets when in the boat or a canoe, but these will do for us."

The lake was perfect—but to her it almost always seemed that way. Ginger commented about how smooth the surface was, then was delighted when a fish came to the surface to catch an insect and ever-widening concentric circles were formed. And, of course, there were the chevron-shaped ones the wake formed behind them.

Raised in Philadelphia, Steven had never paddled a

canoe before but was having a wonderful time. He exclaimed over the water's being so clear that he could see pebbles at the bottom and was surprised that the fish were untroubled by the slow movement of the paddles and canoe.

When they got to the lake's far end, he asked if Christie would change places with him so he could "experience both paddling and steering." As she was getting out along the shore in order to make the switch, she asked if Ginger would like to paddle, also—which she did.

Nate came to the dock to meet them, calling, "I'm impressed, Christie; you got your guests to paddle you around the lake!"

She laughed, but Ginger very seriously explained that she and her husband had asked to do it. When Nate reached for Christie's hand and she climbed onto the dock, the others decided to go back out.

Uncle Bill had called to verify that both they and their son and his wife would be coming in tomorrow evening. And yes, they still planned to again supervise and do things with the kids, beginning as soon as they arrived.

"That's a relief!" she told Nate. "I love children and work with seven- and eight-year-olds all the time, but I've never had much experience with younger or older ones."

"That goes for me, too. But remember that Uncle Bill's always been active in church camping, and Mike and Kathy with scouting."

"And you should have seen what a fabulous job they did with it two years ago, Nate."

He was pleased with how comfortable Christie seemed with hostessing his relatives; seeing how well she handled this many, he was sure she also would with the rest. It was amazing how this woman, growing up with no siblings, handled things so well. Mom had commented about that two years ago, but gave much of the credit to Jerry's being so outgoing.

Several times during these last couple of days Christie had stated that he and Jerry were enough alike to be brothers, both in appearance and personality. He'd been pleased at the time, but he now hoped Christie didn't think of him like that; he wanted her to think of him as *himself.*

Oh, Lord, please let it happen over this weekend.

❧

Hours and days passed so quickly that it seemed impossible to Christie that it was Sunday evening already, with everyone gone except for Nate and the Smiths, the latter to head back for New England the following morning. The sun was going down when Aunt Carol came up on the porch to sit with her. They watched the others making one last canoe trip around the lake. "You've done a wonderful thing this weekend, Christie —far more than you needed to."

"I'm grateful for the opportunity and that everyone helped so much." She hesitated a moment before adding,

"And I'm especially glad Nate was able to get back for it, partly because he so enjoyed it, but also because I don't know how I'd have managed without him."

"Do I detect maybe a little more than just cousinly friendship?"

Christie was not offended by the question; it didn't seem out of place here on the porch after such an enjoyable, fulfilling weekend. "We've been friends since senior high and used to date then. And he's the one who brought Jerry and me together—for which I will always be grateful."

"When he looks at you, or you at him, it's not the teens of the past, Christie, but the man and woman of today whom you are seeing."

"I—never thought of loving again, or even of dating." She turned toward this aunt-by-marriage, seeing the smiling encouragement. "We haven't spoken of our feelings, nor have we even *kissed*, other than—well, like on the cheek. I care about him very much, but the thought of becoming deeply, emotionally involved with him—or anyone—frightens me."

"Because of Jerry?" Her voice was very soft.

Christie nodded. "We were so very close, did everything together. And then he was *gone*—in one horrible moment."

Aunt Carol's hand rested on her shoulder. "*He* is gone, dear, but Nate is here, and he loves you very much."

She didn't ask how their aunt knew that, nor why it seemed so right to be speaking this way. "Although

I've not told him nor *any*one until this moment, I have come to love him—perhaps too much. Maybe God meant it for *me* that Nate had to leave when he did, even when it could have meant his missing out on the reunion—of not getting to see all of you."

She paused for a moment, but Aunt Carol just smiled and squeezed her arm. "I discovered how lonely I was for Nate during those relatively few days—and how wonderful it was to have him return. And that was with no commitments, no shared intimacies on the part of either of us.

"I. . ." She struggled with how to word this. "I've had to face the fear that I'm not strong enough to always be given second place to his time, thoughts, and loyalties."

The older woman nodded, perhaps with understanding, maybe encouragement. Christie's soft voice again broke the lengthening silence. "Jerry and I loved each other so very much, Aunt Carol, but I didn't realize until after marriage that he didn't want children, at least not for a few more years—so I have nothing left of him but memories."

Again there was stillness on the porch. The canoe was pulling in at the dock, and the women stood up and went to meet the others, who were exclaiming over the beauty, quiet, and peace they had just been sharing.

The chairs and tables had been folded and stacked, ready to be returned to the volunteer firemen's building the following day, so the seven ate leftovers together on

Christie's porch. Everything seemed unusually subdued following the happy hubbub of these last days; even the nine- and eleven-year-olds were either played out from all the activities or totally relaxed.

Peggy, their mother, shared memories of being brought here as a child, and Carol told of helping clear away the original trees and brush from the driveway-area and from the house to the lake—and of doing what little she could to help build this lovely log house.

Then the Smiths returned to their camper, and Nate sat beside Christie on the swing, with Trevor at their feet. *I must admit this is why I remained sitting here, hoping Nate would join me.* She had not consciously allowed that thought, but it had sneaked in. . . .

"Are you exhausted, Christie?"

"No." She shook her head. "Not *totally.*"

He drew in a slow, deep breath. "Aunt Carol mentioned as she was leaving that she thought it time that you and I had a good long talk."

Uh-oh! She did not look at him as she asked in as normal a voice as she could manage, "Did she say why?"

"No, but since I've been telling myself the same thing, I figure she was giving good advice."

There was a smile in his voice, and she turned to face him. "So—are we about to have that 'good long talk'?"

"I do hope so." His left hand lifted hers from where it lay on her thigh and clasped it between his. "Can you help me know where to begin?"

Her gaze remained on their joined hands. "I was

talking to her about—us." She'd hoped he would respond to that but, except for a tightening of his hands on hers, he did and said nothing. She drew away slightly, her voice a mere whisper. "Perhaps I shouldn't have done that."

His right hand moved to cup her chin, to turn her head so she *had* to look at him. "Christie, dear, I don't know what you told her, but what I'm desperately hoping is that you love me—or that maybe, sometime. . ."

She had to ask, "Do you love *me?*"

"Of course I do! I have for a long time but didn't want to push you, knowing how much—knowing that. . ."

"Knowing how much I loved Jerry." Her finishing his sentence was not a question—and it didn't give her the stab of pain she'd subconsciously expected. It wasn't too hard to add, "I believe I will always love him."

He nodded. "*All* of us will; he was a fine man."

"Yes. He was." She looked out toward the lake, then back into his warm brown eyes. "I never thought I could love again, not like that, not a man/woman love."

"The thought of being married to me—in every sense of that word—does that upset you?"

This was the first he'd spoken of marriage, and her head tilted slightly as she tried to give an honest answer. "Not anymore—I don't have a feeling of disloyalty or anything like that." His arm had slid around her shoulders, but she tried to resist his gently drawing her closer.

"My problem right now is that—I'm not as tough,

as strong as people seem to think. And I am afraid. . . ."

"Of *me?*"

She smiled just a little, but immediately sobered, knowing she had to make this point. "Jerry and I were always together—in all the years of our marriage, we were apart no more than fifteen or twenty nights—thirty, at the most. And I missed him terribly even then. It scares me to find I had a similar, almost intolerable loneliness while you were away, and yet we had never even. . . kissed."

He did pull her close then, but she buried her face against his neck, from where her admission continued, "To think of being married to you—and having you just *leave* as you have to do. . ." He was trying to interrupt, but she went on, though now looking at him, feeling miscrable. "It will be hard to make the break even now, but I realize how much you love your work and you need to go when they call. . .and must stay as long as they want you to. If we were married, Natc, I couldn't *bear* having you away so often and for such long times."

"Oh, sweetheart, you don't have to cry about that."

She hadn't even realized she was crying! She dug a tissue from a jeans pocket and blotted tears which had begun running down her checks. "I could probably handle a few weeks, knowing you'd come back soon, but for *months*. . ."

"That's what I was trying to say, dear—there probably will not have to be so many any more, not running for months. Anyway, I've accepted these in the past *because*

I didn't have a wife or major family responsibilities. Having seen too many consequences of being apart too much, I've willingly done more than my share of being Mr. Fix-it.

"But I promise it will be different now. In the first place, with all this traveling I've accumulated thousands of air-miles, so if I *should* have to be gone for even several weeks you could come to me, if I can't come to you. . . ."

She felt the smile forming as she repeated as in a nursery rhyme, "Me coming to you, and you coming to me. . ."

"Either would be special, but not nearly so *extra*-special as our being together here most of the time."

She reminded, "Your office and labs are in New York."

"I've been thinking about that."

Christie murmured, "You've apparently been doing a *lot* of that lately."

"Indeed I have!" He laughed. "And I didn't know whether I was making a complete fool of myself when calling the home office to talk this over with them."

"You must have been awfully sure of yourself, Nathanael Mitchell, talking it over with them before me!"

He must have seen through her pretending to take offense, for he raised her hand to his lips and kissed her palm. "I had to be assured of where I stood there before I could propose to you." He was very serious now. "I, too, don't want to be separated for long periods, and you, my love, have the right to know what to expect as to my job."

He drew in a deep breath. "Since almost all my office work is done on the computer, *much* of it could be done right here, keeping tied-in electronically with New York—or wherever else my input's needed."

But then he asked, "I presume you want to keep teaching, right? Until we have children, that is?"

Her cheeks felt as though they were getting warmer, but she nodded her affirmation. "Until we have children. . ."

Suddenly, she was in his arms and the kiss they were sharing was warm and exciting and fulfilling and. . . "Oh, Nate. . ." It was all she could say, for they were kissing again, there on the swing at Lake Lenore.

There was the sound of running feet coming up the steps and the voice of Aunt Carol's younger grandson. "Christie!"

She was on her feet before he got around from the side porch.

"Hey, Christie, have you got antihistamine stuff to put on my leg? Something stung me, and boy, does it itch! And it *hurts*, too."

"Wow, that's quite a swelling you have there, Joshua!" She got an ice cube from the freezer and placed it on the large reddened area on the front of his thigh. Telling him to hold it there, she brought a damp washcloth from the bathroom so he could more easily keep it in position. A few minutes later she dried the area and lightly rubbed the ointment on it.

As he left, she requested, "Joshua, please tell your grandma that Nate and I did have a good long talk tonight. And also say we'll talk with her in the morning."

"Okey-dokey!" he called back. "See you in the morning!"

Christie and Nate stood there together on the porch, watching the child run down the slant to the camper, turn to wave, then climb inside. The three-quarter moon was almost halfway across the sky, bright enough to give marked contrast to the lighted lake, yard, and tops of bushes and trees as compared with the blackness of the shadows. Three deer moved out into the light.

Christie was standing in front of Nate, his arms around her, holding her close. "There's always been a special something here at Lake Lenore," he murmured. "I could never put my finger on it before, didn't recognize what it was."

She turned enough to look up into his eyes. "You sound as though you've figured out the mystery."

"I have." He nodded, cheek against her forehead, arms holding her yet closer. "I finally have."

She, too, had learned the secret and was blessed by experiencing it again. But she did want to hear it from his lips. "You say it first, Nate, and I'll repeat it after you."

But when she did that, his voice was joining hers in affirmation: "That special something of Lake Lenore is love."

EILEEN M. BERGER

Eileen lives in her native state of Pennsylvania and is the wife of a minister and the mother of three grown children and grandmother of seven. She and her husband own a choose-and-cut Christmas tree farm. She worked twenty-five years as a medical technologist, but she wrote on the side and had numerous books, short stories, articles, and poems published. Eileen also became an active member of the St. David's Christian Writers Association, whose annual conference is the second oldest in the country. She has directed and taught workshops and special courses at many conferences and loves helping writers write.

STORM WARNING

by Colleen Coble

Dedication

For my baby brother, Dave Rhoads,
the family daredevil,
whose pride in his big sister has
always been humbling.
Love you, little brother!

Acknowledgment

Special thanks to Lucile Campese. She loved her city of Wichita Falls, Texas, so much that she wrote asking for some stories set in her area and provided books, magazines, and newspapers for research. Thanks, Lucile!

Prologue

Randi Walker hated wedding invitations. They always brought back painful memories of the unused wedding invitations that she'd never had the heart to throw away. She sighed and picked up the thick cream envelope. Ripping it open, she felt almost faint when she read the contents. It wasn't a wedding announcement at all, but an invitation to a reunion. A very special reunion.

Her sister, Lauren, looked over her shoulder at the invitation. "You're going, aren't you?"

Randi stared at her in disbelief. "You've got to be kidding!" Her last two years of college she'd spent with eight other students majoring in meteorology and their professor chasing storms across the Great Plains. She'd fallen in love with the thrill of the violent weather, but that wasn't all she'd fallen for. She carefully sat on the couch and looked at the invitation again. Well, they could count her out. She refused to ever relive her stupidity in front of her former colleagues. They'd seen enough of it then.

"You have let those old memories affect you for way too long as it is. Get over it and get on with your life."

Randi felt like stomping her foot at her sister's condescending tone. Her sister wasn't usually so obtuse. "It would be like pouring salt in the wound. You may enjoy pain, but I don't. I put that all behind me, and I have absolutely no desire to rake it all up again."

Lauren gave an exasperated sigh. "Randi, that was over five years ago. You won't give any guy a chance with you. I don't call that putting it all behind you. You're going to be twenty-eight next month, and you're still afraid to love another man. Besides, there's no reason to even think Brock will be there. You haven't seen or heard anything about him in all these years. He just disappeared without a word and left you at the altar."

"He didn't leave me literally at the altar," Randi protested. The habit of defending Brock was an old one and hard to break. Even if he didn't deserve it.

"A month from the wedding is leaving you at the altar, as far as I'm concerned," Lauren said sharply. "The invitations were even addressed."

Randi flinched at the reference to the invitations. "I saw his name on a piece about Hurricane Floyd several months ago," Randi told her. She wanted to sidetrack her sister from the images she was bringing to mind—images she had thought she would never have to think about again.

The ploy worked. Lauren gaped at her. "You never told me." Her tone was reproachful.

"I knew what you'd say."

"Where is he?"

"Florida. He's working for the Hurricane Center." She spoke quietly, a bit ashamed for anyone to even know she'd still been interested enough to find out where he was.

"See. He's far from Texas. You would get to see your old friends and maybe even see a tornado or two."

Randi gave a derisive laugh. "I'm a meteorologist, Lauren. Remember? July is not the best time to see tornadoes. We might see some thunderstorms or hail, but the chances aren't good for tornadoes. There has to be a major outbreak to get lucky enough to see even one."

"All the same, I think you should go. Maybe if you face it, you'll be able to put all those old memories to rest and get on with your life."

Randi thought about those words long after her sister left. Maybe she was right. Maybe she should go to the reunion. She'd get to see Lisa and Karen again. And Will and Steve. She would show them her life had turned out just fine without Brock in it. Besides, she was due a vacation. She'd worked as WKWB-TV's resident meteorologist for three years and had never taken a vacation. Summer was a good time to be gone. There were generally no hurricanes or tornadoes to report. Before she went to sleep, she filled out the reply card. She was going to do it. Lauren was right. Brock wouldn't have the nerve to show his face.

Chapter 1

Brock Parker tossed his suitcase in the trunk of his professionally restored 1960 MGB roadster and folded his long legs under the wheel. The engine roared to life, and he stomped on the gas and headed west. The beautiful sky blue car turned heads on the freeway.

He still wasn't sure if this was a good idea or not, but when the invitation came to attend a reunion of the storm-chasing lab from Valparaiso University, all he'd been able to do was think about looking into Randi's warm brown eyes once again. He knew all he'd see in them would be contempt, but he had to go. He had to know if she'd ever been able to move beyond the blow he'd dealt her—and if she hated him or just felt indifference. He'd never been able to love another woman and knew he never would. He hadn't made the decision to leave her lightly, but it had seemed the only thing he could do if he loved her. He had loved her then, and he loved her still. But he could never marry her.

Lately, the Lord had been stirring him to confess to her, to ask her forgiveness. He didn't think he could disobey any more. He'd resisted because he didn't want to see the pity in her eyes, but he couldn't do it any longer. She had a beautiful soul, and she would have stuck by him then, but he hadn't wanted that for her. He still didn't. He'd kept tabs on her through Lisa and knew she'd never married. Could that mean she still thought of him at all?

⊗⊚

CHASE LOG: *Saturday, July 22. Clear skies with slight chance of rain in the afternoon. . . .*

The sight of the red clay dirt and wonderfully stark landscape brought the memories flooding back. Randi's heart pounded when she saw the sign that read WELCOME TO TEXAS. Just a few more miles and she would be there. The storm chasers were to meet at the Wichita Falls hotel near the airport. Already the memories of that magical spring and summer were flooding back. Long, sunlit days following the thunderstorms, hoping to see that ultimate sight—a twister just beginning to form. There had been some close calls. One funnel cloud had dropped right behind them and damaged their van with hail.

She forced her concentration back on driving. Lauren had been elated when she learned Randi was going to the reunion. She'd promised to pray for her, but Randi knew the next two weeks wouldn't be easy. But maybe once they were over, she would be able to go home and make some kind of life. Paul Minton was certainly hoping so. He was the news anchor at WKWB. They had dated a few times so far, and Randi knew Paul was already beginning to hope for a permanent relationship. That was the real heart of why she had come. She wanted to be able to love and trust a man again.

She followed I-44 until she saw the exit. She smiled with anticipation when she saw the familiar green hotel sign. Her breath came faster, and her chest felt tight. It had been so long since she'd seen her friends. This had been a good idea. Facing these memories would help her settle her future. She had to wonder if they would feel strange, too. She and Brock had always been invited to do things together. She'd rarely even heard her name mentioned without Brock's tacked on. Randi and Brock, like Laurel and Hardy or Rocky and Bullwinkle.

She pulled into the parking lot and saw the distinctive van parked out front. Bristol Storm Chasers was emblazoned across the side. Lisa and Steve had married after school and started a business several years ago. They took tourists on storm-chasing adventures and made a good living. The prime time was past for the year, and this excursion would be more for fun and memories than for any actual hope of seeing a tornado. She parked in the open space beside the van, grabbed her purse, and got out. The door on the van opened at the same time, and she saw a familiar blond head.

"Randi, I've been watching for you!" Lisa opened

her arms and ran to her.

Randi hugged her. Lisa was still just as pretty and bubbly as ever. They'd been good friends in school and still exchanged the occasional E-mail and cards, but it wasn't the same as seeing her in person. It had been three years since they'd been together at Lisa and Steve's wedding.

"Let me look at you!" Lisa held her at arm's length. "You look marvelous. I don't know how you keep that same slim figure. I can't seem to get off those extra fifteen pounds I've gained since Steve and I got married. Your hair is shorter, but it suits you."

"You always were too thin," Randi said. "You look great! Keep those fifteen pounds." She linked arms with Lisa, and they started toward the hotel. "Who all is here?"

"Everyone except Brock." She glanced at Randi as she said Brock's name.

He wasn't coming. She'd been almost sure he wasn't, but the confirmation was reassuring. Randi relaxed, but she couldn't help feeling a shaft of disappointment. "I wondered if he would come" was all she said. She quickly changed the subject. "I thought you and Steve would be parents by now. You always said you wanted a dozen."

Lisa blushed. "Well, now that you mention it, we are in the family way."

"Lisa, that's wonderful." Randi stopped under the awning and hugged her friend. "When are you due?"

"Not until January. Steve is so excited. He bought me a huge Winnie-the-Pooh for the baby's room. He's eager to see you. The rest of the group is in our suite. Let's go see them."

They turned to go inside, but before they could open the door, a familiar sound stopped Randi in her tracks. Her heart began to thump at the gentle roar that grew steadily louder. It sounded like Brock's MGB. But that couldn't be. She couldn't imagine him driving his cherished antique car clear across the country. She didn't know whether to turn around or run. Part of her hoped it was he, and part of her wanted to bolt in case it was.

Lisa heard it, too. She turned around. "It's Brock," she said. "Let's go meet him."

Randi swallowed hard and stiffened her shoulders. She was shocked he'd had the nerve to face her after what he did. But if he thought he'd see her pining for him after all these years, he would find he was sadly mistaken. She'd meet him, but not yet. She needed to catch her breath. She really thought he wouldn't have the nerve to show his face. "Later. I need to check in." She aimed a cool wave in his direction and went inside.

She paced her room in agitation. She'd made her excuses about freshening up, but she couldn't stay holed up here forever. She had to face him sooner or later. The phone on her bedside table rang. Her heart leaped, and she stared at it. It rang again, and she moved stiffly to answer it. "Hello," she said softly.

"Randi, we're all going out for supper. Meet us downstairs in five minutes." Lisa's voice didn't invite any disagreement.

"I'm really not hungry." Randi clutched the phone in a finger-whitening grip. Her heart began to pound. She'd managed to maintain her composure for a few minutes, but was she really ready for this?

"On second thought, I'll stop by and get you. Be right there."

The phone clicked in her ear, and Randi stared at it. She had to go. The decision to come here and face all of these memories had already been made. Cowardice now would serve nothing. Besides, Brock had probably moved on already. Maybe he even had a wife with him. Her heart sank at the thought. Knuckles rapped on the door, and she moved slowly to answer it.

She opened the door to Lisa's smile. "Let me get my purse," she told her. She would show them all that Brock Parker meant nothing to her. Nothing at all.

They walked down the hall to the elevators, and Randi couldn't help the question that bubbled to her lips. "Is. . .is Brock married?" Somehow she managed to keep her voice from trembling.

Lisa cut a sympathetic glance her way. "No. He asked the same about you. I told him about Paul."

Randi nodded. "Good." Maybe that would help Brock keep his distance. They stepped out of the elevator and walked toward the lobby. She felt as though she might suffocate any moment. Her heart seemed to leap right out of her chest at the sight of Brock's dark head. His hair was still curly and thick. He stood with his back to them and had not yet realized they had arrived.

92

She took a moment to inspect him for changes time had wrought, but he still looked just as good as he ever had. She swallowed hard and tried to compose her face into some kind of cool, disinterested smile.

"I'm starved. Let's go eat," Lisa said.

Brock turned immediately and looked straight into Randi's eyes. Their gazes locked, and Randi felt her smile falter. The lobby faded away, and all she could see was the intensity of Brock's gaze. It was as though the intervening years had never happened. The old chemistry was still there, for her at least. Had she ever really known Brock? She had never expected him to leave her without a word the way he did.

"You haven't changed a bit."

"You haven't, either," Randi managed through a tight chest. He looked just the same to her. He was a bit thinner, maybe, but he looked good. Entirely too good for her peace of mind. With a sinking heart, she realized this trip might fail to put the past to rest at all.

She was suddenly enveloped in a bear hug.

"Give me a kiss, you hussy, you." Will Michaels bent over her and placed a smacking kiss on her cheek.

She laughed and hugged him. "What would your wife say if she knew you went around kissing other women?"

"Ask her. She's right over there." Will released her and tugged her over to see his wife.

His wife, Ann, was smiling. "I'm used to his antics.

He's just a big kid, but he'd never look at another woman seriously. He knows he'd never live to enjoy it."

Will clapped a hand over his heart. "You know you have me around your little finger, my love."

From the expression in his eyes when he gazed at his wife, Randi realized the statement was true. She felt a wistful stab of envy. Would she ever find someone to look at her like that? And even if she did, could she ever really believe it? She found trust hard since Brock left her. If she had just known why, maybe she would have been able to move on.

She hugged the rest of the group. Steve beamed when she congratulated him on his newly expected baby, and he hugged Lisa with obvious pride. Karen Larson seemed reserved. She'd always been jealous of Randi since she'd had an eye on Brock herself. She didn't wear a ring, which surprised Randi. Karen was a lovely young woman with blond hair and big blue eyes. The guys had flocked around her in college. Professor Larry Dials looked a bit older with more head than hair showing on top, but his blue eyes still looked as though he was looking at something no one else could see. The other four had evidently not been able to make it.

"Are you ever going to feed me, or do I have to pass out from hunger right here on the spot?" Will's voice was plaintive. "I've been thinking about Eddie's steaks since we got the invitation."

"And we have a reservation," Lisa added. "We'd better get going."

They all piled into the van, and Randi found herself squashed up against Brock in the backseat. She could smell the spicy scent of his cologne, and the familiar fragrance made her mouth go dry with longing. She fiercely willed herself not to look at him. She would *not* allow herself to feel anything for him. All she wanted from him was to be left alone.

He put his arm up on the seat behind her head and shifted slightly. "Got enough room?"

She nodded, not trusting her voice to be steady. His breath ruffled her hair when he spoke, and she longed for him to put his arm around her shoulders and pull her close. The rest of the group chattered around them, but neither she nor Brock spoke again until they reached the restaurant. Will kept up a constant line of stories that had everyone laughing. He was becoming fairly well known as a meteorologist for a major television station in California, and Randi could see why. His engaging personality and ability to poke fun at himself drew others to him and always had. Lisa and Steve were also successful in their business and seemed happy and content. Only Karen held slightly aloof. She was the only one employed outside her field. She'd started out as a meteorologist but had soon moved up to news anchor on the evening news for her station in Connecticut.

Eddie's Grill had been a favorite spot of theirs whenever they passed through Wichita Falls in the old days. It hadn't changed much. The walls were pale lemon instead of green, but Eddie's steaks were still tender and delicious. In the restaurant Karen seated herself between Brock and Randi. She immediately engaged him in conversation, but Randi told herself she was glad. She didn't want to have to make polite conversation with him herself.

Once, her gaze collided with Brock's. The intensity in his eyes pierced her defenses, and she tried to avoid looking in his direction as much as possible. She couldn't help wondering if he'd come hoping to see her or wishing she'd stay away. Maybe he hadn't even given it any thought. Maybe he felt only indifference. The thought hurt. The moment of their linked gazes seemed to stretch out forever; then Karen touched his hand and drew his attention back to her.

On the way back to the hotel, Randi squeezed into the seat with Will and Ann. She didn't want a repeat of the trip to the restaurant. She felt so tongue-tied and skittish around Brock now.

Will gave her a penetrating glance and hugged her gently. "Hang in there, kiddo," he whispered. "It ain't over till the fat lady sings."

"Yes, I'm afraid it *is* over, Will. It was over long ago. I've just been too stupid to let go," Randi answered softly.

Ann squeezed her hand gently. "Will told me about the broken engagement. We've both been praying that this trip will bring healing to both of you."

Randi looked at her with surprise. "You're Christians? Will, you always said Christianity was a crutch."

He grinned sheepishly. "Yeah, I said that, but I was

blind. That's one reason I wanted to come to the reunion. I wanted to thank you and Brock for the witnesses you were to me in college. Things you said echoed in my mind for years. So, thanks, Randi. You made a difference in my life."

Heat rose in Randi's cheeks. "You're welcome." She wanted to cry with sudden joy. Those college years had accomplished something after all.

The van stopped in front of the hotel, and they all clambered out. Randi started for the door, but Brock put a restraining hand on her arm.

"I'd like to talk to you for a minute, Randi."

The touch of his fingers on her arm left a trail of heat. "I think you said it all five and half years ago, Brock, when you left me with a three-tiered cake to pay for. I really don't care to hear anything more now." She pulled her arm from his grasp and hurried inside. If he thought she cared why he'd left without a word, he would find he was mistaken. That pain was in the past, and she was determined to leave it there.

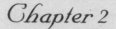

Chapter 2

CHASE LOG: *Monday, July 24. Satellite pictures show possible area of severe activity along a line extending from Joplin, MO, to Childress, TX.*

Randi pulled on her jeans and caught her dark curls up in a clip. Today they would take the van and go out on the road looking for storms. Yesterday they'd gone to church, then had lunch and spent the day around the pool. She'd talked to the women as much as possible to avoid any conversation with Brock. She'd been aware of his gaze several times, though.

She turned on the news, but the only possible hot spot was up into Oklahoma, so they would probably head up that way. Will would have more details on his computer's satellite uplink. She was determined to sit in the seat Brock *wasn't* in.

The rest of the group was clustered around the tables in the hospitality room eating the normal continental breakfast fare of muffins, bagels, and coffee. Randi grabbed an apple and some instant oatmeal and headed toward Lisa. Brock wasn't down yet, and she breathed a sigh of relief. The next two weeks would be a nightmare, she was sure of that.

Lisa smiled when she sat down. "I thought I might have to come drag you out of bed."

Randi took a bite of the crisp apple. "We about ready to go?" She was determined to show Brock and her friends that the past was firmly behind her. Paul had offered to come with her, and she was considering calling him and accepting his offer.

"Looks like we'll be heading into Oklahoma as soon as everyone is ready. It sounds like the weather could get nasty up there."

"We can only hope." Randi wasn't too optimistic, but they might at least get to see a multicell system. She was tired of sitting in a newsroom and looked forward to the opportunity of seeing developing weather of any kind. She caught a movement out the corner of her eye and turned. Brock was standing at the breakfast buffet. His dark hair gleamed from his morning shower, and even from four feet away, she caught a whiff of his cologne. She forced her gaze back to her oatmeal. She didn't want him to see her looking. She prayed fervently that he would sit at the other table.

But her prayers went unanswered. He dropped into the chair beside her. "Good morning."

"Morning," she murmured. She kept her gaze fixed on her bowl of cereal and didn't dare look his way.

"You're the last one up," Lisa told him. "We're going to be pulling out in about fifteen minutes." She got up. "I'm going to look through my room once more to make sure I haven't forgotten anything before I turn in my key."

Traitor, Randi thought when Lisa walked away. What on earth could she talk to Brock about? She sneaked a glance his way and caught him staring at her. He flushed and looked down. Randi struggled to keep her jaw from dropping. He was nervous! Calm, unflappable Brock Parker was actually showing his agitation. Her heart lightened a bit. It was about time *he* felt a little of the turmoil she'd gone through for over five years.

Brock cleared his throat. "So, how have you been?"

"Same as I was Saturday," she said coolly. "Fine. Busy."

He nodded. "I heard you were doing a great job at WKWB. Been there three years, right?"

She stared at him sharply. "How do you know that?"

"I've kept tabs." He stared down into his coffee cup.

She immediately went from nervous to angry. "I fail to see how you could possibly care enough to check up on my situation. You left me a month before our wedding, remember? If you had cared, you'd have at least stuck around and jilted me in person. You didn't even leave a note, Brock. I have not heard a word from you from that moment to this."

"It seemed best at the time." He raised impenetrable gray eyes and met her indignant gaze. "I'd like to explain it to you and ask your forgiveness."

She rose shakily. "Well, it's a little too late for regret now. I've done just fine without you the last five and a half years, and I'm *glad* I found out what kind of man you are before I married you. Marriage is for life, and you certainly showed your commitment colors early enough. For that I'm grateful. I couldn't live with a man I don't trust. I never would have dreamed I couldn't trust you, Brock. You showed me I was wrong." She stormed from the room and stopped by the front doors. Why had she ever come? She didn't want any expressions of remorse from him now. It was much too late for that. The wounds went too deep. There was no excuse for what Brock had done. No excuse whatsoever.

She had regained her composure by the time the rest of the team joined her by the door.

Will rubbed his hands together. "Okay, let's roll out into the wild blue yonder, gang. We're gonna see some action today!" It was the same litany he'd told them every morning of storm chasing in the old days.

Randi smiled at him. "I don't know, Will. Doppler seems to show a fairly calm day with just a chance of something developing up in Oklahoma. Better bring along a book to read."

He wriggled his nose like a rabbit. "I'm infallible, my sweet. The nose never lies. I predict a severe thunderstorm today, at the very least."

She punched him in the arm. "The nose has lied on many occasions."

"That's right," Ann agreed. "What about the time you told me you could smell a storm coming in, and we'd better stay on the island where we went for a picnic? It was all a ploy to have me at your mercy."

"I was a perfect gentleman," he objected. "My nose knew it was the day to propose."

Randi chuckled. Their lighthearted banter would keep her from dwelling on what Brock had said. She glanced at him through her lashes. He stood talking to Karen, and she felt a shaft of jealousy. Their disagreement didn't seem to have fazed him at all. If his insides were churning like hers, he didn't show it. Karen laid a graceful hand on Brock's arm and laughed up into his face. He smiled, and they both started toward the van that already held Lisa and Steve.

Randi stiffened her shoulders; why was she watching this scene? Clearly Karen and Brock were relishing each other's company. And why shouldn't they? They probably deserved one another.

She followed Will and Ann to the van and climbed into the backseat with them. Professor Dials sat beside Karen and Brock in the middle seat while Lisa and Steve took their familiar places as pilot and copilot. The hotel had agreed to allow them to leave their cars there until they got back.

They pulled out of the parking lot and headed north. Lisa popped in a CD, one of the old ones from their college days. It gave Randi a strange sense of déjà vu. The only thing different was that Brock wasn't in the backseat with her. Those days and weeks of storm chasing the summer before they were to be married were like being in a different world. They'd been in the backseat saying the sweet, loving things couples say. Making plans. Kids, professional plans, their dream house. . . Now it was all gone, like the morning mist.

The hours melted away in laughter and music. By lunchtime they were passing under darkening skies near Stillwater, Oklahoma. It was still hot and humid, in spite of the building thunderheads ahead. Will kept consulting his computer data with its satellite link while Lisa listened to the handheld scanner for current weather broadcasts.

"I think we're not going to get much more than a thunderstorm from this system," Lisa said. "I'm hungry. Let's stop for lunch."

They pulled up outside a fast-food restaurant and parked. Filing into the restaurant, Randi was very conscious of Brock following her. Waiting in line, he stood closer than was necessary. Her stomach clenched at his nearness. She remembered leaning back against his chest in other lines they'd stood in. Like the one to apply for their marriage license. She bit her lip and pointedly ignored him.

They got their food and found some adjoining booths near the window. Karen called Brock over to sit with her, and Randi slid in next to Lisa.

"Are you just going to let her monopolize Brock?" Lisa frowned and worked at cutting the pieces of chicken in her salad.

"He's a free man. That's obviously the way he wanted it." Randi popped her fork out of its plastic wrap and stabbed at her salad.

"Aren't you even the least bit curious about what happened? Don't you care enough to find out the truth?"

There was a hidden knowledge in Lisa's eyes, and Randi suddenly felt betrayed. "You know, don't you? You've known all along, and you kept it from me." The incredulous words burst from her lips. Lisa didn't have to answer. The truth was in her eyes.

Lisa hesitated then cast her gaze back to her plate. "I don't want to talk about it."

"You're the one who brought it up." Randi's voice rose, and she clenched her napkin in her fist. "How could you let me go through the agony of not knowing all these years when you knew all along?" This betrayal felt almost as bad as Brock's had.

"You need to talk to Brock," Lisa said. "It's not my place to tell you."

"I thought you were my friend!" She threw her napkin on the table and stalked outside. She couldn't believe it. Lisa had been her best friend in school, and they still kept in touch. How could she have stood by and watched her suffer when she could have at least explained the situation? She still remembered the shock of going to pick Brock up at his apartment and finding it empty. His landlady had told her he'd left the night before. She'd frantically looked for a note or a message, but there had been nothing. Nothing but silence. And Lisa had known all along. The betrayal was bitter.

Randi felt suffocatingly hot, but it wasn't just from the press of humid air. She would just leave. She would catch a train or a bus back to her car in Wichita Falls and head for home. Back to her familiar surroundings, her predictable job, and even more predictable future. She pressed her lips together and marched toward the van to get her luggage. The hot pavement crackled under her feet, and the stench of tar added to the soul sickness she felt. She didn't know if she wanted to cry or scream in anger. This had been a mistake. She should have known she could never go back. The past had been too painful and humiliating.

She jerked on the van door and stamped her foot in frustration when she discovered it was locked. The equipment was much too valuable to leave unlocked, but right now she didn't care. She wanted to get out of here *now*. She bit her lip. She'd just have to go ask Steve for the key. She headed back toward the door, but before she could enter the rest of the group came rushing out talking excitedly.

Confused, she stood in their path. Will saw her puzzled look. "Don't just stand there, woman! Haven't you looked at the horizon since you've been out here?" He gave her a nudge and pointed to the north of them.

The dark cloud he'd pointed out loomed to their northeast. Flashes of lightning lit its underbelly, and its towering height with shafts of sunlight piercing through in places was a beautiful sight. "Just a thunderstorm," she said analytically. "We won't find a tornado in there."

"Since when are you interested only in tornadoes?" Brock gave her a gentle shove toward the van. "I brought my camera to take all kinds of weather pictures. We should get some good lightning shots from this thing. Let's go."

Randi thought of protesting and grabbing her suitcase, but she didn't want to make a scene with everyone there. She climbed back into the van, and they took off in pursuit of the storm. She'd somehow ended up beside Brock. The excitement in the van was running high. She'd forgotten how much fun storm chasing was.

They drove into the fleeing storm and left the sunshine behind them. The van shook with the booms of thunder. Brock had his head and arm half out of the window while he snapped pictures of the storms. "I have a web site for kids, and they love all kinds of pictures of violent weather. Tornadoes are their favorite, of course, but they gobble up lightning, floods, and hurricanes, too."

The rain hadn't begun yet, so they stopped the van. Will and Steve took some readings while the women stayed in the vehicle. Brock slid open the side door and got out. Randi followed him into the storm. She took every opportunity to be out in the elements. A flash of lightning struck a tree about a mile away, and she clutched his arm involuntarily. He glanced down at her, and she caught her breath at the tenderness she saw in his eyes. It was gone a moment later, and she wondered if she'd imagined it.

"Still haven't conquered that fear of lightning, Randi?" A smile tugged at his lips.

She shook her head ruefully. "No matter how hard I try, it still scares me."

"I love it. I sometimes imagine a great battle between the heavenly hosts taking place. The sparks from their swords is the lightning, and their roars echo in the thunder." His smile came then. "Fanciful, aren't I?"

"I never knew you had such a poetic bent," she said.

His smile faded. "There are other things you don't know about me."

"I already know more than I want to know. I've learned some hard lessons in these years, Brock, and you've taught me the hardest ones. I've learned to stand on my own, not to lean on anyone, and that loving words don't mean much. Maybe I should thank you." She dragged her gaze from his and stared up into the clouds.

"You'll have to stop running from this sooner or later, Randi. I'm not giving up until I explain what happened."

She turned back to him then. "You know, Brock, a few years ago I would have given anything, anything at all, to know why you would leave me without a word like that. But I just really don't care anymore. I've put it behind me. I suggest you do the same." The words were a lie, but Brock didn't have to know that. She longed, *craved* to know, but could she stand to hear the truth? There had to have been something wrong with her for him to leave like that.

He paled at her blunt words but answered her softly. "All the same, I have to tell you."

She shrugged. "I had a few things to tell you, too, but since you didn't leave a forwarding address, I never got the chance." She wasn't quite sure how she was managing to maintain her iron control, but she knew that if she gave any indication of softness, she was doomed. She couldn't let any tender feelings for him show through. They had to be dug out and eradicated if she had any hope of ever finding a life with someone else. She didn't trust Brock, she couldn't. The hurt went too deeply.

The lightning moved closer. "We'd better get back in the van."

He nodded. They had just climbed back inside when the rain started. It pounded down on the roof of the van, making further conversation impossible without shouting. Randi was grateful for the respite. She needed some breathing space to marshal her defenses again. She drew as far away from Brock as possible and huddled against the wall of the van. Leaning her head against the window, she fell asleep to the sound of the rain.

She awoke with a start. The van had stopped outside their hotel, and her head rested comfortably against a warm shoulder. Brock's shoulder. She jerked away, her face flaming with mortification. Brock was still asleep. She studied his relaxed face a moment. The tension was gone from his jaw, and his lips were curved in a partial smile. He looked content. Randi felt anything but content.

"Hey, sleepyheads, we're home," Will called from the seat in front of them. "Everyone but me and Steve slept all the way. I think you'll have to pay a penalty. A match to the death of Trivia Chase."

"Oh, no," Karen groaned. "Not Trivia Chase."

Will rubbed his hands together with relish. "Ann and I will beat you so badly, you'll wonder why you ever agreed to play."

"We haven't agreed to play," Randi pointed out. She brushed her curls out of her face and stretched. "I haven't played since, well, since college."

Will pointed a finger at her. "You are ripe for the picking, my girl. Pick your partner, and the tournament will begin over supper. We're ordering in pizza."

"I pick Professor Dials, then. I need someone who knows something."

"That won't save you, my girl." Will gave a fake evil laugh. "You're doomed."

Doomed was how she felt, and it had nothing to do with playing the game. They got out of the van and ran through the drenching rain to the hotel. They departed to their rooms to change into dry clothes and meet back at Steve and Lisa's suite. Randi kicked her wet sneakers off then noticed the message light was blinking on her phone. She punched the button to listen.

Paul's deep voice came on. "Hey, sweet thing. I'm being sent on location to Dallas on Wednesday and wondered if I could tag along with you tomorrow. If I

don't hear from you by noon, I'll be there by six tonight.
I'll rent a car and meet you at the hotel. See ya."

She glanced at her watch. It was already 5:30. He'd
likely be here any time. She felt a sense of relief that he
was coming. It would be easier to avoid Brock if she had
Paul to entertain. And he was lots of fun. She hurried
to the bathroom and fluffed her dark curls then quickly
pulled on a pair of dry jeans and a T-shirt. Maybe Brock
would take a hint when he saw Paul was interested
enough to come here to find her.

At ten after six Randi's phone rang. She snatched it
up. "Paul?"

"I'm here, darling girl. I'm in room two twenty-
five. Where are you?"

She laughed. "I'm right across the hall. Are you up
for a game of Trivia Chase and pizza?"

He groaned. "Isn't that a bit juvenile? I hate games."

His tone put her back up immediately. These were
her friends, and he was showing up uninvited. What
right did he have to criticize? "I'm going in fifteen
minutes. I can call you when I get back." She felt a bit
deflated. She'd been looking forward to showing him
off to her friends, even if it was only a way to deflect
Brock's determination to talk to her.

He sighed. "I'll go with you. I'm ready now."

"Be right there." She hung up the phone and went
across the hall. Paul opened the door at her first knock.
He stood five-ten with light brown hair and dark blue
eyes; he looked terrific to Randi. He always dressed

with meticulous care, and today was no exception.

He swept her into a hug. "I've missed you."

Randi hugged him back. Why didn't she feel the same way in Paul's arms that she did in Brock's? Just sitting beside Brock in the van had been like coming home from a long trip. She pulled away. "It was nice of you to come."

He kept his hands on her shoulders and studied her face. "Something is different. What's wrong?"

She gave a light laugh. "Nothing's wrong. Whatever do you mean? I've only been gone three days. You're imagining things." She pulled out of his grasp and turned to the door. "Let's go. You'll be odd man out, but you can play with me and Professor."

He groaned again. "I hate Trivia Chase. It just shows you how crazy I am about you." He gripped her arm and pulled her back around to face him again. "Have you thought any more about our talk?"

"Paul, you just got here. Don't start badgering me already!" Randi couldn't help the defensive tone that crept into her voice. He'd asked her to marry him over a month ago, and she had told him she had to think about it. But she'd done everything *except* think about it. She didn't want to even face the thought of making preparations for another wedding.

He put up his hands defensively. "All right, I'm sorry. But you have to give me an answer sometime, Randi. I won't wait forever." His back stiff with anger, he opened the door. "After you," he said distantly.

Randi sighed and led the way down the hall. She stopped at room 247 and knocked. The laughter didn't stop, but the door swung open.

"Randi, it's about time. I need reinforcements." Lisa's smile faded when she saw Paul behind Randi. "Oh, I'm sorry. I didn't know we had a visitor."

"This is Paul Minton," Randi announced.

Brock's head shot up at the name, and he gave Paul a penetrating glance. Randi was thankful Paul didn't notice. She introduced him to everyone, while Lisa ordered the pizza.

"It will be here in forty-five minutes. We should be able to get a round of Trivia Chase in before it gets here," Lisa announced. She sat on the edge of the bed and patted the space beside her. "Sit here with me, Steve. We're married, so it's legal if we sit on the bed together." Her husband obeyed with a grin.

"My team claims the couch," Randi said. She flopped down into it, and Paul sat beside her. Professor Dials decided to read the questions since there was an odd number of players.

Brock and Karen went first.

"How many days elapsed between the bombings of Hiroshima and Nagasaki?" The professor pushed his glasses up on his nose and smiled. "I know this one."

"Three?" Brock asked Karen.

"I was thinking one," she said.

"One," Brock told Professor Dials.

"You had it right, Brock. Three."

The rest of the group groaned, but Brock just grinned and shrugged. "Better luck next time. It was a good guess, Karen."

"Randi, your team gets to go next. Here, roll." Professor Dials tossed her the dice, and she rolled. "What Wild West marshal died in his sleep in Los Angeles in 1929?"

Behind him Brock began to hum a quiz show theme song.

"Don't rush me! It has to be either Wyatt Earp or Bat Masterson," she said.

"I think it was Wyatt Earp," Paul said.

"I think it was Bat Masterson." Randi sucked on her bottom lip. "Bat Masterson," she said decisively.

"Sorry, you lose. You do not pass Go, you do not collect two hundred dollars," Brock said. "It's Wyatt Earp."

"I *told* you the answer, Randi!" Paul said sharply.

And the evening progressed downhill from there. Paul forcefully expressed his opinion on every answer, and when he was wrong, became defensive. The rest of the group tried not to let his attitude spoil their fun, but Randi could tell Paul's presence put a damper on the evening. She couldn't help comparing Brock and Paul. She'd forgotten how even-tempered Brock was, how quickly he gave encouragement. Paul became red-faced and angry as they fell behind. She'd never seen that side of him before. No wonder he hated games. She made her excuses as soon as the last game was over.

Paul was still sulking as they went down the hall

toward their rooms. "Are you going to come in for a while?" he asked.

"I'm tired," she said. "What time do you leave in the morning?"

"I had planned to go with you to do a bit of storm chasing tomorrow." A scowl darkened his face.

"There isn't room in the van for another person," she said. "I'm sorry to be abrupt, but I have an answer, Paul. The answer is no, I can't marry you."

Color surged into his face, and he scowled. "Why? Is it that Brock person? I saw the way you looked at him."

Was she that obvious? She shook her head wearily. "Don't blame anyone, Paul. I just realized tonight that I couldn't marry you. I want someone who keeps smiling when the times get rough, who doesn't blame others for every little mistake. That's not you."

"You'll regret this, Randi," he said through gritted teeth. "I have clout at the station. You can't toy with my affections like this, then toss me aside."

Randi suppressed a smile. That sounded more like a line a woman would say.

He saw the suppressed merriment, and his face went beet red. "I wouldn't count on a job when you get back! Then we'll see what you have to smile about."

"Is he giving you a hard time, Randi?" Brock had materialized out of nowhere. He took a step closer and addressed Paul. "I think you'd better back off."

Paul gave him a frustrated shove. "*You* back off, hotshot."

Brock stood his ground. He didn't shove back or get angry but answered Paul quietly. "I'll see Randi to her room. I think when you've had time to consider your manners, you'll want to apologize to her." He took Randi's elbow and guided her down the hall. At the end of the hall, he turned and added a parting shot. "Oh, and I'd think again about getting her canned. I was a witness to your sexual harassment. I don't think the station would take kindly to dealing with a lawsuit."

She felt numb. She would never have imagined there was a side like this to Paul. On their dates and at the station he was urbane and solicitous of her comfort. She felt sick at the thought that she had been actually thinking of marrying him. They stopped at her door, and she unlocked her room.

"Thanks," she said. "It was getting ugly, and I didn't know how to end it."

"A soft answer turns away wrath," he said with a grin. "Glad I could help."

She stood staring up into his eyes for a moment. In a bolt of illumination, she knew she still loved Brock and always would. She didn't know what had happened, and she was afraid to find out. Afraid he'd left because she was inadequate in some way. He wanted to tell her, but she didn't think she was ready to hear about it yet. She wished it could be for some reason that could be worked out, but she knew Brock wasn't a quitter. If it could be fixed, he would have fixed it.

She shut the door behind her and leaned against it.

Another moment and she would have flung herself into Brock's arms and begged him to love her again. She couldn't do that. He could never know how much he had hurt her.

Chapter 3

C HASE LOG: *Tuesday, July 25. Hot and humid with no chance of rain in the forecast....*

The next day was sunny and warm. The rest of the group looked gloomy when they met in the lounge for breakfast. Against her will, her gaze found Brock. He looked back with those impenetrable gray eyes.

"What's everyone so glum about?" Randi asked. "It's a beautiful day to spend together. Let's get going!"

Brock smiled. "No storms in the forecast. Not even a smidge of rain. Nada. Not even my suggestion was met with enthusiasm after that daunting news. They only want a storm."

"What was your suggestion?"

"Here we are in Wichita Falls. What better place to find a dude ranch and go horseback riding?"

"That's a great idea! Come on, guys, it will be fun. When was the last time you were on a horse?" Randi was immediately enthusiastic.

"Uh, try never," Karen said. "But I'm willing to do whatever the group wants."

"Oh, all right," Will grumbled. "We'll give in gracefully. I'll check at the front desk and see where they suggest." He went off to find directions.

An hour later they were heading out of the city and down a dirt road. They passed under a crossbar that read TRAVIS RANCH. A quaint ranch home with paddocks and several barns and outbuildings sat at the top of a knoll overlooking a small valley.

A rangy man of an indeterminate age welcomed them on the porch. "The name's Murphy," he said. "You must be the weathermen bunch. How many of you have ever ridden a horse before?"

Two hands went up, Brock's and Randi's. "Hmm. Well, I'll give you some gentle ladies then."

He led them to the barn and helped them mount. Randi was thankful they were all able to hold their laughter when Professor Dials needed a step to get into the saddle. He was mounted on a huge mule. Murphy swung onto his buckskin and led the way down the trail.

"There's an advanced group leaving for a trip in ten minutes. You're welcome to join them while I take these tenderfoots out," Murphy said, looking at Brock and Randi. "I can tell you're no strangers to the saddle."

Randi wanted to stay with the group where she felt safe, but before she could refuse his offer, Brock broke in. "Thanks. Where do we wait?"

"Over by the tree yonder." He pointed one gnarled

finger toward a twisted mesquite tree on the other side of the corral. "Sam will be along right shortly."

Randi watched them go with a feeling of both dread and exhilaration. Karen looked back with an expression of displeasure on her lovely face. She'd managed to monopolize Brock pretty well the past few days.

"Let's wait in the shade," Brock said. He urged his horse across the corral, and Randi followed. He rode his horse easily, his knees hugging the mare's belly.

"You look like you still ride a lot," Randi said. She bit her lip at the impetuous words. She didn't want to bring up the past. It would be best if Brock didn't know she still remembered everything about him.

He didn't seem to notice her discomfiture. "I do. I try to take kids out one Saturday a month. I'm involved in the Big Brothers/Big Sisters group in Tampa. Kids love to ride."

Randi nodded. "I've been meaning to volunteer, but there never seems to be time." She knew the words sounded lame. She needed to make the time to help others, but she'd been too lost in her own misery to care much about others. Brock had obviously moved on. She needed to do the same.

The prescribed ten minutes came and went with no sign of Sam. "I think we've been left," Brock said. "Want to explore on our own?"

She hesitated. "We might get in trouble."

"Hey, we're paying for the horses by the hour. I'm tired of sitting here." He wheeled his mare around and started down the trail behind the tree. "Where's your sense of adventure? There are new horizons to discover."

She smiled and relaxed in spite of herself. She was willing to call a truce for the day, if he was. "Lead on, Wild Bill Hickock."

He stopped short at the familiar nickname and grinned. "I'd forgotten you called me that."

She looked away quickly. "Old habits die hard." She followed him across plains of rocky red clay scattered with yucca and creosote bushes. The hot sun felt good on her arms at first, but she was soon perspiring and wishing for a tall glass of water. The temperature had to be over one hundred.

They rounded an outcropping of rock, and Brock reined in his mare. "Look! A dust devil."

From out of clear blue sky a funnel of dust and debris swirled in front of them. This was the closest Randi had ever been to one. It was a large one, as dust devils go, and spun crazily toward them.

Brock dismounted. "I've always wanted to try to get inside one. You game?"

Randi stared at the vortex doubtfully. "Is it safe?"

"The wind velocities can't be high enough to hurt us. Come on, Calamity Jane."

Now it was her turn to smile at the nickname. She couldn't remember anymore how they started calling each other Wild Bill and Calamity Jane. It had been years since she had thought of it. She stared at the dust devil then back at Brock again. "Okay, but if I get hurt, you have to pay the doctor bill." She slid to the ground, and they approached the dust devil slowly.

Close up, it looked even bigger. Brock took her hand, and she curled her fingers around his instinctively. He was smiling that daredevil smile that used to bring her heart to her mouth. Time hadn't diminished her reaction.

"Ready? Let's run right through the dust and into the center." He waited for her nod, and they dashed into the dust devil.

Tiny pellets of sand and dust stung her skin, then they were through the outer wall and in the center. There was no wind resistance in the hollow eight-foot cylinder. An eerie orange hue illuminated the interior. It was suffocatingly hot, and Randi looked up to see the vortex twisting like a long snake until it disappeared into the clear blue sky. A sound like wheat being beaten pounded in her ears, and in the circulation wall around them she saw tumbleweeds and newspaper, as well as the ever-present red dust. She looked at Brock and saw him smiling widely. He was totally in his element. Beads of perspiration had popped out on his forehead from the heat, and Randi could feel droplets on her own brow. It was difficult to breathe.

He drew her with him and walked around the center a few moments. "Awesome, isn't it?" He had to raise his voice to be heard above the noise of the vortex.

She nodded. She looked up again, awestruck at the sight of the vortex disappearing into blue sky. She felt as though she could almost see into heaven. The dust devil made a zigzag, and one wall crashed into them. Randi's mouth was full of dust, then suddenly, they were free of the vortex and it dissipated, leaving only debris behind it. She was still clutching Brock's hand, and she quickly dropped it.

Brock stared down at her then tucked a stray curl behind her ear. "I really want to talk to you, Randi. Are you ready to listen yet?"

No. Yes. The conflicting emotions gripped her throat, and she couldn't speak. She swallowed hard and nodded. She couldn't avoid it forever.

✧

They rode out to the Red River and dismounted. Brock dropped onto a nearby flat rock under an overhanging mesquite tree and patted the one beside him. He was reminded of the words of the song, "Red River Valley." *Come and sit by my side if you love me.* He had to tread carefully. She must never know how much he still loved her, how much he yearned to make her his wife. It could never be, but she did deserve as much of the truth as he could tell her.

She dropped beside him and sat with her hands in her lap. That was the first thing he'd noticed about her —her stillness. She didn't fidget or complain during those long days of storm chasing. Her dark brown eyes were huge with trepidation, and he smiled reassuringly. "Don't look so scared. I'll try to be brief."

She nodded and waited quietly for him to begin.

"I was a fool to leave without an explanation, Randi.

I was in an emotional tailspin and just wasn't thinking clearly." He raked a hand through his hair.

"What you did was inexcusable, Brock," she said when he fell silent. "It was cowardly and crushing."

He nodded. "I realize that now. Please, just hear me out. I had been keeping a secret from you, and I realized I couldn't keep it any longer."

She raised her eyebrows at his admission. "Well, you certainly have kept it all these years. I never got one word from you, let alone a confession."

"I have leukemia." He decided to cut right through to the heart and quit skirting the issue. Maybe she would listen to the whole story then.

That stopped her. Her mouth dropped open, and she gasped. Her expression changed to shock and disbelief. She gripped her hands together and terror raced over her face. She started to speak, but no words came. She swallowed and tried again. "How long do you have?"

He gave a short laugh. "Actually, I'm in remission. I responded well to the treatment and went into remission almost immediately."

He didn't get the reaction he expected. She stared at him for a long moment then stood. Her face white with rage, she shoved him off the rock. He landed in the red dust and looked up in bewilderment. He'd expected tears, sorrow, and pity.

"You just decided for me, is that it?" she demanded. "I can see it now. You wanted to spare me, right? You idiot!" Arms waving in agitation, she paced around him.

"The great Brock Parker was too big to need help. How dare you make a decision like that on your own!"

Too shocked to do more than watch her stalk around him, he finally got to his feet. "I didn't want you to have to nurse me as I got sicker and sicker. I thought leukemia was a death sentence and you would be a widow in your twenties. I thought the kindest thing would be to make a clean break and let you get on with your life."

She gave a derisive laugh. "A clean break? Is that what you call it? I would have said you left a gaping wound. Did you have so little faith in me and in our love that you could just walk away without giving me a chance to decide what I wanted?"

"I'd just gotten the doctor's diagnosis and wasn't thinking clearly. And you would have stayed with me," he said. "You know you would have."

She nodded. "Yes, of course. And you're still here. We would have had at least five years together. For how long have you been in remission?"

"Five years."

"Five years. Does that mean you're cured?"

He shook his head. "I don't know. That's what the doctor says. After five years, they call it a cure, but they'll always have to monitor me to see how I'm doing. I'll probably have to take medication the rest of my life. However long or short that may be."

She stared at him. "So what you're saying is that you wrecked our lives and now you're not even dying?"

"You sound disappointed." She had him totally

bewildered. He'd expected tears, at the very least. He'd been prepared for tears.

"Of course, I'm glad you're doing so well. But you destroyed our lives on the mistaken notion that you were dying. Don't you find that just the least bit ironic? And you've been in remission five years. Why are you just now looking for forgiveness?"

"I've started to pick up the phone many times but wasn't sure what to say. And to be honest, I wasn't ready to tell you about the leukemia. I didn't want pity, but I do want your forgiveness for the way I hurt you."

She stared at him and shook her head. "I don't know, Brock. I've asked God over and over to help me to forgive you, forget you, and get on with my life. I just haven't been able to do it yet. Are you asking me to take up where we left off? I don't think I can do that."

"No!" He saw her flinch and softened his tone. "I mean, I'll always care about you, of course, but we've both changed. I just want us both to move on from here and forget the past." He had to make sure she didn't suspect he still cared. Although, she seemed to have nothing but contempt left for him, anyway.

She nodded slowly. "I guess I'm still in shock. Of all the reasons I thought you might give, something like this never crossed my mind. I thought you'd gotten cold feet, or another woman had returned from your past, or even maybe you'd been called away by an emergency and had grown away from me, but nothing like this."

He squeezed her hand and fought the impulse to

take her in his arms. He couldn't show his love. The future was too uncertain. After all the pain of the past five and a half years, he couldn't put her back into the same situation. "We'd better be heading back. They'll be wondering where we are." He held her hand and walked her to the horses. They mounted, and he led the way back to the ranch.

❧

Randi felt as though her smile was frozen in place. When they reached the ranch, the rest of the group was waiting on the porch with glasses of lemonade. No one seemed to notice the pain behind the smile. Even as she laughed and talked with her friends, she tried to get her thoughts around the reality of what Brock had told her. *Leukemia!* The very word was terrifying. She would have insisted on staying with him, she knew that. But would she have been strong enough to handle the day-to-day medical problems, the pain of seeing him suffer? And she was smart enough to know that even remission didn't usually last forever. Tears stung the back of her throat. The thought of Brock's dying took her breath away. How did you watch a loved one suffer?

She'd actually asked him if he wanted to take up where they left off! Squirming inwardly with mortification, she castigated herself for practically throwing herself at his feet. He'd denied that idea quickly. What would she have done if he'd said yes? She needed to think very carefully about all of this. One thing she did know, he should have told her. She was no child, to be spared every heartache. If that was Brock's idea of love, it was a good thing they had not married.

They were all tired when they piled back into the van. Only Lisa seemed to realize something had taken place. A question in her eyes, she kept glancing at Randi. When they reached the hotel, Randi told them she had a headache and went to her room.

She took some aspirin and lay on the bed, but she couldn't sleep. She lay there with her eyes open, staring at the ceiling. Was Brock going to die? She couldn't bear the thought. She was just so confused. She felt a mixture of sorrow and rage. She should have been there for him all these years, but he had robbed her of that. He should have talked to her about it, but if he did it because he truly loved her and wanted to spare her, she had to let it go. It hadn't been because he didn't love her. The knowledge brought some relief. She hadn't been able to allow herself to love another man because she thought there was something wrong with her. For the first time in over five years, she felt free of the chains that had bound her.

Tears leaked from her eyes, and the ceiling fixture grew blurry. Sometimes she had felt her life was blurry and without meaning. Walled off from the possibility of hurt, she was also barricaded against future joy. She knew it but had seemed helpless to change it. The familiar adage, "The truth will set you free," was right. Someone knocked at the door, and she swiped at the tears with the back of her hand. Getting to her feet, she smoothed her unruly hair and hurried to the door.

"Hi," Lisa said. "Can we talk for a minute?" She didn't wait for Randi's invitation but brushed past her. She walked into the room and sat in the chair at the table by the window.

Randi shut the door and followed her slowly. She was in no mood to talk, but Lisa hadn't left her with a choice. She sat in the other chair.

"Brock told you, didn't he?"

Randi nodded.

"I knew it! You looked different when you came back. Are you all right?" She leaned forward and touched Randi's hand.

"I don't quite know what to think," Randi admitted after a long pause. "I'm still reeling from finding out he has leukemia. He looks so healthy. And I'm angry that he would make the decision for our lives without even talking to me about it."

"You still love him." The statement wasn't a question.

Randi stared down at her hands. "Yes," she whispered after a long moment of silence. "I probably always will. But maybe he was right. I don't know how I could watch him every day and wonder if the cancer would come back, if he would be gone by this time next year. It would be hard."

"How do any of us know how long the Lord will give us?" Lisa said. "Every breath we take could be our last. We live every day to the fullest and try to leave a mark for God. What more can we ask?"

"I don't know if I'm strong enough," Randi admitted.

"What you say is true, but maybe Brock recognized something in me and knew I couldn't handle it."

Lisa gave an exasperated sigh. "You two were meant to be together. It has to mean something that neither of you has been able to forget."

"I don't think Brock was looking. He seems determined to deal with this alone."

"Then you have to change his mind."

"I don't know if I can, or if it would even be for the best. I'm going to have to pray about it. Going back may not be the best thing for either of us." Only God could untangle this mess. What was the right thing to do?

Lisa nodded. "God will tell you what's right for both of you." She stood and walked to the door. "Let's go to supper."

They went out to a local Mexican restaurant. Randi found her gaze straying to Brock too often for her peace of mind. She didn't like the feelings of jealousy that rose when she saw Karen's blond head close to Brock's dark one. She forced herself to laugh and chatter with Will and Ann as though nothing were wrong.

Chapter 4

CHASE LOG: *Wednesday, July 28. High probability for severe weather in a line extending from Oakey, KS, to Albuquerque, NM. . .*

The next day Randi awoke to sunshine. She hurriedly showered and dried her hair. The rest of the group was waiting at the front door. Ann thrust a paper plate with a warm bagel at her, and Will handed her a cup of coffee.

"Let's go!" Brock said. "We're missing the good stuff. Wait till you see the forecast. You can eat breakfast in the van."

They hurried to the van. Randi climbed in and found Brock right beside her. Karen got in and sat beside Brock, too.

"Where are we headed today?" Randi balanced her paper plate on her knee and took a bite of bagel. "Um, it's warm. Someone toasted it for me."

"I did," he said. "And I put strawberry jam and

cream cheese on it."

"You know me too well," she said.

He smiled slightly and looked away.

So much for trying to see how he really felt. She still wasn't sure what she should do. She'd spent the night tossing and turning. Near dawn she'd decided she would try to determine exactly how Brock felt before she made any decisions. Once that was decided, she drifted off to sleep for a few scant hours before the alarm went off.

Lisa turned up the CD player. One of her favorite Christian artists was singing. Randi felt like she really was going on a great adventure into the glorious unknown this morning as Steve and Lisa sang along. Life seemed fresh and new again. Funny how things changed just knowing Brock hadn't left because he had found he couldn't live with her. And the doctor said he was cured, whatever that meant.

They headed west toward Amarillo. Will downloaded some data from the weather satellite. "Looks good for this afternoon. We have a moderate risk for some severe weather developing toward New Mexico." He stretched. "We've got a long day ahead of us. You up for our game?" He didn't wait for an answer. "I'm going on a storm chase, and I'm bringing a barometer."

Brock groaned. "I haven't played that game since school. Do we have to?"

"Yep," Will said. "Your turn, Ann."

"I'm not a meteorologist," Ann said. "You can skip me. Your turn, Professor."

"I'm going on a storm chase, and I'm bringing a downdraft," he said.

Karen yawned. "How juvenile."

"Come on, you gotta play," Will said. "You just can't think of anything. You've been too busy playing glamour girl to the camera to remember your training."

Karen bristled. "Fine. I'm going on a storm chase, and I'm bringing an anemometer."

Brock grinned. "Good one. You can still pronounce it." He looked at Randi. "Your turn."

"I'm going on a storm chase, and I'm bringing hail," she said.

"Oh, you think so? Pretty optimistic, aren't you?" Brock put his arm along the back of the seat. "I'm going on a storm chase, and I'm bringing a van full of meteorologists."

They spent the rest of the morning in easy camaraderie laughing when Will and Brock began to say they were bringing things like pool balls and underwear. By noon they were on the other side of Amarillo. The sky to the west was beginning to darken.

Brock peered out the window. "Looks like a classic supercell storm. Inflow looks good and there are some scud cloud fragments. We may see some hail soon."

He had no sooner said the words than the hail started. It thudded against the top of the van, and wind gusts shook the vehicle. Steve pulled to the side of the road. Thunder rumbled overhead, and lightning flashed then struck a tree about fifty feet away.

Will jerked the earphones for the scanner out of his ears. "That was close. I got interference from that." He didn't put the earphones back in.

"Look!" Brock pointed. "The wall cloud is lowering. We'd better get out of here. It looks like it's changed direction and is coming right over us."

Steve nodded and gunned the engine. The tires squealed and the van fishtailed before righting itself and shooting ahead. Overhead, the storm raced toward them.

Looking out, Randi could see a pair of "Saturn rings" circled the body of the storm, indicating rotation. The huge anvil-shaped cloud towered up, its thick edges lined with knuckle-like features. "The wall cloud is rotating!"

Wind rammed the van, and Steve fought for control. Then suddenly, every piece of paper began to float as though suspended in zero gravity. The pages of the chase diary in Brock's lap began to turn one by one as though by an unseen hand.

Horror gripped Randi's throat. They were directly under a forming tornado. She looked at Brock and saw the knowledge in his eyes, too.

"Steve, get us out of here! Now!"

Steve gunned the engine again, but the van responded sluggishly as the wind buffeted it further. Suddenly, a thin appendage reached down from the wall cloud and kicked up red dirt.

"There's a ditch! We need to get to cover, Steve!" Brock shouted.

Steve screeched to a halt, and Brock slid open the door. "Go, go!" He grabbed Karen and Randi's arms and thrust them toward the deep ravine along the side of the road.

Randi ran with the wind to her back and fell into the ditch. She buried her face in her arms then looked up to see that the rest had made it out of the van. Steve and Lisa lay five feet away, and Professor Dials was just beyond them. Will, Ann, and Karen were on her other side. The small twister was now only about one hundred feet away. Frantic to see what Brock's position was, she got to her knees.

"Get down!"

Seconds later, Brock's body bore her to the ground and covered her. Grass and dust filled her mouth, and she turned her head. Brock's lips were against her ear.

"Don't worry. You'll be all right," he whispered.

The roar of the tornado nearly deafened his words, but he held her down firmly and protectively. In that moment, Randi knew he still loved her. He had given her up because he loved her, and he loved her still. Her heart sang with the knowledge.

Moments stretched to eternity, then the tornado was past them and spinning harmlessly off into the field. Another minute and it lifted back into the wall cloud. Brock sat up then helped her to her feet. They turned to look at the departing twister.

"Where's the camera when you need it?" Brock asked.

One by one, the rest of the group stood, brushing

the dust and debris from their clothes. They all looked shaken. Steve had his arm around Lisa, and she was holding her stomach.

"Are you all right?" Randi hurried to her friend.

"I don't know," Lisa admitted. "I'm having some cramps."

"We'd better get you to the doctor." Randi tried to hide her alarm.

"Is the van okay?" Steve looked around for his vehicle. It had been pushed several yards down the road, and was a bit battered, but seemed to be in one piece. He helped his wife into the front passenger seat and hurried to the driver's side.

The rest of them piled in quickly, and Steve turned the key. The engine turned over and sputtered, but then caught and roared to life. He floored the gas pedal and sped back toward Amarillo.

Randi leaned forward and gripped Lisa's hand. "Hang on. We'll be there soon."

Beads of perspiration on her brow, Lisa nodded. She held tightly to Randi's hand and bit her lip. "I'm losing the baby, aren't I?"

"Maybe not," Randi said soothingly. "Don't borrow trouble. We'll see what the doctor says." She was afraid Lisa was right. Praying fervently as the battered van sped through the traffic, she asked for the Lord to spare Lisa and Steve this grief.

Steve braked outside the emergency room of the hospital. Brock jumped out and ran inside for an aide.

When they had wheeled Lisa away, the rest of the chasers went to the waiting room.

"Let's get a cup of coffee," Randi told Brock.

"Anyone else want anything?" he asked.

"You could bring me back a cola," Will said.

"Anyone else?"

No one else seemed interested. Ann and Karen were talking quietly in the seating by the window, and Professor Dials looked through a magazine. Randi and Brock walked down the bustling halls. Nurses, their shoes squeaking on the tile floors, hurried by, and aides slipped past them with rattling trays of medicine.

"I hate hospitals," Brock remarked. "It seems most of my life has been spent in waiting rooms."

"I'd like to hear what it's been like for you," Randi said.

He made a face. "It's not interesting conversation," he said. "Lots of drugs and needles."

They got their coffee and found a secluded table in the corner. Randi pulled her chair closer to his, and he looked at her with his expression hooded. "Just what do the doctors say?"

He shrugged. "No one really knows. The survival rate has been steadily rising for leukemia, but every person is different. The chances are pretty good since I haven't come out of remission since I went in. My blood counts have been pretty stable."

Just being in this medical environment brought home to Randi what life would be like with Brock's illness.

The antiseptic smell and clinical feel would become very familiar, as familiar as her own home. She thought she could handle it, but how could she be sure? That moment in the ditch when she had feared they might all die, she had realized that whatever time they had left on this earth, she wanted to spend it with Brock. She knew it would be a battle to convince him, though.

She reached out and placed her hand on his cheek. He flinched as though she had struck him.

"Don't," he said softly. "I don't want your pity." He took her hand from his face and laid it on the table. "I'm all right, Randi. I'm not a stray dog who needs a home. We've grown away from each other. We can't go back, even if we wanted to. And I don't."

"Why did you cover me in the ditch, Brock?" His words stung, but she was determined to make him admit he still cared.

"It was just instinctive when you started to get up. Don't read more into it than it meant." His words were cool. "I would have done the same if it had been Karen or Ann."

Randi flinched at his words. Had she read more into it than the act warranted? She just didn't know. But she had to know the truth. She had to know if there was any hope for them at all. The chase would keep them together for the next week. She had until then to probe the old feelings and uncover what remained.

◈

Brock escorted Randi back to the waiting room. Steve

was still back with Lisa, so he sat beside Will. He had seen where Randi was headed with her questions and was thankful he'd been able to deflect her curiosity. He hoped that's all it was. She couldn't still care, could she? Not after what he'd done. If she did, he had to find a way to help her get on with her life and leave him as a fond memory. Coming here had probably been a mistake. He picked up a newspaper but found his thoughts drifting and put it back down restlessly.

The door opened, and Steve came out. His face was white with strain. Sinking into a chair beside Brock, he buried his face in his hands.

Brock put a hand on his shoulder, and the rest of the group huddled close around him. "How's Lisa?"

"She lost the baby," Steve said.

He raised his head, and the agonized expression on his face broke Brock's heart. "I'm sorry, buddy. How's Lisa taking it?"

"Like you'd expect." He raked a hand through his hair. "We're going to have to cut our storm-chasing days short, guys. I need to get Lisa home to recover. I hope you understand."

"Of course," Brock said. He squelched the stab of disappointment. It was best this way all around. Randi could put him behind her.

"Can I see her?" Randi asked.

"She was asking for you. Go on in." Steve rubbed his eyes wearily.

Randi touched his shoulder then hurried from the

room and slipped back into the emergency area. "I won't be long," she said before shutting the door behind her.

"Man, it hurts," Steve said. "We wanted this baby so much."

Brock had heard well-meaning people point out to other couples that they could have another baby. That didn't help now. *This* baby had meant something special to them. He just put his hand on Steve's shoulder. "You'll see the little one in heaven someday, Steve. I know that's not a lot of comfort right now. But the baby is with Jesus."

Steve looked up with a surprised look on his face. "You know, you're right. I really hadn't thought about it. With our culture, we get into the habit of forgetting the baby is already a person." He laid his hand over Brock's. "Thanks."

Randi was back a few minutes later. "She wants you, Steve."

He shot to his feet and hurried to his wife. Randi took his seat. "She doesn't want to go home yet," she told Brock. "She says she can't face the empty nursery yet. She wants to continue the chase."

"I think we've seen all the tornadoes we're going to see this trip," he said. "That small twister was more than I had even hoped to see in July."

She nodded. "But I hated to go back to work myself. If I even have a job, that is."

"What do you mean?"

"You heard Paul threaten to get me fired. He

could probably do it, too. He has a lot of clout with the producers."

"You don't sound worried."

"Oh, I'm not. I might quit it anyway. Anyone in your area hiring?"

The words were innocent, but Brock's heart began to thud in his ears. What did she mean? Was she really intending to continue to see him after this chase was over? He looked at her uncertainly and saw the twinkle in her eyes. He relaxed but couldn't help a niggle of disappointment. Disgusted with himself, he picked up the paper again. What did he want, anyway? For her to throw her life away on a man who didn't know from one year to the next how long he had to live? What kind of love was that?

❧

They were all tired by the time they got back to the hotel. Lisa cried most of the way. She sat in the second seat with Randi and Ann while Brock took the copilot seat. Randi and Ann offered what comfort they could and prayed with her several times. Randi knew it would take time to heal. Lisa wasn't very far along, so she would heal quickly, at least physically. The emotional scars would take longer. The doctor had said they could try again in a couple of months.

It was nearly eleven by the time Randi got to her room. She shut the door wearily and kicked off her shoes. Her message light was blinking, and she grimaced. Surely it wasn't Paul again after the way they'd parted.

She picked up the receiver and punched the button.

Her sister's voice came on. "Hi! I just wondered how it was going and if Brock had the nerve to show up. Call me."

Her sister was a night owl, so Randi went ahead and dialed her number. The phone was picked up after only two rings.

"Hey, Randi."

She laughed. "How did you know it was me?"

"Who else would call at midnight?"

"It's only eleven here. I forgot about the time difference or I would have waited until morning."

"And make me wait another night for the news? Shame on you! Tell me everything!"

"He's here, Lauren."

Lauren gasped. "I can't believe it! He's got a lot of nerve!"

"He had a good reason. He has leukemia." She heard Lauren's quick inhalation. "He's in remission, though. The doctors say he's cured. But he didn't want to put me through the pain of dealing with it."

"Huh. Maybe it was for the best, then."

"Don't you start! I think he still loves me, but he won't admit it."

"Randi! You're not thinking of going back into a relationship with him, are you? What about a family and your future? It's best to leave it alone."

She hadn't considered the thought of a family. She thought about it a moment. "Brock would make a great dad. If the treatments left him unable to have children, we could adopt. We could take whatever God gives us as long as we were together."

"Does Brock feel like this, too?"

"I don't think he's thought that far ahead. He won't even admit he still loves me. At least he won't admit it to me. But I intend to force the truth out of him somehow." She didn't know how just yet, but she had a week to find a way.

Chapter 5

CHASE LOG: *Thursday, July 29. Moderate chance of thundershowers south of Wichita Falls along a line extending from Fort Worth to Laredo, TX....*

The next day Lisa was still in bed when Randi went downstairs.

"I think she's going to stay close to the hotel all day and rest," Steve told them all. "She told me to go ahead and go out chasing, though."

"I'll stay with her," Randi said immediately.

Steve looked at her gratefully. "That would be great, Randi. I hate to leave her, but she was adamant."

"I'll stay with you," Karen said. "I'd like to soak up some sun around the pool today."

Randi stared at her in surprise. "Are you sure?" She would have thought Karen would take this opportunity to get Brock to herself. Although, now that she thought about it, Karen hadn't been chasing him quite so hard as she did earlier in the week.

"I need to make some calls back to the station, too. It was a tiring day yesterday, and I need the rest," Karen said. She walked back toward the elevator.

"Well, the rest of us might as well head out," Will said. "We might catch some good lightning around Fort Worth, if we get a move on."

"I think I'll stay here, too," Ann put in. "The pool sounds heavenly. Then it will just be a trip for you guys."

"What? No women?" Will punched Brock in the arm. "I'm stopping for some powdered donuts and soda pop. My wife can't nag me about my health today."

Ann smiled. "I'll make up for it tomorrow, honey."

Will sighed. "The trials of marriage." But he looked anything but unhappy about it. He kissed Ann, and the men filed out of the hotel.

Randi waved and turned to Ann. "What do you want to do now? It's too early for the pool."

"We could take some breakfast up to Lisa."

Randi nodded. "I want to see how she's doing, anyway."

Lisa was still in her nightgown when she came to the door. Her face brightened when she saw them. "I was starving, but I didn't feel like getting dressed and going downstairs. I'm surprised the crew hasn't left for the day."

"We girls stayed behind today," Ann told her. "We wanted to be with you."

Tears filled Lisa's eyes. "Thank you," she whispered. "I was hating the thought of being alone, but I didn't want Steve hovering, either." She hugged them both. "Now give me that food before I perish of starvation."

They laughed and talked as they ate their bagels and juice. "I think I'll go back to bed for a while," Lisa said. "What are you going to do?"

"Probably hang out at the pool. Karen stayed behind, too," Randi told her.

Lisa raised her eyebrows. "Really? I'm shocked."

Randi chuckled. "She had some phone calls to make and wanted to soak up some sun."

Lisa rolled her eyes. "I should have known."

"We'll be by the pool if you want to join us later," Ann said.

"I might."

Ann and Randi walked down the plush hall to their rooms. "Let's change and meet at the pool," Ann suggested. They parted at Ann's door. Randi hurriedly changed into her one-piece suit and threw her wrap and sandals on.

A blast of heat struck her in the face when she went through the exit to the pool. She shielded her eyes from the glare of the sun on the water and looked around for Karen or Ann. Ann was nowhere to be seen, but Karen was in a skimpy two-piece in a secluded corner.

She looked up at Randi's approach. "How is Lisa?" Her tone was almost bored.

"Tired. She might join us later."

Karen nodded and leaned back against her lounge chair. She closed her eyes and raised her face to the sun.

Randi studied the perfection of the other woman's face. The chiseled features made Randi feel dowdy and plain.

Karen opened her eyes and caught Randi staring at her. She sat up and smiled lazily. "I think I'm going home this afternoon," she remarked.

Randi threw her a wide-eyed gaze. "So soon?"

"The chase isn't worth it. And I'm not just talking about the storm chase. I had hoped to find Brock wholehearted and ready for a new relationship, but nothing has changed." She gave a slight smile. "You've won again, Randi. Just like before." There was a bit of grudging respect in her words.

"What do you mean? Brock has made it clear he isn't interested in a relationship with me." Randi's pulse began to hammer in her throat. Had Brock said something to Karen?

"He's just hiding it. It's obvious to anyone who cares to look. And I looked." She stood and stretched her long limbs. "Good luck, Randi. I think I've given up for good this time. There are other fish to fry. I've wasted enough time pining over Brock Parker." She slung her wrap over her shoulder and walked away without a backward glance.

Randi stared after her numbly. What could it all mean? Was there any chance that Karen was right? Had she seen something in Brock's manner?

The afternoon dragged by while Randi waited for the men to return. She had listened to the radio, but there had not been much weather news. The men had probably had a fruitless day. Around six she changed into a gauzy flowered skirt and top and curled her hair. If Brock didn't want Karen, perhaps there was some hope for her. She knew one thing: She wasn't going back to Wabash without exhausting every avenue. She'd spent enough time living in the past.

She hugged herself at the thought of what the evening might bring. If she could just get him to admit he cared, she could win him over. She just knew it.

She had just gotten to Lisa's suite when the men came in.

"Man, you should have seen it," Will said after kissing his wife. "Brock got some awesome pictures of lightning, and I got some terrific readings for research."

"Are we ever going to eat? I want you to take me on a romantic dinner to some fancy Mexican restaurant," Lisa told Steve.

"And I want seafood," Ann said. "You are all mine tonight, Will."

Both men looked surprised. "We aren't going together?" Will asked.

"I think I'll order in room service," Professor Dials said apologetically. "I'm rather tired tonight."

"We've had enough togetherness. We want a little attention," Lisa said.

"What about Randi and Brock?" Will looked confused by the turn of events.

Randi's face burned when Brock didn't immediately offer to take her out. When he finally spoke up, she was sure her face was scarlet.

"We'll be fine by ourselves. You old married types go keep your wives happy."

Will grinned. "My pleasure." He held out his arm to Ann, and they turned to the door. "See you all tomorrow."

"Where do you want to eat?" Brock asked.

Randi shrugged. "I really don't care. Anything sound good to you?" She knew what he was going to say. It was what he always said.

"How about Italian? It's right across the street." He saw Randi smile and grinned. "I can't help it if I love Italian food. Don't look at me like that. You never used to complain."

"I'm not complaining now. It's just funny that you're still so predictable." She took his arm and waved to Lisa and Steve.

The noise of the traffic mingled with the sound of crickets when they started across the street.

Brock took a deep breath. "I can smell that lasagna from here."

"Quit salivating." She punched him in the ribs when he paused outside the entrance to the restaurant. "It's not attractive."

"I never claimed to be," he said, protesting.

"You can't help it," she said. "You'll always be the most attractive and fascinating man in the world to me." Randi tightened her grip on his arm.

He stopped and looked down at her. Was it her

imagination or was there a tender twist to his mouth? His gaze probed her own, and her breathing quickened. She reached up and touched his cheek. He swallowed hard, and she felt his arm tremble. "Kiss me, Brock," she whispered.

His gaze grew tender, and he started to bend his head, when a group of laughing teenagers brushed past and startled them. He drew back and cleared his throat. "Let's go in."

The anticipation fled and left Randi feeling drained. Why was love so hard? Why couldn't she penetrate that shell of his? Blinking back tears, she walked inside with him. The hostess seated them at a booth in the corner, and they ordered their meals. Some old habits never change. She ordered chicken fettuccine and Brock ordered his beloved lasagna.

When the waitress brought their salad and breadsticks, Randi tightened her grip on her courage and reached across the table. "We have to talk, Brock," she whispered, touching his hand.

"What about?" He avoided her gaze and picked up a breadstick.

She bit her lip. This wasn't going to be easy. "About us."

His shield was back in place when he looked at her. "The only 'us' we have is as friends, Randi. That's the way it has to stay."

She drew in a deep breath. It was now or never. "Does it? I still love you, Brock. I'll always love you. No matter how I've tried to eradicate you from my heart, I can't do it. God put us together. I really believe that. You used to."

Brock's pulse began to throb in his throat, and Randi thought she saw a look of joy in his eyes. He quickly veiled his expression. "You'll get over it, Randi. Just give it some time."

"Look at me." He raised his eyes to hers. "Tell me you don't love me."

A muscle jerked in his cheek, and he looked away.

"You can't say it, can you?" she demanded. "You still love me, Brock, I know you do."

"Don't do this to us, Randi," he said in a low, tortured voice. "It's best this way. Believe me, it's best."

"No, it's not! Our love is a precious gift from God. Will you throw it away like so much trash?" The waitress brought their meals, and Randi fell silent a moment, then continued her impassioned plea. "Neither of us knows how long we will stay healthy. I could come down with cancer tomorrow; you could get hit by a car. There are no guarantees in this life, Brock." She drew an exasperated sigh. "I'm not giving up on us, I'm not! Will you promise to pray about it?"

He looked at her gravely. "I have, Randi, don't you know that?" His voice was low and intense. "I felt I had to tell you the truth, but I can't let you share my life. I love you too much for that."

Randi closed her eyes at his words. He'd finally admitted it. She'd known it in her heart. Opening her eyes again, she smiled at him tremulously. "We'll work it out, Brock. I know we will. You take some time to pray, and you'll see."

"I wish it could be, my love, but it can't," he whispered. "Believe me, it can't."

They ate their meal in silence. Brock paid the bill and Randi took his arm. They walked outside into the muggy evening air. Randi didn't know how to reach him, what words to say to make him see. Lost in thought, she didn't see the curb and stumbled on the shadowed walk.

Brock caught her before she could fall. He looked down into her upturned face then buried his face in her curls; she twined her fingers in his hair. She pulled his head away and pressed her lips to his. At first he was stiff and unresponsive then drew her closer and returned her kiss.

It had been so long since he had held her. Randi was struck with the rightness of it. With Brock was where she belonged. She had to make him see that. Somehow, she would make him see.

❧

Brock shut the door behind him and sat on the bed. He'd been so stupid! How had he let himself be put in a position where he had to admit he still loved her? He should have found a way out of taking her out to supper. He castigated himself for being a weak fool.

Her perfume still lingered around him. Holding her again had been the best thing that had happened to him in the last five years. He hadn't wanted to let her go but had forced himself to thrust her away and walk her to her door. Maybe he should just pack up, climb back into the MGB, and head back to Florida. He contemplated the thought, but he knew he couldn't do that to her again. He'd taken the cowardly way out once.

They spent the next two days futilely chasing storms around the plains. Brock tried to avoid being alone with Randi as much as possible, but it wasn't easy. She sat in the same seat with him every chance she got. She forced him to look at her and talk to her. His resolve became more and more tested. Professor Dials had to get back to the university. That left three couples: Ann and Will, Steve and Lisa, and him and Randi. The pairing up came naturally to all of them.

They'd had a hard day of driving all over the plains and were ready for a break by Monday.

"Let's do something fun," Ann grumbled. "I'm sick of sitting in the van and watching the clouds."

Randi laughed. "We forget you're not a nut about weather like we are. But to be honest, I could use a break myself. I'm not as young as I used to be. These old bones are getting stiff from sitting."

Brock grinned. "You sound like you're Methuselah."

"I feel like him today."

When she smiled at him like that, the sun seemed to shine brighter. He dropped his eyes and pretended to look at the rack of attractions in the display in the hotel lobby. "What do you ladies want to do?"

"I want to go shopping," Lisa announced.

Ann clapped her hands. "Wonderful idea!"

Will and Steve both groaned. "Not shopping! Anything but that. Pour hot coals on my back, drive slivers of wood under my nails. . . . Don't make me go shopping." Will clasped his hands piteously.

Ann patted his back. "You'll survive it. You and Steve can sit at the coffee shop while Lisa and I shop, or you can check out the sporting goods store."

Will sighed heavily. "Don't ever get married, Brock. The things we do for these women."

Brock couldn't keep the smile in check. "I'll keep that in mind."

"Well, I don't want to go shopping," Randi said. "I can go shopping at home. I want an adventure."

Brock's head swiveled toward her, and his eyes lit up. "Adventure? What kind of adventure?" He knew he shouldn't ask—that he should make some excuse about taking care of errands, but he knew this was his last day with her. He was going to live life to the fullest this one last time.

She pulled an amusement park brochure out of the rack. "I want to go to here."

Brock began to shake his head. "Huh-uh, no way. You know how I feel about amusement parks. I hate roller coasters." He backed away with his hands in front of him. "I'd rather go shopping."

Will groaned. "You don't know what you're saying, man! Hey, you can take Ann shopping and I'll ride the roller coasters with Randi."

"Nope," Randi said firmly. "It's about time you learned that amusement parks can be fun. You haven't been to one since you were twelve."

So Brock found himself driving toward Arlington in his MGB with the top down. Singing to the radio, Randi's smile lit the interior of the car. He grudgingly decided it was worth it to see her that happy. He followed the line of traffic to the park and found a parking place. He slipped on sunglasses and sighed. "Let's get this over with."

Randi had her curls pulled back in tiny clips. She was dressed in jeans and a white Valparaiso University T-shirt. She looked altogether too adorable for his peace of mind. It was going to be a hard day, in more ways than one.

"We'll break you in gently," Randi told him. "Let's go to the 3-D movie first. That'll whet your appetite for something more adventurous."

"Don't count on it," Brock muttered. He followed her through the crowds to the line for *The Right Stuff Mach 1 Adventure*. After a wait of about half an hour, they were seated and strapped into cockpit seats. The seats moved and twisted with the action on the screen, and Brock found himself enjoying it more than he expected.

Randi's cheeks were pink when they exited. "Are you ready to try a roller coaster now?"

He wanted to say no, but he couldn't refuse when she looked at him like that. Dread congealed in his stomach as he followed her to the first ride she had picked out. It had its own mountain.

"This one is in the dark, so maybe if you don't see what's happening it will be easier for the first ride," Randi said.

"Can't we go on a nice, tame Ferris wheel first?" Brock begged.

She laughed at him. "Survive this, and I'll go on the Ferris wheel with you."

And he did. Randi screamed beside him and about broke his hand as they went through the twists and turns. When they got out, he had red marks on his wrists.

"Why do you like to go when all you do is scream and close your eyes?"

She blushed. "I don't know, but it's fun. Did you enjoy it?"

"Do you enjoy having the skin ripped from your arm?"

She looked alarmed. "Did I hurt you?"

He grinned. "If I say yes, do I have to go on another?"

She punched him. "Let's go do your Ferris wheel." On the way, he bought her some cotton candy and a soda. She looked like a kid with her mouth red from the candy and her hair a tangle of curls. He was suddenly glad he came. The memories of this day would last him a long time.

There wasn't much of a wait at the Ferris wheel. They got right on and sat down. Brock decided if this day was a memory-making one, he would enjoy it for all it was worth. He put his arm around her and pulled her against him. She smiled up at him with happiness in her eyes and leaned her head against his shoulder. A small voice whispered he shouldn't encourage her to think he was changing his mind, but he pushed it away. They were together for the day, and he intended to make the most of it.

The day went much too quickly. They were both exhausted when they made their way to the car. He held her hand and walked through the parking lot. Saddened that they had to return to reality, he didn't have much to say, and neither did Randi. He opened the car door for her, but she didn't get inside.

She leaned against his chest. "Thanks for a super day, Brock."

He held her and kissed the top of her head. "I enjoyed it, too." He could hear the finality in his words, the remoteness. Already he was withdrawing, back to his safe position. He knew she understood for she stiffened and pulled away.

"You're so stubborn," she said softly. "But so am I." She got in the car without another word, and they drove back to the hotel in silence.

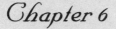

Chapter 6

CHASE LOG: *Tuesday, August 2. Possibility of two storm outbreaks. One along the Wyoming/ Nebraska border and the other along New Mexico/ Colorado border.* . . .

Randi peeked into the lounge looking for Brock. He'd been so distant when they got back to the hotel. It had been a wonderful day, but as they drove back, she could feel him withdrawing to that secret place where he wouldn't let her come. She was beginning to despair. What would she do if he refused to budge on his position? She pressed her lips together. She wasn't beaten yet. If she had to, she would go see his doctor and find out for herself what he said about Brock's marrying.

When she finally found him, he was talking with Will and Steve. "Where are the girls?" she asked.

"They'll be down shortly," Steve said. He continued his discussion with Will and Brock. "I think the chance is better up toward Wyoming. I really think we should head up there."

Will shook his head. "I don't know, guys. The computer stats sound like New Mexico might be a better bet."

"I vote for New Mexico," Randi put in. "Wyoming is too far."

"I vote with Randi," Brock said. "Let's do it."

Steve shrugged in resignation. "I'll let you call it today."

The women joined them, and they piled into the van. It was dirty and battered from the many miles and the close encounter with the small twister their first week. Steve took Highway 287 west and pointed the van toward Amarillo. This was their last chance for a good storm. Tomorrow they had decided to spend the day seeing more of Wichita Falls.

They were all a little quiet on the trip. When they neared the New Mexico border, Lisa grew quieter when they passed the site of the encounter with the small twister. Randi knew she was remembering the loss of the baby. With the site about an hour behind them, a large cumulus cloud began to build ahead of them. Randi looked it over. It was a nice multicell with a decent rain shaft under it. There were other shafts to the north.

They stopped and checked wind velocity. It was out of the southeast at about ten to fifteen knots. "Let's park and watch," Brock said. "I want to take some film of this."

They pulled to the side of the road, and Brock got out his tripod and camera. By the time he got it set up, pea-sized hail had begun to fall. Then the lightning came.

"Get in the van!" Randi shouted at him. Fear gripped her. She was terrified of lightning.

He nodded and gave one last adjustment to the tripod. Overhead a lightning bolt leaped from cloud to cloud. Brock gave a yelp and fell away from the tripod.

"Brock!" Randi screamed. She launched herself from the van into the storm. Kneeling beside him, she touched his chest.

He sat up with a dazed expression on his face. "I'm okay," he said. "The lightning electrified the tripod and shocked me. Good thing it didn't make it to the ground."

Randi helped him up, and they hurried to the van, hail crunching under their feet. The storm raged for about fifteen minutes, and Brock was elated. "I'm getting some terrific footage," he exulted.

Randi was shaken. She didn't care about the footage, but she realized that it was only by God's protection that Brock hadn't been killed. They drove back to Wichita Falls somber from the experience. Brock may have escaped the lightning, but could he escape the leukemia forever? She had managed to forget his illness for the last few days, but now the terror of it preyed on her mind. If there was any hope of a future together, she had to face it and leave it in God's hands. She did just that as she prayed. He would take it and make it right.

❧

Brock felt out of sorts and morose when he went down

for breakfast. This was their last day together. Tomorrow they would all go their separate ways again. He would probably never see Randi again. She had been distant yesterday, and he wondered if she had finally realized he was right.

Will joined him at the breakfast table. He was scowling.

"What's wrong?"

"Great chance of storms today and we're going sightseeing," he grumbled.

"How good?"

"Moderate."

Brock relaxed. "That's all we've had this entire trip. We'll maybe see an afternoon thunderstorm. That shouldn't spoil our fun."

Will nodded reluctantly.

The rest of the group joined them. Brock found his gaze drawn to Randi. She had an odd expression on her face. It was almost one of peace and contentment.

She saw him staring and smiled. She leaned forward and kissed him right in front of everyone. "Good morning," she said.

He stared at her. What was she up to now? She got a bagel and slid it into the toaster. She seemed unaware of his curiosity.

"So, what are we doing today?" she asked when she sat beside him.

"We're going to tour Kell House and visit the railroad museum. Then we're going to go out to Sheppard

Air Force Base and watch the pilots train. Did you know this is the only place where NATO pilots train?" Steve asked.

Brock nodded. "I'd heard that."

They hurriedly finished their breakfast then went out into the sunshine.

"It has to be at least eighty already," Ann grumbled. "I hope we're going to be inside today."

"Quit whining, woman," Will said. "You're married to a weatherman. You're supposed to enjoy the weather, no matter what it does."

Randi slipped her sunglasses on and climbed into the seat. Brock glanced at her several times, curious as to what had changed her mood so dramatically since yesterday, but she just smiled at him serenely.

They toured the Kell House and marveled at the fine furnishings and exquisite detailing of the structure. Next, they went through the railroad museum, which the men enjoyed tremendously. Brock was particularly interested in the World War II troop sleepers.

They ate lunch at a pizza parlor then went shopping. Steve parked, and they all got out.

Randi nudged Brock. "Look at the sky." Her voice was filled with suppressed excitement.

They'd been inside most of the day and hadn't been monitoring the weather. Large clouds filled the sky to the west. The storm clouds sprawled over the landscape like a twenty-mile blanket. The mass of snow-white clouds that formed the main body were so dense they looked like huge cauliflower. At the top of the towering cloud, an anvil-shaped cloud spread outward in a circular pattern with a domelike cloud protruding over the top.

Brock's breath whooshed out in excitement. "Look, Randi. You can actually see it expanding, almost like lungs inhaling."

Will craned his head out the window. "Get the camera, Brock," he said in an awed voice. "The wall cloud is lowering."

"The wall cloud is rotating," Lisa whispered. "It has appendages."

The muggy air gave way to an onrush of cool air. The bottom of the cloud was ringed with low-hanging, slowly rotating scud clouds. Brock watched breathlessly then with growing alarm. "It's changing directions!" He knew that right-movers like this storm were extremely dangerous. There was no time to get out of the path of danger in the van in the middle of city traffic. The best they could do was watch from here and get to safety in one of the stores if necessary. Only a handful of storms ever reached this intensity.

He opened the van door and retrieved his camera. He caught a glimpse of Randi's expression. She looked exalted, and he suppressed a grin. He supposed he looked the same. This storm was a rare sight for a meteorologist to see. He quickly snapped a half dozen pictures then ran to the end of the street for a better view. The rest of the group followed him. He suddenly remembered the hand scanner.

"Randi, would you grab the hand scanner and see what it's saying? There may have already been some tornadoes develop out of this baby."

She nodded and ran back to the van. Moments later she was back with the scanner. "A tornado was reported on the ground just west of here. All of Wichita Falls is to take cover," she said.

"There it is," Will shouted. He pointed, and they all turned to see.

Brock heard Randi's swift intake of breath. He felt as though he couldn't breathe himself. The tornado was massive, easily a mile across. Black as midnight, it tore toward them. "Everybody inside!" he shouted. The storm was moving fast and would be here within moments. He felt paralyzed for a moment then grabbed Randi's arm and raced for a nearby candle shop.

The clerk looked up in alarm when they barreled into the store.

"Do you have a basement?" Brock asked urgently.

The clerk nodded. "Back there," she said, pointing to the back of the store. "What's wrong?"

"Tornado," he said succinctly. "A big one."

The clerk paled. "This way." She led the way through the aisles of candles, their aroma somehow sickeningly sweet in the face of the danger racing toward them. Before they could reach the door to the basement the windows blew out, and the tornado's roar filled the air.

Randi cringed beside him. He could see the frightened faces of his friends past her terrified face. They were running for the basement door. A certainty of death gripped him in the seconds before the walls were ripped away. He shouted Randi's name, then she was ripped from his arms.

He flew through the air with debris flying around him. Landing against a table, he managed to crawl under it and covered his head. He squeezed his eyes shut as the roar of the storm grew to an unbearable pitch. Then just as quickly as it came, the wind diminished, and he heard the roar move away. Dazed, he raised his head. Where was Randi? Where were the rest of his friends? He crawled out from under the table and staggered to his feet. The store had been leveled and all that was left was debris. He could see that the entire neighborhood no longer existed. It looked like a bombsite.

"Randi!" Praying all the while, he began to shove debris aside. He felt a sickening sureness that she was dead. Why hadn't he realized that their time together was so precious? Why had he been so stiff-necked and proud? He couldn't let her stay with him, and they had wasted these past five years. Now she was dead, and he was still alive. How ironic.

He heard movement from what used to be the back of the store and looked to see Will and Ann emerging from the cellar door followed by the clerk and Steve and Lisa. They had made it to safety. Maybe Randi was with them. That hope was dashed by Will's first words.

"Where's Randi?" Will looked dazed, his eyes unfocused.

"She was ripped from me. I can't find her." Brock

wasn't aware he'd actually spoken the words until Lisa gasped and tears sprang to her eyes.

She began to frantically dig through the debris. "Randi!"

The rest of them began to dig in earnest, but the search was futile. Randi was nowhere to be found. Despair flooded Brock, and he struggled to keep back the tears. He had decided if God gave him a second chance, he would take it and never let her go, but it didn't look as though he would have that opportunity. She was gone.

∾∞

Where am I? Randi opened her eyes and shifted. Every part of her body hurt. Cuts oozed blood all over her legs and arms. She touched her head, and her fingers came away bloody. *What happened?* She sat up slowly, groaning with the pain the movement brought. Darkness clothed the area and nothing looked familiar to her. The terrain was littered with debris, ripped boards, pieces of drywall, a doll with one eye, half a couch, and other curiously twisted shapes.

The tornado! She tried to get to her feet, but the pain was too great. Looking down, she saw a broken edge of bone poking through the skin on her left leg. Seeing the condition of her leg brought the pain in exquisite waves. *Brock!* Where was he? Looking around, she had no idea how far she'd been thrown. Were her friends dead? Crying weakly, she buried her face in her arms and prayed for God to send someone.

When the storm of tears had ended, she lifted her head and wiped her face. Crying would do no good.

She had to find help. Brock might be lying somewhere under a pile of debris. "Help!" she cried. The sound was barely more than a whisper. She gathered her strength and tried again. "Help! Somebody help me!" This time her voice carried a bit more. She heard voices to her left and tried again. "Help!"

"Did you hear something?"

Was that Lisa's voice? Hope filled Randi's heart. "Over here! Lisa!"

"Brock, she's here!" Lisa's voice came closer. Randi could hear the tears and relief in her friend's voice.

She heard the sound of feet crashing through the debris, and then Brock's strong arms were around her, his breath upon her face.

He showered her face with kisses, muttering, "Thank You, Lord, thank You, Jesus," under his breath. His face was wet with tears, and he held her as if he would never let her go.

If she had ever doubted the strength of his love, those questions were swept away in that moment. She clung to him and returned his kiss, the pain of her leg forgotten in that moment.

"I'm sorry, Randi, so sorry," he muttered. "I'm never letting you go again. You were right, and I was wrong. We have to stay together for whatever time we have. We'll leave the future in God's hands and take what He gives us today. I'm marrying you as soon as we can get a license." He turned and shouted for Steve and Will to find a board to use as a stretcher then gathered her close again.

She looked at him with a teasing smile. "Will you put that in writing?" she asked before she drew his head down for a kiss.

❧

Birdseed showered over Randi's head and lodged in her veil and the lace of her wedding gown. Brock laughed and helped her brush it off. He looked carefree and extremely handsome in his black tux. She still could hardly believe the wedding had gone without a hitch. They'd even used the original invitations. They'd just changed the date. It had seemed like the right thing to do, and their families and friends had loved it. It was as though nothing had changed; just a little time had elapsed.

"Hey, come on, you two lovebirds. You'll have all next week to cuddle on the beach at Maui." Will stood with his hands on his hips beside the Bristol Storm Chasers van. The rest of the wedding party, Steve, Lisa, and Ann, were already waiting in the van to take the newlyweds to the airport.

Brock didn't seem to care that everyone was waiting. "Well, Mrs. Parker, you're stuck with me now," he whispered.

"That's right." Randi caressed his cheek. "You're not to listen to the weather the entire week. It will just say the same thing anyway. Warm and sunny, a perfect day for the beach."

"A perfect way to begin a marriage," Brock said. "No storm warnings, not even a watch."

COLLEEN COBLE

Colleen and her husband, David, raised two great kids, David Jr. and Kara, and they are now knee-deep in paint and wallpaper chips as they restore a Victorian home. Colleen became a Christian after a bad car accident in 1980 when all her grandmother's prayers finally took root. She is very active at her church where she sings and helps her husband with a young marrieds Sunday school class. She enjoys the various activities with the class, including horseback riding (she needs a stool to mount) and canoeing (she tips the canoe every time). She writes inspirational romance because she believes that the only happily-ever-after is with God at the center. She now works as a church secretary but would like to eventually pursue her writing full time.

TRUTH
OR DARE

by Denise Hunter

Dedication

In memory of my grandmother,
Vickie Louella Waters,
whose life was a beautiful reflection of God's love.

Prologue

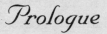

The pathway from the picnic grove to the entrance of Sycamore High School stretched before Brianna like a par five fairway. Her gaze clung to the twin marble columns, proudly propping up the entranceway. In her peripheral vision, an American flag atop its pole whipped at the mercy of the wind, its metal clip producing a lonely ping.

Brianna's sandals dug into the ground, stirring up dust, which obscured her Passion Red polish, a remnant of her recent pedicure. Her long, graceful limbs swung in rhythmic precision and, as her skirt rode high on her tanned thighs, she wished for the first time it wasn't quite so revealing.

Would she ever reach those glass doors? It had never taken this long before. But then, Jake Volez had never stared her down from behind. And she knew he was. She could feel the hot, prickling laser of his gaze burning into the back of her head. He was probably still perched arrogantly on the tabletop with his bronzed arms crossed over his muscular chest.

Her gaze darted to the second-story landing, where her three friends huddled together over the railing. Excited giggles wafted out through the treetops and hovered around Brianna's ears like a pesky mosquito. She faked a cocky smile and gave a thumbs-up, carefully concealed from Jake's view. Her friends' eyes grew wide, their smiling mouths converted to gaping holes of awe. She wiggled her brows twice, for good measure, hoping the girls weren't close enough to see the tears.

One thing was for sure. She'd never set herself up for that kind of rejection again. Who did Jake think he was anyway? A nobody, that's what. Just an arrogant, dirt-poor jerk from the wrong side of town.

Now he'd actually think she was interested in him! As if she couldn't do better than a guy like him. Why, she'd had four different invitations to the prom! More than any other girl she knew. And they were all from good families, besides. It chafed her pride to let Jake think he'd gotten the best of her.

Maybe she couldn't tell him what she'd been up to, but she'd never let him know how his rejection had stung. Never let anyone else know either. She'd think of something to tell the girls. She straightened her spine and raised her chin a notch.

Go ahead and watch me, Jake Volez. See if I care.

Chapter 1

Five years later

Brianna Van Allen swung her van around the circular drive of the Circle Q Ranch. Excitement raced through her blood, replacing the fatigue from hours behind the wheel. As she looked at the brick estate, warm memories surged to mind, welcoming her home.

She slipped out of the van, stretching as she walked toward the house. The door flew open and her mother glided down the brick steps, followed by Max. "Brianna, darling, you're home at last!" her mother said.

She lovingly embraced Celia, inhaling the expensive perfume that was her signature scent. "It's so good to see you! And you, too, Max!" She hugged her stepfather.

Her mother draped an arm around her waist and escorted her inside while Max retrieved her luggage. "You mustn't wait so long to come home next time! I can't believe you stayed away for five years!"

"It's not as if we haven't seen one another in all that time. And you have to admit, you enjoyed your visits to Los Angeles. Why, you bought out half the shops on Rodeo Drive! They had to close down for weeks."

Celia tapped her daughter on the waist. "Oh, you! It wasn't that bad! Max hardly even blinked when he saw the bill!"

Brianna laughed. "That's only because he'd bought a new car!"

"Well, true, but we did save the airfare home!"

Brianna shook her head. How she'd missed her mother! They seated themselves in the parlor.

"You did remember to bring all your samples and catalogs, didn't you?"

"The van's packed full of them. I can hardly wait to start decorating the cottage! What finally made you decide to do it?"

"Our foreman J.C. is living there now, and he'll soon be celebrating five years at the Circle Q. We thought we'd have it redecorated to show our appreciation. Besides, it still looks just the way it did when your Aunt Gertrude lived there."

"J.C.'s not the doily type?"

"Hardly!" Her mother laughed. "Oh, Megan called to say she'd pick you up for the reunion at nine o'clock in the morning."

"I'm so glad we're going together. She's the only one I've kept in close contact with."

When Max came in, they settled around the kitchen

table and munched on homemade banana bread. After they'd caught up, the conversation turned to the foreman's house.

"Speaking of the cottage," Brianna said, "I was hoping to get a look at it tonight so I can get some ideas going. Do you think your foreman is home and would let me walk through?"

"Oh dear, he usually goes to Bible study on Friday night. I doubt if he locks up, but I really don't think it would be right to let ourselves in."

"No, you're right. I think I might just walk around the place, though. I'll knock anyway. Who knows, he may be home. Want to come?"

"You go ahead, darling. I've got some final plans to make for the charity auction."

Brianna stepped out the door and walked along the path on the north side of the house. When daylight beckoned from the other side of the woods, she entered the clearing where the cottage was perched on a mound of lush, green grass. The screen door hung ajar on the enclosed porch, so Brianna walked in and tapped on the white painted door. After knocking a second time, she decided he must have gone to his Bible study.

Her eyes scanned the large porch. Except for a pair of dirty work boots, everything was exactly the same as when Aunt Gertrude had lived here. Even the same floral cushions padded the swing and chairs. She'd spent hours on that swing listening to stories. Her aunt had not been able to get around well, but she'd been able to weave a story like a spider spins a web.

I wonder if Aunt Gerdy's china cabinet is still in there? And that big deer head over the fireplace. . . She looked in the window through the curtain's narrow slit but saw only murky shadows in the house's dark interior.

Her gaze darted toward the door. Maybe if she had just a little peek. She wouldn't go inside or anything, she'd just look in and get a better idea of what was still there, what she had to work with.

Her hand closed around the warm metal knob and she turned it. Sure enough, it clicked open. The door squeaked open and her gaze settled on an unfamiliar tattered rug. She flicked on the light, careful to refrain from stepping inside. She had standards, after all. Yep, there was the deer head above the mantle, staring right back at—

"Hey! What do you think you're doing?" A male voice boomed from behind her.

Brianna sucked in a breath and spun around. Then her eyes widened. Adrenaline pumped through her body and her legs weakened. She felt her jaw go slack.

Glaring at her from the doorway, arms crossed over his chest, was Jake Volez.

Chapter 2

J ake?" Her eyes could scarcely believe what they were seeing. A ghost from the past standing right in front of her. She felt almost faint from the adrenaline rush and put a hand to her chest as if to still her heart.

"Brianna." His face brimmed with recognition. That, and something not so pleasant. She wondered if she were safe here alone with him. "You didn't answer my question." His eyes narrowed as he propped a foot on the porch.

Brianna recalled how he'd found her, feet planted on the threshold, leaning inside the house. Heat crept up her neck. "I was just, um...that is. . . ." She watched Jake arch an arrogant brow, and she narrowed her own eyes. "Maybe I should ask you the same question, Jake Volez."

"Go ahead."

She crossed her arms, imitating his pose. "You're trespassing. This is private property. *My parents'* private property."

"Is that so?"

Smug man! "Yes, that's so. Either I can get my step-dad or you can clear off the property and go home. Your choice."

"Afraid I can't do that."

His insolence caused her to worry less about her safety and more about his. "And why not?"

"You're standing in my way."

Standing in his. . . Reality hit slowly, but thoroughly, as her mind processed the information. *Oh, please, God, tell me it's not so. . . .* "You're not the—"

"Foreman." He finished the sentence and punctuated it with a smirk.

"You can't be the foreman. His name is—"

"J.C. As in Jacob Christopher Volez. Haven't you noticed everyone at the Circle Q goes by a nickname?"

"Of course I did, I just didn't. . . Mother didn't mention—"

"Look, if you don't mind, I've had a long day, and you're blocking my way."

She snatched her hand from the doorknob and stepped away. She straightened to her full height, her posture tall and regal, and gestured grandly for him to pass her. "Be my guest."

❧

Branches slapped Brianna's face and shoulders as she plodded down the path to her parents' house. Shock still fed her mind as she relived the last few moments.

Jake Volez, living here on her parents' property!

Why hadn't someone told her? *Because they don't know anything about your silly little crush on him.*

Good point, she conceded to the inner voice. *They don't know I made a fool of myself. No. How Jake made a fool of me!* There were some moments in life you wish you could undo or, at least, erase from your memory. Since Brianna couldn't undo the moment, she'd decided five years ago to abolish the incident from her memory. And she had, until tonight.

She sucked in her breath and skidded to a halt. The cottage! She'd forgotten all about her promise to her mother. There was no way she was going to spend her whole month's vacation with him! Maybe she could get permission to access the cottage, so she could come and go freely. Brianna resumed her walk. Jake would be more than willing to comply. After all, it was clear he didn't want her company now any more than he had in high school.

∗

Jake had caught a whiff of perfume as he passed Brianna on the porch. *I'll be. . .the same stuff she wore in high school.* He clenched his jaw, fighting the pull of the sweet, subtle scent. As he entered his house, he heard her heels clicking across the porch and down the step. Only Brianna VanAllen would wander around a ranch in heels. Jake closed the door behind him and dropped his Bible on the end table, feeling a moment's guilt. Some Christian he was. He'd been rude enough to make a saint mad. Something about her brought out the worst in him.

Jake pulled off his boots and sank onto the floral sofa, all thoughts of dinner disappearing. He'd known there was a chance she'd come home for the reunion, but since Max hadn't mentioned it, he'd assumed she couldn't get away from Los Angeles. He hoped she wouldn't be staying long. At least he wouldn't have to see much of her around the Circle Q; he couldn't see her mucking out stables and riding the range. He'd just avoid her at the reunion, which should be easy enough since they hadn't exactly run in the same social circles in high school.

His mind whirled back to that day five years ago. She'd been tempting when she'd sidled up to him and run a finger down his bicep. Those years in Drama Club had almost paid off for her. She'd even added a convincing tremble to her voice, as if she'd been unsure of herself, and he'd almost fallen for her act. Except, when a breeze had parted the leafy branches, he'd glimpsed her friends off in the distance, snickering behind their hands. He suppressed the wave of humiliation.

She looked different now than she had in those days. She'd gotten her long, blond hair cut in a sleek, shoulder-length bob, and she wore less makeup than she used to. He didn't know if he'd have recognized her at all, if she hadn't been standing on her parents' property. She looked all grown-up and professional. A rich city girl if he'd ever seen one.

Just the kind he needed to avoid.

Later that night as Brianna prepared for bed, her mind drifted back to the conversation she'd had with her mother after she'd returned from the cottage. Her spirits sank all over again, filling her with dread. *Be sure to give Jake a say in all the decisions,* her mother had said. She'd already promised she'd do the cottage, but that was before she knew who lived there. And before she knew Jake was supposed to pick out everything! *So much for avoiding him. We'll be shopping together, looking at pattern books together. . . .* She sighed.

The only good thing about this was that her mother insisted on paying her for the job. She'd feel funny charging her own parents, but she knew how her mother was once she dug in her heels. Besides, she could use the money. She desperately needed a new mattress. It had a valley in the middle that pulled her to the center, no matter how often she flipped it.

And she needed a new computer for her office. She'd bought hers secondhand three years ago, and now it was a proverbial dinosaur. When she'd started up her business, she'd realized it was important to project a successful image, so she'd done up her showroom with top-notch taste and purchased stylish business suits from a designer outlet. She'd even invested in an almost-new minivan and had paid to have the name of her company, Interior Motives, painted on both sides. Although the ritzy image seemed shallow to Brianna, she knew the clientele she sought wouldn't trust her instinct for design if she didn't look the part.

Brianna laid her toothbrush in her cosmetic bag, then withdrew her baby blue skort from her garment bag and hung it in the closet. She was too tired to unpack tonight, so she slipped under the covers of her canopied bed, knowing she needed a full night's sleep. After all, who wanted to go to her reunion with dark circles under her eyes?

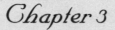

Chapter 3

Megan turned the car into the park and followed the winding, hilly curves to the main pavilion at the back of the park. "Nervous?" she asked.

"You betcha!" Brianna admitted. Her stomach had been jittery all morning.

"Me, too. Wonder what we're going to do all day."

"The registration form said something about games and activities."

Megan glanced at her watch. "Half hour late. Right on time."

They laughed, remembering their habit of arriving fashionably late. Since the event was an all-day one, Brianna knew others would undoubtedly be late. The parking lot was already crowded, and Brianna saw clusters of people spread across the park site and playing volleyball on the sand courts. A large canvas banner in their class colors of red and gold hung from the pavilion rafters, flapping in the wind.

After signing in, they scanned the group for familiar faces.

"Look, there's Cassandra by the grills," Megan said.

They headed in that direction and, in moments, Cassandra spotted them and came running over for a big embrace. "Brianna, you rotten friend! Staying away all this time with hardly a phone call."

"Hey, what am I, chopped hamburger?" Megan pouted.

Cassandra gave Megan a squeeze. "It's *chopped liver,* goofy, and I just saw you last week!"

Laurel arrived with her husband, Mark, and there was another round of embraces. Other casual acquaintances from school came over to say hi periodically, but the friends had so much to say, they spent over an hour huddled together on a picnic table.

When a luxury SUV pulled into the parking lot, Megan and Brianna watched to see who it was. Moments later, a golden head appeared.

"Evan Pierceton," Megan sighed. "Be still my heart!"

Brianna watched him stride over to the courts and greet a few classmates.

"Or should I say, 'Be still *your* heart'?" Megan said. "You're the one who dated him. Man, could that guy write a killer love letter!"

"Megan!"

"You're the one who let me read them. Mm mm mm, smooth as satin."

"That's *smooth as silk,* and he was smooth all right.

184

If you'll recall, I caught him making out with Patricia Olinger!"

Megan tucked in a corner of her lip. "Oh, yeah." She frowned. "On the other hand, maybe we should give the guy a break. He was just a seventeen-year-old kid, you know."

While she chatted with her three friends, Brianna became aware of Jake's arriving in an older model pickup. Although she participated in the conversation, she was keenly aware of Jake's whereabouts through it all. First he'd mingled, then he'd settled on a tabletop with several other denim-clad classmates. *Good grief! I'm tracking him like a hound!*

Just then, Stephanie Gillis, class president, called everyone into the pavilion. When they arrived, she welcomed them. "We have a variety of activities planned for today, but we thought we'd do something a little different." She shared a conspiratorial grin with the class vice president.

"Uh-oh," Brianna whispered to Megan.

Stephanie continued. "We'll be picking a partner for each of you, and you'll compete in all the activities with your partner." The crowd groaned in response.

"Stop it, you party poopers, this will be good for you!" Stephanie's dimple flashed. She explained the rules, stirring slips of paper in the basket. "After lunch, we'll start our first activity, the scavenger hunt, then we'll have another activity every half hour, which will give you a chance to mingle with everyone between games. Okay, here we go!"

She drew two names and read them aloud, then proceeded quickly through the slips.

"I hope I get Evan," Megan said, wiggling her brows, but a few minutes later she was paired with a girl Brianna remembered as being very studious and quiet.

As the names were called, a flicker of apprehension surged through Brianna. There were not many left, and Jake had not been paired with anyone.

"Brianna VanAllen and Jake Volez," Stephanie read mechanically.

Brianna froze. *No, no, no! This isn't happening!* She forced her lips into a polite smile and felt Jake's piercing gaze from across the room. She wouldn't look.

"Well, aren't you the lucky one?" Megan nudged her in the ribs.

She didn't hear the rest of the names. *Paired for the whole day! What did I do to deserve this?* Brianna struggled to pull herself together after the drawing ended. Lunch was next, at least, so she could put off the inevitable for a few moments.

She numbly followed Megan to the line and proceeded to stack food on her plate. So much for this day! She'd looked forward to it for months and now it was ruined. She'd spend the whole day with the person who'd caused her worst high school memory. The one who had mortified her in the cruelest way.

❧

Jake shoveled the last bite of potato salad into his

mouth. He hadn't tasted one bite of the lunch, but he'd eaten it slowly enough to be one of the last with a plate in his hands. He glanced at Brianna. She didn't seem to be in a big hurry either.

Stephanie announced the start of the scavenger hunt and began passing out the lists and bags. Jake tossed his plate in the trash and walked toward his partner who was now sitting alone at a picnic table. *Might as well get this over with.*

She stood as he advanced, reluctance in every line of her body. "Well, this is going to be boatloads of fun," she said.

Jake crossed his arms. "Look, I didn't want to be your partner, and you didn't want to be mine, but this is the way it is, so let's just get on with it."

"Fine."

"Fine." He took the list and skimmed the page. "Something with our class year on it." His gaze darted to the banner hanging in the shelter.

"Don't even think it." She held up the bag. "It wouldn't fit." She scanned the area. "Hey, the plates and napkins had the class year on them!"

"They did?"

They walked to the serving table, but all the table-ware had already been packed away.

"There'll be some in the trash." Jake walked to the trash barrel and Brianna followed.

Brianna looked in and wrinkled her nose. "Eeew."

Oh, for pity's sake. "I'll get it." He swatted away the

hovering bees and reached in for a napkin. "Here." He handed her the partially wrinkled, but relatively un-stained, napkin, and watched her pinch it delicately be-tween finger and thumb and drop it in their collection bag. *Good grief!*

He scanned the list again. "A linden tree blossom. I know where we can find one."

He started off toward the woods, leaving her to traipse behind. There was no path, but the undergrowth was low, so he trudged ahead at a brisk pace. When he reached the linden tree, he realized Brianna had fallen behind, and it was no wonder, the way she was trying to step over the undergrowth rather than go through it. He forced himself not to roll his eyes as he waited.

☙

Brianna caught up to Jake, slightly out of breath. "How are we going to get it?" she panted, pointing at the blos-soms which were well over his head. He scanned the ground, swiping at the brush to see if any fallen flowers lay underneath. No such luck. The lowest tree limb was above his reach. "You'll have to climb on my shoulders."

"Excuse me?"

"Weren't you a cheerleader?" he challenged.

"I was, but you weren't. It takes two, you know."

Jake sighed. "How hard could it be? Just get on." He turned his back to her, squatted down, and waited.

She stood contemplating his shoulders. *If he thinks...* "Are you going to get on already?"

All right, wise guy. She kicked off her sandals and

settled one leg on his shoulder. He grabbed it around the shin before she swung her other leg around and tucked her feet behind his back.

Brianna's palms grew slick as Jake wrapped his arms around her bare legs and rose easily to his feet. What was wrong with her? She wasn't afraid of heights.

She reached up toward the blossoms. "I can't reach them." Even she could hear the pout in her voice.

"You're going to have to stand up."

She braced her hands on top of his head, noting the soft texture of his nearly black hair. Pushing against him, she attempted to get her foot up to his shoulder.

"That's my head you're pushing on!"

"Well, what do you expect me to do? I haven't anything else to hold on to!"

One more push proved to be futile. She sighed.

"How'd you do it in cheerleading?"

"That takes practice! You won't be able to do it the first time."

"Just tell me what to do," he gritted out.

"Give me your hands. No, keep them shoulder-high." She put her hands in his and felt the roughness of his skin. "Now, when I count to three, bend your knees, then pop up, straightening your arms."

"That's it?"

She counted, he popped, and before she knew it, she was standing on his shoulders. "Hey, that was pretty good! You missed your calling, Volez. Should've been a male cheerleader."

His snort told her his opinion of male cheerleaders. She carefully straightened her legs and reached for the nearest branch, plucking a yellow flower. "Got it!" she said, stashing it in her pocket.

"Give me your hands and you can jump down. Anybody ever tell you you've got bony feet?"

"I can't jump down, I'm barefooted."

He huffed. "Fine, Princess, just sit down and I'll lower you."

She resisted the urge to smack him on the head.

After she sat, he squatted down, and she was soon slipping back into her sandals. "Sheesh, I hope everything doesn't take that long."

He withdrew the list from his pocket. "There's a few more things we can find easily in the woods. Can you recite the school fight song?"

"Can't you?"

"I only went to Sycamore High for my senior year, if you'll recall."

"I remember it." Brianna jotted down the words as they hiked. They stopped and picked up various items along the way.

"What did our senior float look like?" He read from the list.

"It was a commode, and it said, 'Flush the Falcons.' "

"You've got to be kidding." Jake stooped to retrieve a leaf, then they were off to find the next item. It was a good thing he knew the various species of trees, because she didn't know one leaf from the other. She remembered their senior prom theme, but couldn't recall whom they'd played for their homecoming game.

Jake dug in his pocket for a 1968 penny, the last item on the list. "That's it. We've got everything."

They headed back toward the reunion site, Brianna taking two steps for every one of his. Finally, they reached the clearing and saw their classmates gathered around the pavilion. Everyone turned, then the group broke into applause.

Stephanie took the mike in hand. "Well, it looks like our last pair has finally completed the scavenger hunt! What took you guys so long?"

Brianna smiled good-naturedly and shrugged dramatically.

"Maybe they were pursuing other interests in the woods!" Craig Weaver yelled.

Their classmates laughed, and she felt heat climb her neck and settle on her cheeks. She didn't dare look at Jake as she turned in the bag and took a seat next to her friends.

"You have about half an hour to mingle before the next event, volleyball, begins."

The group discussed the scavenger hunt, laughing when Brianna described her and Jake's struggle to get the blossom. Eventually, the others wandered off, leaving Brianna and Megan perched on the table.

"So, *was* there anything going on in those woods with you and Jake?" Megan asked, wiggling her brows.

"Megan! I don't even like him!"

Megan cocked her head skeptically. "Please! I know you had a crush on him in high school."

"That was then. Things change."

"Nonsense. You're attracted to him, admit it. I could always read you like a sign."

"A book. And maybe I did have a crush on him at one point, but that was before I found out how mean he was. Remember that game of Truth or Dare we played our senior year? He rejected me flat out. You wouldn't believe how cold he was."

Megan blinked. "I thought he kissed you."

Brianna's gaze slid to the table before bravely meeting Megan's stare again. "I lied to you guys. I'm sorry, I was so mortified, I went home and cried after school."

Megan's face softened. "Oh, Brianna, I wish you would have told me. I would have kicked him in the shins!"

Brianna laughed. "Well, anyway, now you can see why I'm less than thrilled to be his partner."

"Bree," a deep male voice said from beside her.

Brianna turned to see Evan's athletic form. "Evan!" She stood and Evan embraced her in a massive bear hug.

He held her away from him and let his gaze wander over her face. "I didn't think it was possible, but you're even more gorgeous."

Evan and Megan exchanged greetings, then Megan suddenly found someplace else she had to be.

"Say," Evan said after they'd chatted awhile, "how about trading partners. Donald won't mind being Jake's partner, then you and I could spend the day catching up."

"Are we allowed?" she asked hopefully. Anything to avoid Jake.

He winked. "Rules are made to be broken, Bree. Why don't you go tell Jake."

"All right, be right back."

Brianna walked toward Jake, who was watching a volleyball match. The sun glinted off his hair, shooting tiny white twinkles around his head. *Look at those broad shoulders. No wonder I didn't have any trouble balancing up there.*

He didn't turn as she arrived at his side, but she sensed he knew it was she. How could she word this without offending him? She lifted a hand to her mouth and started to chew on her nails before she remembered the three coats of Perfectly Pink she'd applied the previous night and slipped her hands into her pockets. What was she so worried about? He'd be as eager to get a new partner as she was.

Brianna put an amiable smile on her face. "Say, Jake, I have a proposition for you."

He turned, obviously not at all surprised to see her there, and lifted a brow. "Another one?"

Brianna's smile froze on her face as his words oozed their way to her brain. Her smile faltered, then she sucked in a deep breath and narrowed her eyes. How dare he refer to that day! Hadn't he the least bit of shame over the way he'd treated her? She clamped her lips together and fought for composure. If she wanted a new partner, she'd need his cooperation, and getting angry was no way to accomplish that.

"I was just wondering if you'd like to trade partners." Her smile felt stiff and unnatural.

His gaze shifted to some point behind her, then back. "Chicken?" he asked.

Arrgghhh!

"Or just used to having your own way?"

His smirk sent her temper into overdrive. "For your information, I thought you might want a different partner, too! Donald Keeley is willing and the two of you might have more in common."

"You mean, being from the lower class."

"That's not at all what I—"

"Listen, we were drawn as partners fair and square, and it's my policy to play the hand I'm dealt without working things around to suit my whims. I know that may be a new concept for you, but—"

"Never mind!" She whirled around and left him mid-sentence. That man! He thought he knew everything—thought he knew *her,* when clearly, he didn't have a clue who she was!

Brianna joined Evan at the refreshment table and grabbed a can of soda pop from the cooler. She told him she couldn't be his partner, and he pouted his disappointment before returning to his flirty ways. Only when the volleyball games were announced did she return to the sand courts, this time staying far away from her partner. Rules and instructions were given, then the first teams took to the courts.

She and Jake teamed up with another pair as they played four-on-four. It didn't take long to figure out they were mismatched. The other team had eight points before Brianna's team scored. She had to admit Jake was a good player, which the other team quickly figured out, but Brianna had never quite gotten the knack of hitting a volleyball. The years had not improved her skills and every time Brianna hit the ball, it went flying off in some unforeseen direction. It was no surprise when they lost and were eliminated from the tournament.

When the tournament ended, with Megan's team winning, her friends munched on chips and chatted until Stephanie took up the microphone and instructed partners to sit together, since the next activity was a quiz to be completed as a joint effort.

Brianna glanced at Jake, who was still talking quietly to a friend. Since he was making no effort to find her, she walked toward his table.

Chapter 4

Jake glanced up to see Brianna standing beside him. Duane took his cue and trotted away to find his own partner, then Brianna lowered herself to the bench across from him. Papers and pencils were being passed out, but they were instructed not to start until given instructions. A breeze carried Brianna's perfume to his nose. The scent didn't suit her at all. Sweet and subtle. The exact opposite of her.

The class president took the stage again, and Jake rolled his eyes at her overly enthusiastic mannerisms. She told them they'd have a five-minute time limit to complete as many answers as they could, then gave them the signal to start.

Brianna reached out and flipped over the paper, drawing the pencil eraser to her lips. "How many were in our graduating class?"

She turned her fringed blue eyes toward him. "I think there were about one hundred and forty. Do you know the exact count?"

"No."

She wrote the number and continued. "Name one thing your occupations have in common. Hmm." She chewed on the inside of her lip, apparently trying to think of something and coming up with nothing.

"It would help if I knew what you did," he hinted sarcastically.

"Well, excuse me." She narrowed her eyes derisively. "I thought you knew. I'm an interior designer."

He surveyed her pompous expression and couldn't stop from muttering his opinion.

"What did you say?" she asked.

"I said, 'It figures,'" he stated plainly.

"What's that supposed to mean?" She crossed her arms on the table and set her jaw.

If she wanted it spelled out for her, so be it. "It means your career is as shallow as you are." He heard her suck in her breath. "It means while other people have meaningful jobs, you do something so froufrou, only someone of your kind could possible appreciate it."

"Froufrou. . . !"

"It means it's typical for you to be absorbed with how things look and how much they cost." *There. Take that.* Her mouth hung open. He'd obviously shocked her speechless. Jake took a deep breath and boldly studied her face, attempting to calm down and rein in his tongue. If the deep breaths didn't do it, the look on her face did. She was angry, he could see that, but there was hurt in those eyes, too.

Maybe he'd gone too far. *If any man among you seem to be religious, and bridleth not his tongue, but deceiveth his own heart, this man's religion is vain.*

Okay, he'd gone too far. He bridled his tongue.

She loosened hers. "For your information, what I do is more than just beautifying someone's home." Her voice quavered with anger. "I make their home comfortable and warm, a place they want to spend their time. If that's not so noble as some jobs, well, I'm sorry. There's a place for everyone in this world; and if God gave me an eye for color and design, then I reckon He expected me to do something with it!" She lowered her voice to a harsh whisper. "You have no idea what you're talking about."

Suddenly her expression transformed from one of hostility to one of smug satisfaction. She knew something that he didn't. "But you will soon."

"I will soon what?" he asked, feeling a strange sense of dread.

"You'll know exactly what I do."

Her smile bothered him, and he grew irritated with her games. "Just say what you have to say and be plain about it!"

She propped her feet on the bench, clearly enjoying the moment, then she met his eyes. "For the next month, Volez, you're going to have your very own interior designer."

He scanned her features. *What in the world is she talking about?* "What?"

"My mother hired me to redo your cottage. During the next month, you'll go shopping, pick out froufrou patterns, and look through sample books, and all in the delightful company of yours truly."

She looked utterly smug, and it was at his expense. She didn't want to be around him any more than he wanted to be around her. "The cottage is fine. I'll tell your mother I like it just the way it is."

"Floral chairs, doilies, and all?"

"Look, I'm not spending the next month with you under my feet, and that's final."

Brianna's smugness was replaced by indignation. "I'd love nothing better than to drop this project like a hot potato. However, I promised Mother I would do it, before I knew you lived there, by the way, and she's doing it as a gift for you! She went on and on about what a splendid employee you've been and wants to do something in appreciation, so if you dare offend her by rejecting her gift, I'll personally make you miserable for the whole month I'm here!" She slammed the pencil on the table.

Jake digested the information, his countenance going from obstinacy to defeat. He rubbed his hand across his stubbly chin and sighed. "A gift, huh?"

"I don't want to be around you either, but this means a lot to Mother, and I'll not disappoint her."

The microphone screeched as Stephanie picked it up. "Oops, sorry! Time's up! Turn your sheets in to Stacy." She gestured toward the woman. "We'll meet over in the field in half an hour for the last event, the three-legged race."

Brianna snapped up the sheet and turned it in. Not that there was much point—they'd answered only one question. Jake watched as she joined her friends at the courts for a game of pickup volleyball, where they all jokingly argued over which team had to take her. For the moment, at least, it wasn't him.

※

Later that night as Brianna lay in bed, her mind whirled with the day's events. The three-legged race had been a disaster from the start, with two falls and a last-place finish. And the silly rope had rubbed her ankle raw. She recalled the words they'd slammed back and forth like a tennis ball at Wimbledon. What made her so short-tempered with Jake? It wasn't her nature to be so easily riled.

Forgive him.

The inner voice startled her from her drowsy state. Had she not forgiven him for rejecting her? Nonsense, it had been five whole years ago, and she couldn't have carried a grudge for five years.

I have, though, haven't I, God? Why else would I be so defensive and touchy around him? She pulled the quilted comforter around her shoulders. *All right, God, I'm willing, but I'm not sure about able, so this is going to require some heavenly intervention.*

Brianna snuggled under the covers, suddenly feeling very weary.

200

Chapter 5

Brianna stepped through the cottage door and scanned the room with a trained eye. An early morning phone call to Jake had granted her permission to access his home during the day. He'd even been pleasant once he'd known what she'd wanted, probably relieved she could do some of the work solo.

While lying in bed the previous night, she'd decided to treat Jake like any other client. She'd maintain a professional distance, simply refuse to be provoked. How hard could it be?

The cottage had lost the mildewy smell it'd had under Aunt Gerdy's residence and had assumed a more manly scent. She inhaled deeply. Jake.

She meandered to the bookcase and browsed the titles. Nonfiction mostly, books on ranching techniques and cattle, with a few mainstream titles. But what struck her was how neatly the books were shelved. The spines of the books were flush in the front and, when she tilted her head to the left, all the titles ran from the bottom up. She arched her brows. In alphabetical order, even. Brianna's gaze skimmed over the orderly room. Even his shoes were lined up against the wall, toe first. *Not only is he irritatingly smug, he's compulsively organized.* Brianna tended toward organized piles herself, but she could find anything at a moment's notice.

Walking across the room, she whisked a finger across the entertainment center. Not a smidge of dust. Atop the unit was a chessboard, its figurines posed randomly in squares. She wouldn't have figured him for a chess player, but apparently he had a running game with someone. She wondered who. . .

Come on, Brianna, get to work. She'd intended to begin right after breakfast, but her mother had wanted to talk, and Brianna hadn't been eager to start on the cottage anyway. Now it was nearing lunchtime, and she hadn't even begun.

After several trips to the van for sample books, she sat on the chintz sofa and made a list. What style did he prefer? She noted the beamed ceiling and stone fireplace. It would make sense to go rustic but, since money was no object, they could reface the fireplace and vault the ceilings if he preferred contemporary. Somehow she suspected he'd like a rustic or traditional style. He was very earthy himself, rugged and natural. Would he like to keep the hardwood floor or have it carpeted? Which pieces of furniture would he like to keep? Wallpaper or paint? What about color preferences? The familiar questions came easily and, by the time she finished, two pages were full. She started flipping through samples, marking various pages.

Suddenly the door opened, and she turned as Jake entered the house.

"I saw your van outside. Thought you'd be finished by now."

Brianna closed the sample book and began gathering up the ones without marked pages. She'd leave the others for him to consider later. "I didn't expect you until tonight."

"It's lunchtime." He removed his hat and ran his fingers through his hair, giving it a disheveled look.

Brianna consulted her watch. One o'clock already. "Max always took his with him; I guess I assumed you did, too." She walked to the door, struggling with the oversized books. "I'll get out of your way."

He moved aside to let her pass, but she stopped on the threshold. "Are you free tonight to go over some things?" She noticed the five o'clock shadow on his jawline and upper lip. Did the man ever shave?

He spoke, but she didn't hear. Her gaze settled on his eyes, and she noticed for the first time they were the color of dark chocolate. "I'm sorry, what did you say?"

He quirked a brow, clearly amused by her perusal. "I said, give me a chance to eat supper, then you can come over around seven."

"Oh, okay, that's fine. See you tonight." Brianna hurried through the door before she could surrender to the crazy urge to fix his tousled hair.

Jake shrugged on a black T-shirt and finger-combed his damp hair. Returning to the bathroom, he swiped at the foggy mirror, then peered at his reflection. *No time to shave,* he thought, running his hand over his prickly chin. He grabbed his cologne and unscrewed the lid, before stopping cold and replacing the top. *Shaving cologne. . . What is this, a date? Get a grip, Volez. She's just like your mother.*

Before he could brush his teeth, a rap sounded at the front door. He padded barefoot through the living room and opened the door. Brianna stood on the porch looking rich and sophisticated in an ivory pantsuit.

"Good evening, Jake."

Jake stood back and let her pass, then shut the door. She stood just inside the door with a clipboard held against her chest like a shield. She was acting funny. Stiff, formal, not at all the feisty female he knew.

He invited her to take a seat, then sat across from her and propped his feet on the coffee table. He watched Brianna's gaze skitter to his feet and saw a brief flicker of disapproval before she snapped a pen from the clipboard and met his gaze.

"The first thing we need to do is decide what style you'd like to go with: contemporary, rustic, Southwestern, country, etcetera, etcetera. Do you have a preference?"

He knew he didn't like that modern stuff, but what in the world was Southwestern? He knew what he didn't want. A bunch of frilly stuff. And none of that fake cowboy nonsense either.

"The general architecture of your home goes in the rustic or country direction. But we can change some of the features, like the beamed ceiling, for instance, if you'd like to go with a more contemporary style."

"No." The last thing he wanted to do was prolong the process. Better to keep it simple. "Rustic's fine." If she could be distant and professional, so could he.

She made a note. "What about color?"

What about color? He shrugged. "Color's fine."

He saw the corner of her lips twitch. "No, I mean, what kind of color scheme do you want to go with? Do you have a color preference?"

"Oh," he muttered, feeling incredibly stupid. "I like blue. Or green."

She took more notes, her blond bangs falling in her eyes. "How do you feel about the floor?"

He looked down at the shiny planks. "I like it fine."

"Would you rather have carpeting? If you'd like to keep the wood floor, we can find a large area rug to cover most of the living room, and place others in strategic locations."

"Fine." *It's a floor, for pity's sake.*

She continued to go through her list asking question after question. He couldn't believe all the detail involved, and they hadn't done anything yet. He'd been perfectly happy here for nearly five years and couldn't see the point in all this. And some of the questions confused him. He was a rancher, for crying out loud; how was he supposed to know whether wallpaper or paint would be more appropriate?

"How about the kitchen? Wallpaper or paint?"

He huffed, getting more impatient by the second. He was missing the baseball game he'd wanted to watch. "Paint." *Who cares? And even if I did care, I wouldn't know which was better.*

"Fine. Paint." She made a notation, her pen scrawling in angry jabs across the paper.

It would appear Miss Professional is getting a little miffed. He smothered a smirk.

"Bathroom. How do you feel about the sink and tub?"

How does anyone feel about a sink and tub? Water runs, you wash, end of story. "They're fine."

She slapped down the pen and crossed her arms. "Jake, everything can't be fine. This place hasn't been touched in thirty years."

He planted his feet on the floor and leaned forward. "Fine, not fine? How am I supposed to know? I'm a rancher, not a decorator, I don't have a clue what needs to be done!"

"That's what *I'm* here for. All you have to do is ask my opinion and, if you weren't so stubborn you would—"

"Stubborn—!"

"—you would've asked for it an hour ago." She leaned back against the sofa, looking smug and superior.

Heat surged through his limbs. "I didn't ask your opinion," he grated, "because I just want to get this over with. I don't care if I have drapes or blinds, and I especially don't care about my tub and sink. I've had a long day, I'm tired, and this is not the way I want to spend my night!"

"Do you think *I* want to be here?" An angry flush stained her cheeks.

Jake settled back in the chair, attempting a casual look. He tilted a smile, wanting to provoke her. "Isn't Mumsy paying your usual rate?"

Her eyes flashed with anger. "This isn't about money!" She took a deep breath, obviously struggling for control.

It made him want to set her off, put her over the edge. "I thought everything was about money, Princess."

Silence boomed around them for a moment before she stood in one swift motion, clipboard hugged against her body. "I think we're finished for tonight."

By the time he stood, the door was slamming shut. He stared at the door for a minute before snapping up the remote and flipping on the ball game. Who else but a pampered princess would storm out the door when the going got tough? She had no idea what it was like to live in the real world. In her world, luxury was the norm and every whim was granted.

He propped his feet on the table. What about Brianna riled him so? Every time they were together things escalated until they were yelling. He knew what he didn't like about her. It was that richy-rich attitude she sported. She looked down on him as a working-class nothing and, if he ever forgot, all he had to do was remember how she'd played him for a fool in front of all her spoiled friends.

It was her prejudice that made him want to provoke her. It certainly had nothing to do with her looks. Or the way she smelled.

Chapter 6

"H ow about a truce?" Brianna stood on Jake's porch the next evening, clutching her catalogs to her chest. She'd decided to suggest a truce first thing, before her temper flared, and from the look on Jake's face, he was stunned. "We'll be working together nearly every day for the next month, and I don't know about you, but I don't want to be arguing all the time."

"Me either."

"I know we have our differences, but can't we just put them aside for a while?" She looked him square in the eye and waited.

He stepped aside to let her in, then held out a hand. "A truce, then."

She put her hand in his, feeling his warm, rough palm against hers. "A truce," she repeated.

"Sorry I goaded you last night," he said.

His compelling eyes held her motionless. She hadn't thought him capable of a sincere apology, but she knew she owed him one as well. "Sorry I left abruptly."

He released her hand, and as they settled themselves opposite one another in the living room, she was uncomfortably aware of the tension hovering around them. She set the catalogs and magazines on the coffee table with a thump. "All these contain pictures of interiors. I thought if you looked through them and noted things that appeal to you, I'd get a better idea of what you like."

He picked up one from the top of the stack. "Fine."

She gave him a pointed look.

His lips twitched. "I mean, okay."

While he browsed, she looked through sample books, stopping occasionally when he showed her something he liked. As they worked, she glanced at him through a fringe of bangs. His feet were flat on the floor, and his legs were so long that his knees were elevated above the level of the chair. His hair was cut short on the sides and back, but longer on the top, where it lay back in careless waves. It was not quite black, but too dark to be—

"Like it?"

Her gaze snapped to his eyes, heat filling her cheeks. He'd caught her staring shamelessly. Then she noticed the picture he held. *He's referring to the dinette set.*

He waited expectantly. The table was light oak with tapered legs, and the chairs had a handwoven rush seat with an arched ladder-back. Simple, elegant, rustic. "Perfect. I like it. That company makes good, solid furniture. Why don't you mark the page?"

They resumed browsing, but she kept her eyes on her book this time. For all their sparks and verbal sparring, she admitted she was still drawn to him. She remembered the first day she'd seen him. It had been the first day of classes her senior year, and she'd taken a seat in Trig when he'd waltzed in at the ring of the bell. He carried an aura of mystery about him like an invisible cloak. She stared, magnetized by the attraction, until he met her gaze and arched a brow as if amused by her perusal.

That semester, their schedules required them to pass twice a day in the crowded halls. She never looked at him as he passed, but was intrinsically aware of him each time. He was always alone, and she with her friends. Maybe that had been part of the draw, that loner quality he had.

He was sitting alone in the picnic grove when she and her friends were playing Truth or Dare on the open balcony during free time. She couldn't even remember the question she'd passed on before taking the dare. But she remembered Cassandra scanning the area, devising a good dare for Brianna.

She watched Cassandra's gaze settle on Jake before turning back to her with a mischievous grin. She knew at that moment what Cassandra's dare would be, and her heart raced in anticipation. The other girls giggled nervously when Cassandra announced the dare, but Brianna was in her own world, her mind awhirl with the possibilities.

Maybe Jake was attracted to her, too. Maybe he wanted to go out with her. Maybe he was just shy and afraid to approach her.

She pep-talked her way to the picnic grove. Her nerves rattled, but she pretended she was on a stage acting out a character. Someone with courage.

She saw the surprise on his face when she approached. They were alone under the canopy of leaves, and she was glad no one else would witness her boldest move ever. When she spoke, her voice trembled uncontrollably before she remembered to speak from the diaphragm, like she'd learned in Drama.

His surprise transformed into confusion, and his gaze darted around as if he was expecting someone. Then his eyes narrowed at some point beyond her shoulder, and his face grew taut, his lips thinning into a straight line.

She stopped mid-sentence. What had she said? His gaze drilled into hers, animosity spewing from the fathomless depths of his eyes.

She shook herself from her reverie, but found it hard to clear the fuzz from her head. She wasn't acting herself, she knew. Her mind was befuddled with that awful event five years ago. Why had he reacted that way —first receptive, flattered even, then cold and cruel?

She wrapped up things as quickly as she could, unsettled by Jake's presence tonight. This truce had taken away her shield, her means of defending herself from what she knew was the beginnings of attraction.

Whatever had drawn her to Jake in high school was still there.

Later that night Evan called. They chatted casually for a while before he asked her to dinner Saturday night. She hesitated a moment before telling him yes. Although she suspected a relationship between them was futile, she hoped the distraction of another man would eradicate her confusing feelings about Jake. Maybe she was just lonely and needed to date more often. At any rate, she could catch up with Evan on Saturday and get her mind off Jake for a while.

Jake watched Brianna skitter out the door. He'd thought they'd work late and had even bought steaks to grill, but she had other plans. And plans on Saturday night generally meant a date.

He didn't have to speculate who her date was. He'd seen Evan Pierceton flirting with her at the reunion, trying to convince her to trade partners. Although Jake hadn't joined Sycamore High until their senior year, he knew that Brianna and Evan had been an item the year before. And why not? They were perfect for each other. Wealthy, spoiled, beautiful. They could probably talk all night, with the things they had in common.

He went to the kitchen and started a pot of decaf. Later, as he stared out the window sipping his coffee, Evan's SUV passed on the main drive. So, his instincts had been correct. There was no satisfaction, just a dull, empty feeling in the pit of his stomach.

He turned and set his mug on the counter with enough force to slosh the brew over the rim. Why was he sulking about Brianna's plans? What should he care?

Jake walked across the room, then snatched up the cordless and dialed his parents' house.

"Hello?"

"Hi, Pop, it's me."

"Jake! Nick and me were just talking about you."

"Good to see the two of you can get a word in edgewise."

Pop snorted. "Your mother's not here. She went to that spa she fancies for the weekend."

Jake frowned. "I thought your cards were maxed out again."

"She got a new one."

Silence echoed across the line. What could he say that Pop hadn't heard before?

"Well, you didn't call to talk about my problems. Wanna talk to Nick?"

"Sure, put him on."

The phone rustled in his ear, then his brother said hello.

Jake reached up and fingered a discarded pawn. "Got plans tonight?"

"Nope. Is that an invitation?"

"Only if you feel like getting whipped." Jake smiled.

"It's not me about to get checkmated!"

After bantering for a few minutes, they set a time and said good-bye. Jake carefully moved the chessboard from the entertainment center to the coffee table then went to make a pot of regular for Nick.

His sudden desire to keep busy had nothing to do with Brianna. Or her date with Evan.

❧

Brianna unlatched her tennis bracelet and dropped it in the shell-shaped porcelain dish she'd bought on her senior trip to Florida. Her parents hadn't changed a thing in her room since she'd left, and it gave her a weird sense of nostalgia to be back.

Evan had taken her to one of Denver's finest restaurants. She'd dressed for it, knowing Evan's tastes ran to the extravagant, and everything had been perfect, from the wine-braised beef to the delicious chocolate mousse. She should have had a wonderful time.

But Evan's bragging had grated on her nerves. He hadn't been that way in high school. Or maybe he had, and she just hadn't noticed.

Oh, for heaven's sake, it probably wasn't Evan at all. Her emotions were messed up, and she wasn't giving him a fair shake. All night she'd caught herself comparing him to a certain foreman with almost-black hair and chocolate eyes.

Chapter 7

Where's your chess game?" Brianna asked as she passed the TV unit on her way to the kitchen table where Jake sat looking through samples.

"We finished, so I put it away," he answered distractedly.

"You and your girlfriend play chess?"

Jake, seated across from her, lifted a brow in amusement. "Is that your subtle way of asking if I'm attached?"

"Of course not! I just assumed that's whom you played with, that's all."

His lips twitched, making her burn with irritation. "My brother Nick and I have a running game. He came over Saturday night."

"Who won?" Brianna dog-eared a page.

"He did." His words rang with displeasure. "So, how was your night out?"

"Fine." She'd be every bit as specific as he was.

His eyes darted to her face and back down to a

sample of plaid-textured wallpaper. "Did you go to some fancy-schmancy restaurant with *Bevin*?" he mocked.

"It's *Evan*," she said, her eyes narrowing. "And how did you know whom I was out with?"

He shrugged nonchalantly, but a telltale flush crept up his neck. "I saw him drive by." He avoided her eyes. "He's a good match for you, actually."

"What's that supposed to mean?" She didn't know why the statement irked her, except maybe she was remembering how unappealing she'd found Evan the night before.

He met her gaze with amusement. "Do you find that offensive?"

He had her there. She knew he'd meant it as an insult, but it was her own thoughts that indicted her. "Not at all, but coming from you I assumed it was an insult."

He let the comment slide, and they resumed working in quiet. Was Jake bothered by her date with Evan? She couldn't imagine that he would be, since he'd made it clear he couldn't stand her. Unfortunately, she was attuned to her own feelings enough to know that the thought of Jake having a girlfriend had bothered her. Ridiculous! How could she be attracted to someone who loathed her?

One week down, three to go, Brianna thought dejectedly. Then she could return to Los Angeles, to her real life and job.

❧

The week passed with agonizing slowness. Evan called

to ask her out, but she politely declined. She'd tried to convey disinterest toward the end of their date, hoping to dissuade him, but Evan had never been good at reading people, and this time was no exception. She could tell by the surprise in his voice when she'd said no.

Brianna spent every evening at Jake's, except Friday when he had Bible study. She'd ordered the dinette he liked and a tan leather recliner with nailhead trim. Confusion and dismay welled up, forming a tight little ball in her stomach. She found herself noticing little things about Jake. The way he held a pencil in his left hand, the way he used whipped cream in his coffee instead of creamer, the way he frowned when he concentrated.

Their truce was working. Too well. Instead of being irritated by him, she was being attracted to him. She found herself looking forward to his company during the day, then mentally slapping herself. What sense did it make to indulge these feelings? She lived in a different state, had a separate life, a viable business.

Besides, he didn't return her feelings. She'd caught him staring at her several times, but she was astute enough to realize he was just wondering what planet she was from. They *were* very different. Perhaps that was why she felt this absurd attraction. Opposites and all that. If she wasn't careful, she'd end up right where she'd been in high school, setting herself up for a big, fat rejection. And there was no way she was going to let that happen. But the Jake of today seemed so different from the one who had been cruel to her. If she asked, would he tell her why he'd said those things? Would she even have the courage to ask?

⁂

Brianna tapped on the door for the second time, and Jake opened it. He held a cordless against his ear and motioned her in, holding up one finger, to indicate he'd be with her in a minute.

She toted her satchel into the kitchen and withdrew the bulky ring of countertop samples. Taking a seat at the bar, she flipped through the chips while Jake continued his conversation.

"She's always been that way, and she always will be."

Brianna tried not to listen, but her ears tuned in regardless.

"Why don't you come over tonight, get away. I have some steaks in the freezer I could thaw out."

She took a marbled chip off the ring for Jake to consider later.

"That was blind luck." She heard the smile in his voice. "This time, your goose is cooked."

After more ribbing, he said good-bye and turned off the phone with a beep.

"Sorry about that. My brother called just before you got here." He poured a cup of coffee. "Want some?"

"Sure. Everything all right?"

He turned with a sarcastic smile. "At home? As all right as it ever is. My folks are at each other's throats."

She shuffled through the samples. "I'm sorry, it must

be difficult watching them go through a rough time."

He breathed a laugh. "Their whole marriage has been 'a rough time.' " He added skim milk to her coffee, sprayed a glob of whipped cream on his, then set the cups on the bar.

Brianna noted that he'd remembered the way she took hers. "That's too bad."

Later that night, having decided on a countertop, they moved into the living room to discuss the fireplace. The small stone fireplace had an arched opening lined with rectangular stones. The railroad tie mantle, elegant in its simplicity, underlined the deer head above it, which they decided to get rid of.

As she sat on the hearth taking notes, she wondered why he'd been so cruel five years ago. Had he changed that much, or was there some other explanation? The longer she stayed that evening, the more she was driven to find out just why he'd done it. It would be humiliating to relive the event, but she wanted to know. Needed to know.

Twice she'd tried to gather the courage to ask, but each time she'd chickened out. Finally, having had it with her own cowardice, she set her clipboard in her lap and called his name.

"Hmm?" he asked nonchalantly from his place on the sofa, not even looking up from the sample book.

She opened her mouth, then closed it. *Just spit it out, he isn't going to bite you.* "Why did you do it, five years ago? Why did you say those things to me?" Her heart quaked, sending ripples of anxiety through her.

Her gaze darted to his, away, then back. She watched his whole demeanor change from mellowness to anger, evident in his expression and the way his body stiffened. The muscles in his jaw twitched, and his eyes turned cold. She didn't think he was going to answer, but finally he spoke.

"If you want to keep that truce of yours, drop it."

He turned his attention back to the sample book, flipping through the pages, albeit more roughly than before.

Brianna fiddled with the pen cap, removing and replacing it with a click, over and over. So that was it. She'd finally worked up the nerve to ask, and that was all she got.

Well, that wasn't good enough! He'd treated her horribly, and now he was acting as if *she* had done something wrong. She had nothing to be ashamed of and if he couldn't handle a discussion of his disgraceful behavior, that was just tough!

She crossed her arms and tilted her chin. "I don't want to drop it! You owe me an explanation, and I'm not leaving here until I get it."

He settled back against the sofa pillows and crossed his own arms. "Oh, is that right? You think I was too harsh with you, is that it? You think, 'How dare he treat me that way.' " He shook his head, shooting daggers at her. "You have some nerve," he snarled. "Being bitter about that, when the whole time you were playing me for a fool!"

Numb shock zinged along her nerves. "What are you talking about?"

He laughed bitterly. "As if you don't know. What kind of idiot do you think I am? I saw your friends laughing at me while you were putting on your little show."

Her jaw went slack. *That's* what he'd thought? That she and her friends had set him up for a good laugh?

"Let me tell you something, Princess, in case you don't know it yet: Men don't like to be played for a fool. Come on, did you really think I'd buy your little act? Rich, spoiled girl like you coming on to a lowly, working-class guy like me?" His eyes spewed hostility.

She blinked, stunned, as she mentally rewound the tape of her memory, seeing what Jake must've seen. Megan and Cassandra up on the terrace, nervously snickering behind their hands. She'd seen them herself as she'd approached the school. And Jake had seen them, too. Had concluded that they were. . .

"That's not the way it was," she whispered.

He slammed the book shut and tossed it on the coffee table. "I saw what I saw. Why don't you just admit it?"

She tried to swallow the lump that had formed, but shock had sucked the moisture from her mouth. "It's not true." She absently shook her head. "That's not what happened."

He stared back skeptically, stubbornly.

"We were playing Truth or Dare. It was my turn.

222

Cassandra, she dared me to. . . ," she grew hot remembering how she'd acted that day, ". . .to do that to you."

"Then I was right. You were all laughing at me."

"No! That's not it," she defended herself. Her friends, knowing she'd had a crush on Jake, had been trying to help things along.

And then she realized what she'd done. She'd dug a hole for herself. If she tried to tell him how it had been, she'd have to admit that she'd had a crush on him! And yet, if she didn't explain, he'd go on thinking she'd made a joke of him. She couldn't do that.

All right, Brianna. It was just a silly little high school crush. You didn't even know him, for goodness' sake. She glanced at Jake and read the disbelief in his face that accused her of lying, of trying to avoid responsibility for her supposedly cruel behavior. She wouldn't let him think that. It was worse than the truth.

She studied her sapphire ring as she twisted it on her finger. "I. . .I had a crush on you. . .in high school." Her blood pounded, her face burning with embarrassment. "The girls knew it; they were just trying to help." *There. I said it.*

Her gaze darted to him, then away, just enough to know he was staring, and her skin prickled. She was humiliatingly conscious of his scrutiny.

"Right." The word dripped with sarcasm.

She met his gaze. "It's true!"

"Sure it is." He smirked. "Prom queen Brianna had a crush on dirt-poor Jake. Why is it so hard for you to admit the truth?"

Her temper flared. "I have admitted the truth! Why is it so hard for you to believe it?"

Their gazes battled in a war of wills, hers angry and stubborn, his sarcastic and prideful. Gradually, her words and determination seemed to penetrate his wall of obstinacy, and he appeared to waver. She pushed for the goal. "Do you think I'd say that if it wasn't true? Do you think I like admitting it?"

He blinked, her last words of reasoning seeming to sway him. His gaze bore into hers, as if he could read the truth there. Brianna held his stare steadily without flinching, hoping to convey sincerity.

His gaze skittered away, then back again. "If it's true, why were your friends laughing? Don't tell me they weren't, I saw them."

"They were just giggling like high school girls do. They were nervous for me." She snorted. "Not half so nervous as I was." Her cheeks burned in remembrance. She'd really laid it on him. She recalled the surprise she'd read on his face back then. He hadn't seemed angry or dismissive at first, and the only reason she'd been able to continue her role was because he'd seemed responsive.

And then he'd seen her friends! And that was why. . .

"That's why you said those things," she said in wonder. "Because you thought we were—"

He tucked in the corner of his mouth. "Playing me for a fool."

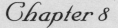

Chapter 8

Jake rubbed a hand over his face. "I can't believe this . . .all this time I thought. . .and you were. . ." The harsh words he'd spoken that day played in his mind, incriminating him. He saw the red patches on Brianna's cheeks and knew she was remembering, too.

"Oh, man." He'd had a filthy mouth in those days. "I'm sorry. . . ." The words seemed inadequate. She'd meant all those sweet things she'd said, and he'd thrown the words right back at her, belittling her, cursing her. No wonder she'd been so snippy with him.

"I always wondered what I'd said."

He shook his head. "It wasn't you. I thought it was just a game. I wanted to put you in your place."

She laughed nervously. "Oh, you did. Believe me, that's the last time I made a move on a man."

He flinched. His apology seemed lame. "I wish I could take it back." He needed to make it up to her. "How about I treat you to your favorite restaurant?" *What are you doing, Volez? Setting yourself up for trouble?*

"Oh, no, you don't have to do that. I understand, really."

"It'd make me feel better. Just pick the place."

She stopped twisting her ring and stared into the kitchen as if the local restaurants were listed on the cabinet doors. "Well, I haven't been to Casablanca's in years—"

"Done. Next Saturday?" Then he remembered the previous Saturday. "Unless you have a date, that is."

"Yes. I mean, no, I don't have plans, and next Saturday will be fine."

Later that night, he wondered what he'd done. As if he weren't spending enough time with Brianna, now he was taking her to a fancy candlelit restaurant. And his reason for disliking her was gone. Now the attraction he'd been feeling all along had no buffer. Thinking of her as a spoiled princess had been easier. Safer.

Attraction aside, they were still wrong for each other. She was born wealthy, just like his mother had been. He knew all too well what happened when affluent and working class mixed: a bitter explosion. In his father's case, one that lasted year after miserable year.

⟨⟩

On Monday Brianna ordered more furniture and wallpaper and bought paint for the scuffed walls. She smiled as she recalled the dainty knickknacks that lined every shelf in the cottage. They'd been fine for Aunt Gerdy, but the pieces practically screamed "old lady." Jake had even admitted his brother harassed him for having porcelain tea sets and miniature music boxes. When she'd pressed him for a decision on the figurines, he'd admitted that he'd rather have no knickknacks at all, which would save her hours of shopping. One less thing to do in the limited time that remained.

Her mother had told her they'd be having Jake over for dinner the night before she left, in celebration of his five years with the Circle Q. Given the way Brianna had been feeling toward him lately, she wondered how she'd feel on the eve of her departure. Last night she'd been stunned to hear what he'd thought all these years. Stunned and relieved. It explained why she'd been able to develop an attraction to him, that he wasn't a cruel person at all, just a man who'd been hurt and had retaliated in kind.

If she hadn't forgiven him already, it would be easy to forgive him now. She breathed a laugh. Wasn't that the way it worked sometimes? Perhaps God had delayed the disclosure of the truth so she'd have to forgive him when she still thought the worst. She had to admit, it had stretched her faith.

She wondered where last night's discussion would lead their relationship. Did he feel the same attraction? Was it even wise to indulge her feelings when her life was in Los Angeles? *Help me, God, to know what's right. I don't want to make a mess of this. Guide me and give me wisdom, and don't let this relationship progress, don't allow my feelings to grow, if Jake's not the one You have for me.*

She opened her eyes and glanced at the cherry

mantle clock. Time to go to Jake's. She grabbed her case containing all her notes and slipped out the door. Before she knew it, she was knocking on his door, holding her breath like a teenager on a first date.

The door swooshed open, revealing the reason for her heart palpitations. *No wonder he makes your heart flutter! Just look at him.* T-shirts and jeans had never done so much for a man, their plainness drawing attention to his well-defined physique. The inky black of the shirt coordinated with his dark eyes and hair, drawing attention to his features.

"Hi, come on in."

Has his voice always been so deep? she wondered. A jazz instrumental floated through the air from across the room. He'd played it before, but his taste in music still surprised her. Country she would have expected, but not the lazy tunes of a saxophone.

She set her case on the counter and snapped it open, withdrawing a tape measure. "Have you decided which print you want for the hall?"

"I've narrowed it down to two. Maybe you can help."

She entered the hall and began measuring. "Sure. Could you pull this to the end?"

His form shrunk the hallway to half its size as he grabbed the metal tip and pulled it to the corner. She read the tape, then jotted the number on her clipboard. Next, she hooked the tab under the woodwork and pulled the tape measure up the wall. Even on tiptoe she couldn't reach the top. Jake took the metal casing from her hand and extended it easily to the ceiling. *My, this hallway is getting cramped,* she thought, swallowing hard. She forced herself to note the number, as he jarred the tab with his foot, freeing the tape to zip up the wall and into its case.

Jake handed her the tape measure but didn't let go until she'd met his gaze. A cocky grin tilted his lips, and his brow was arched at a jaunty angle. "So, you had a crush on me in high school, huh?"

Heat stole into her face with renewed humiliation. He looked entirely too self-satisfied. Irritated, she narrowed her gaze. "I was just a teenager. What did I know?"

His mouth twitched, but before he could comment, she scurried back to the kitchen where she used her calculator to figure how many rolls of wallpaper they'd need. "Why don't you find those two samples, and I'll have a look at them?" she asked, wanting to draw his attention away from her. *Well, he'd recovered quickly from Saturday's discussion! Straight from shock and remorse to conceit and delight.* He'd probably never let her live it down.

Jake set the oversized books on the counter, and she glanced at the samples. Either pattern would fit the rustic style, but she suspected one of them was too dark. She picked up the book and carried it to the hallway. "I think this one will darken the space too much." She held the sample against the wall. "See how the color seems much darker in here?"

"You're right," he said over her shoulder, making her

aware of his proximity.

She closed the book and handed it to him. "Let's try the other one."

He returned with the other oversized book and opened it to the sample he'd chosen. Brianna held it on the wall with both hands and stepped away as far as her extended arms allowed. Straight into Jake's stomach. "Sorry," she mumbled.

He extended his own hand over her shoulder and held one side of the book in place. She dropped one arm, forcing herself to focus on the muted leafy pattern. The colors were great, the pattern was well sized. . . .

And those shoulders. How could she concentrate when those shoulders draped around her like a warm embrace? Every muscle stilled except her heart, which pounded an erratic rhythm. Her breathing constricted, making each breath a concentrated effort. If she turned her head, his lips would be inches away. She longed to lean back into the solid warmth of his chest, inhale the scent that was entirely his own. She inhaled it now, feeling faintly dizzy, either from the sudden rush of oxygen or from the overwhelming emotions his nearness induced. She didn't know which, didn't care.

The music crescendoed in the background, and she suddenly realized her arm had grown heavy. *Just another minute,* she thought, reluctant to leave the security of his arms.

His breath stirred her hair, tickling her ear, and she slowly turned her face until her gaze locked with his.

She saw there what must be reflected in her own eyes. Attraction, desire, promise. The book slid down the wall and onto the floor with a thunk.

His fingers curled under her chin, his thumb caressing in a slow, hypnotic motion, and her breath caught in her throat. His gentleness endeared him to her. His eyes promised a kiss, and she leaned ever so slightly forward, anticipation building to an unbearable degree.

Then his hand fell away, and he cleared his throat. She blinked as he broke eye contact, retrieved the book, and disappeared through the arched opening to the living room. Frozen in place, her numb mind reviewed the last several moments. Had she imagined the whole thing? No, her limbs were shaking, her mouth was dry. She hadn't imagined it, the look in his eyes. She'd seen the look before, the one that preceded a kiss, but she'd never wanted it so badly.

Why had Jake deserted her, leaving her leaning like the Tower of Pisa? She sagged against the wall and wrapped her arms around her midriff. *Get it together, Brianna. He's acting like nothing happened, so can you.*

❧

Jake set the wallpaper book on the counter, then plopped on a bar stool and ran a hand over his heated face. What was he doing? A spontaneous move like that could get him only one thing. Trouble.

Hadn't he told himself repeatedly she was all wrong for him? Hadn't he reminded himself of his parents and their pathetic relationship? Hadn't he been listening?

Apparently not when at the first opportunity he makes a move on her!

He glanced at the doorway to the hall. What was she doing? *Probably wondering what in the world you were doing in there.* What would he say when she returned? He'd like to pretend nothing had happened, but he owed her an explanation.

He propped his elbows on the bar, cupping his lower face with both hands. Seconds ticked by, painfully silent seconds, while the CD player switched CDs.

Finally, she rounded the corner wearing a generic smile and timidly avoiding his eyes. "I think it'll work," she said, opening the book from across the bar. She smacked the pattern. "It's a good choice. Pattern is a good size, colors are perfect."

She was going to pretend nothing had happened.

"I'll order it tomorrow," she said, jotting down the pattern number.

"Brianna—"

"It'll take several weeks to get here, but I'll set an appointment to have it hung."

"Brianna—"

"I know a very reputable man in Denver who hangs paper, and he—"

"*Brianna.*" He clamped his fingers around her wrist. She looked up at him with wide wary eyes, reminding him of the *Whos* of *Who*-ville. "We need to talk."

"About what?"

"Come on, Brianna. You know very well what just

happened. What almost happened."

"It's nothing, Jake, don't worry about it." She twisted a strand of silken hair around her index finger.

"We're all wrong for each other, you know." He waited for her to agree, and when she didn't, he continued. "You're rich, I'm working class; you're all city, I'm all country; you live hundreds of miles away, we have nothing in common. . . ." He ticked them off one by one, but she remained silent, her eyes downcast. "You know I'm right."

Finally, she looked up. "Let's not make a federal case of it, okay? It was nothing."

It was nothing. He released her wrist, his fingers tingling with warmth, and watched her busy herself with her notes. Apparently he'd made a big deal over nothing.

❧

Brianna lay in bed that night, her eyes closed and her mind spinning. She couldn't believe what he'd said tonight. So they were different. Lots of couples were different; everybody knew opposites attracted. And lately, she was very sure of its accuracy. True, they'd had a rocky start, but ever since their talk the other night, she thought they'd put their hard feelings aside.

What had he said? She was wealthy and he was poor? *Hah!* she thought, picturing her pathetic little flat in Los Angeles. After she'd finished design school, she'd decided to start her business right there, wanted to stand on her own two feet and not be tempted to accept help from her parents. She managed, but just barely.

Jake's cottage was nicer than her apartment.

And he'd said something about the distance that separated them. Of course, he had no way of knowing how she'd missed the mountains rising in the distance, or the rolling hills, or the clear, crisp air. The shopping in Los Angeles was great, but who could afford to buy anything? And the traffic and smog weren't much to write home about either.

She'd love to get to know Jake, to find out if this attraction was of any substance. *It's more than attraction, Brianna, admit it.* She rolled over, untangling the sheets from her legs. It was true. Her feelings had gone way beyond the crush she'd had in high school, but she was reluctant to put a name on those feelings just yet. And he obviously felt something. If she hadn't known before, she surely knew it after tonight. Which just proved her point. If they were both attracted, why not see where it led? If her intuition was correct, it would be worth it, differences or not.

She decided to do just that for the remainder of her visit, with or without Jake's participation. She had less than two weeks, but it was better than nothing, and if her feelings were anything to go by, she suspected they were in for the ride of their lives.

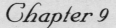

Chapter 9

Brianna winced as she inserted her sapphire studs. The week had gone incredibly well, both in terms of the cottage and her goal to get closer to Jake. He'd really let loose the last few days, letting her see a carefree side of him she hadn't known existed. One evening he'd attempted to teach her chess, and they'd both ended up in stitches at her difficulty remembering each piece's moving capabilities. She'd always been more of a right-brained person. She'd teased him relentlessly about his neatnik habits.

Jake had talked about his family and had even mentioned the source of his parents' problems. No wonder he'd objected to their relationship; his parents had come from different economic backgrounds and had suffered years of problems because of it. But she still thought he was wrong. Perhaps his mother had been a spoiled debutante, but Brianna had been making it on her own for five years. She and his mother were not the same. Now all she had to do was convince him of that.

She wound her hair into a French twist, tucking under the ends, and inserted a decorative comb to secure it. It had been two days since she'd seen him. Last night he'd had Bible study and today he'd had to work. Brianna had gone shopping with Megan and Cassandra, and they'd had a wonderful time.

Her nerves rattled as she readied herself for their. . . she hesitated to call it a date, yet that's how she viewed it. She'd missed him over the last two days and wondered if he missed her.

After pulling a few strands loose to frame her face, she misted her hair lightly with spray. The doorbell rang just as she was slipping on her sandals, and since her parents were out, she descended the stairs anxiously and answered the door.

Jake's typical T-shirt had been exchanged for a gray plaid shirt, and his work boots had been replaced by newer, cleaner ones. His black jeans lent a dressier look than his typical blue ones.

"Ready?" he asked, his smile revealing his own anticipation.

"Sure, just let me get my purse." She pivoted to the foyer table and grabbed it. "Ready."

They walked to his truck, the silence creating an awkward tension. Once there, he opened the door for her and she smiled her thanks. While he walked around, her gaze scanned the interior of his truck. Neat as a pin, of course. He even had a coin sorter, each denomination having its own stack. She teased him about it when he entered, and suddenly they picked up where they'd left off.

The restaurant was crowded when they arrived, requiring a long wait, but they found a bench in the courtyard and settled in. Conversation flowed from their respective days to the churches they attended, then finally to the moment when they'd accepted Christ. Brianna had been only seven and had just a faint memory of her conversion at vacation Bible school. Jake's experience had been only three years ago.

She could hardly believe how time had passed when his name was called and they were led to their table. After a quick perusal of the menu, they ordered. Somehow the conversation turned to grandparents, and she learned his paternal grandparents lived in Denver, but he'd never met his maternal grandparents. It was a sad, vague tale, but apparently his mother had had a falling-out with them years ago and they weren't on speaking terms. He wasn't even sure if they knew of their grandchildren.

Somewhere along the way, Brianna noticed Jake had shaved for their evening out. She'd never seen his chin so smooth, and her fingers ached to caress his jawline. The globed candlelight flickered erratically, casting a golden glow on his skin and a shimmering light in his dark eyes.

When their food arrived, he said a brief prayer, warming her heart considerably, and the conversation became sporadic as they enjoyed the food. After they finished, they refused dessert, too stuffed from the hefty dinner portions, and started back to the Circle Q.

All too soon, the darkened house came into view. He pulled around the circle drive and shut off the engine. As they walked up the porch steps, Brianna realized she was loath to end the evening. "Would you like to see Mother's garden? Or have you already?"

"I've seen it from your patio door, but I've never actually been through it."

She unlocked the door and flipped on a light, going straight through the foyer and great room to the French doors. "Mother had all the excavating done professionally, but she planted the garden and tends to it herself." They walked peacefully along the curved stone walkway, the landscape lights guiding their steps. Brianna led him onto the footbridge which passed over a shallow fish pond.

"Wow. She went all out, didn't she?"

"She's very passionate about her garden and spends a lot of time out here weeding and replacing the annuals."

When they reached the white gazebo, they climbed the steps and took a seat in the glider. Built for two, it forced them to sit closely, a fact that thrilled Brianna. The dim lighting and sway of the glider lulled her into a peaceful, tranquil state. Crickets chirped, adding to the serenity, but her heart jumped when he took her hand in his. For the first time of the evening she could think of nothing to say, but wished desperately she could as the moment stretched into awkwardness.

She knew the instant Jake looked at her, could feel it in the tingles that raced along her spine. She turned slowly to meet his gaze, and her breath caught at the depth of emotion she saw there. How she wanted him to lean forward and touch his lips to hers. If she could will it with her eyes, he'd be kissing her even now.

She drank in the comfort of his nearness, reveling in the heat of his arm alongside hers, the warmth of his hand, the gentle caress of his gaze. The prolonged anticipation was almost unbearable, but she wouldn't initiate the kiss, wouldn't need to, if only he'd read the invitation in her eyes.

Finally, he lowered his head and brushed his lips against hers. The soft, gentle motion evoked a clamor within her heart, stirring her to the depths of her soul. One brief meeting of their lips, then he withdrew an inch before claiming her mouth again with gentle urgency. Time stopped, and the rest of the world shrank to nothingness. If only she could stay here forever in the arms of the man she loved.

The thought startled her, and she must've jumped, for he withdrew, leaving her bereft. Only their hands bound them together when he settled back in his seat, much too far away from her. But the thought echoed in her mind, and she knew it was true. She loved him.

He turned then, wearing a sheepish smile that made her want to kiss him all over again. "It's getting late, I should go."

Her heart cried "no," but he was right, and truth be

told, she needed some time to explore these new feelings. "I'll walk you out."

They rose as one from the glider, still joined by the hand, and meandered back to the house. When they reached the front door, he paused on the threshold, then turned, his eyes shining brightly from the foyer light. She watched his gaze fall to her lips, and her heart lurched madly.

His thumb caressed the back of her hand while his gaze skittered over her face. His longing was there for her to see, and she knew he wanted to kiss her again. That's why she was surprised when he dropped her hand and stepped back.

Her lips twitched involuntarily. "Coward," she murmured.

An easy smile played at the corners of his mouth. "You'd better believe it."

He backed away then, their gazes breaking only when he had to turn and negotiate the steps. With a soft "good-bye" he was in his truck, and Brianna was watching the red taillights recede.

⌘

The next two days dragged as Brianna anticipated seeing Jake. She was tempted to call and invite herself over on Sunday but was afraid he'd say no. It seemed a shame to waste even one day apart, when they only had seven days left. A mere week. And just when she was beginning to realize the extent of her feelings. Whether or not his feelings equaled hers, she couldn't say. But there was definitely interest; and if he could just keep his feelings about their backgrounds in the, well, background, she knew she could convince him to give the relationship a fair try.

Monday afternoon he called and asked her to come early and have dinner with him, and she was elated he seemed to be following his heart. When she joined him, he'd already put steaks on the grill so she shredded lettuce for a salad. The ever-present jazz hovered in the air, adding to the intimacy of the evening. Very little work was accomplished, but they packed the knick-knacks, rolling them carefully in newspaper, before tucking them in boxes for her mother.

He was different tonight, more open, often staring at her, his gaze raking boldly over her face. That they'd endured the entire evening without touching amazed her, when she felt so attuned to him.

When they'd delayed their good-bye as long as they dared, he walked her to the van, each of them carting a heavy box. After depositing them in the back, Jake opened the driver's door. She turned, one hand on the steering wheel, willing him to step closer. He didn't disappoint.

"Tomorrow night?" he murmured.

"Wouldn't miss it."

"Come for dinner again."

"All right."

His face glowed from the van's interior light, and she saw his intent written there. His mouth covered hers, tenderly at first, then more insistently, until she feared he'd feel the wild thumping of her heart. The kiss lingered, his hands finding her waist, the only thing keeping her upright. Too soon he stepped away, and she entered the van, her legs trembling with every movement. Then they were saying good-bye, and it was she who drove away, leaving him to stare after the taillights.

❦

The painters were scheduled to arrive on Wednesday, so Brianna met them and showed them which colors went where. After opening the windows, she left them and spent the day with her mother, returning to the cottage every few hours to check on the painters.

That night Jake picked her up, and they headed for town, where she'd found a painting suitable for hanging over the fireplace. Although they were hungry, the gallery closed at six, so they rushed there first.

She led him through the first showroom to the back of the studio where the painting hung over a row of decorative mirrors. It had a rustic wooden frame and portrayed mountain peaks looming over a lazy river. She'd seen many paintings depicting the same thing, but this one captured the mood and theme of the cottage's new look.

"Well, what do you think?" she asked.

"Umm. Beautiful."

A satisfied smile formed on her lips, but as she started to turn to him, she caught his gaze in the ornate mirror in front of her. Her breath caught at the compelling, magnetic look in his eyes. "I meant the painting," she murmured, feeling the heat of his chest against her back.

A saleslady with bad timing approached them, and they were forced to turn their attention back to the landscape. Moments later the woman was wrapping the piece in brown paper and locking the door behind them, smiling at the commission she'd earned.

After stowing the piece in the truck, they walked two doors down to a café that specialized in gourmet coffee. Jake seemed skeptical but went along when she insisted they had wonderful sandwiches.

They were in line when Cassandra's mother entered the shop. Spotting Brianna, she glided toward them wearing a wide smile. "Brianna, what a delight to see you here! I must say, I've taken your advice on those pieces for the foyer, and they look simply wonderful!"

"I'm so glad to hear it." She put a hand on Jake's arm. "I'd like you to meet Jake Volez. Jake, this is Cassandra's mother, Mrs. Loughton."

He extended his hand, which she shook daintily with her jewel-clad hand. "Nice to meet you, ma'am."

"A pleasure. Brianna, you must come by before you leave and see the changes I've made, and I'd love your opinion on a fabric for the divan."

"I wish I could, Mrs. Loughton, but Mother has me doing Jake's cottage, and I'm afraid we're in a bit of a rush to finish it before I leave on Sunday."

"Oh, dear, I didn't realize you were leaving so soon."

The line pushed forward, and she and Jake ordered their food. Mrs. Loughton continued talking to Brianna until the employee placed their tray in front of them. It was embarrassing the way the woman had all but ignored Jake, and she was glad Mrs. Loughton had purchased her coffee to go.

While they ate, Brianna attributed the lull in conversation to their hunger, but when Jake remained quiet on the ride home, she began to wonder if something was wrong. When she asked him questions, his answers were stilted and brief. He pulled through the circular drive to drop her off, and she asked him in, but he declined. The quick peck he placed on her lips further convinced her that something was wrong, as did the tight smile he offered when she exited the truck.

⌘

Jake watched to make sure Brianna got in the house then pulled away. A raw, nagging feeling churned in the recesses of his mind until he forced it to the forefront. Somehow, over the past week, he'd let himself forget their disparate backgrounds. He'd followed his emotions, and now he'd grown to care for her.

But their encounter with that lady tonight had reminded him of their obstacles in a big way. She'd reminded him of his own mother, from the way her expensive perfume preceded her into the shop, to her diamond-encrusted jewelry, to her easy dismissal of him. Sure, his clothes were dirty and worn, he'd come straight from work, but that didn't make him any less of a person. It had in her eyes, though.

She and Brianna had talked nonstop about figurines and divans—whatever those were—and seemed to speak each other's language. It had been an eye-opener, one that hurt like mad when he realized what it meant.

He'd been right thinking the relationship would never work. His parents were proof that wealthy and working class didn't mix, and Jake had always planned to avoid the situation at all costs. Unfortunately, one gorgeous, special woman had made him forget those convictions. Those flashing blue eyes and sweet, curved lips had erased the thoughts from his mind, replacing them with something that felt wonderful, overwhelming.

What was overwhelming now was the realization that he'd have to end it. He'd gotten in deeper than he'd ever intended, and that had only made things worse, especially now that he would have to end it. His heart ached at the thought. One way or another, she was leaving on Sunday, but he wouldn't make things worse by getting closer. He'd tell her tomorrow, and hopefully, she'd see the wisdom in his decision.

∽∾

On Thursday Brianna aired out the freshly painted cottage. The colors they'd chosen had really warmed the home, but it was disappointing that she wouldn't see the finished product before she left. She hung the giant painting they'd purchased the night before, as well as the other wall hangings they'd acquired over the past few weeks. The change was good, and she thought Jake would be satisfied.

Maybe she'd drive back when the furniture was delivered and the wallpaper hung. Now that there was something between her and Jake, she'd have a good reason to come back. She'd even been toying with the idea of moving Interior Motives here. Denver was close enough to provide a client base, and their family had many contacts that could start her off. Well, she'd have to wait and see how things went with Jake. But the way it was progressing and the way she was feeling, she expected something serious to come of it.

She'd realized this morning when she'd awoken that his distance the night before was because he dreaded her departure. Of course he'd be worried and hurt at the thought of her leaving, but that was just because he didn't know she'd consider moving back to Valley View. Maybe she'd tell him tonight—put his mind at ease.

When she arrived at his house he was a flurry of activity, shoving catalog after catalog before her, showing her the items he'd circled. The shutters, the countertops, the sink—everything they needed to finish the job. She marked the pages, wondering about his rush. They still had Friday and Saturday to finish, but he seemed intent on finishing tonight.

Finally, she pushed the stack aside. "What's going on, Jake?"

He avoided her eyes, flipping through the next catalog. "I'm just picking out stuff. You said we needed to get this done."

Maybe he wanted to finish it so they could devote the next two days to each other. "We have two more days. You're acting like tonight's our last night." She breathed a laugh at her last words and noticed the way his hand paused briefly over the pages before continuing. Her stomach dropped to the floor, and her heart skipped a beat. "We do have two days left, don't we?"

He closed the catalog, his gaze darting to hers then away again. "I've been thinking maybe we shouldn't spend any more time together."

Icy fear coiled around her heart, squeezing the breath from her lungs as panic swept through her.

"You'll be leaving in a couple days, so what's the point in pursuing this? It wouldn't work anyway."

"What do you mean, it wouldn't work?"

His gaze met hers, brimming with passion. "Come on, Brianna. We're from two different worlds; we've said so all along, and nothing's changed."

Rising anger burned in her throat. "*You've* said so all along, I don't agree."

His impatient sigh ignited her fury. "What's this past week been about, then?" she asked. "Where were your convictions then, when you were kissing me? Was it just a game, something to break the monotony, have a little fling while Brianna's here, then move on when she's gone?" Her voice rose, and she felt the hot sting of tears.

Jake rubbed a hand over his face. "You know it wasn't like that. I just forgot—wanted to forget—the reasons it wouldn't work. But it wouldn't. I've seen what happens firsthand—"

"I'm not your mother! And you're not your father. Just because they have problems doesn't mean we would!"

He leaned back in his chair and crossed his arms, a gesture she'd learned meant he was not budging. "I'm not changing my mind, Brianna. I'm sorry I let things get out of hand. I never should've. . . . But I think it's best if we go our separate ways."

Unpleasant tingles zinged across every nerve in her body. Her heart was a painful mass, and her throat ached with a dry lump that wouldn't budge. "You don't mean that," she whispered.

His eyes brimmed with regret even while his body language shouted his resolve. "It's for the best."

She sat there hurting for a stunned moment, then forced herself to calmly gather the catalogs on the table. There would be no histrionics, and pride forbade her to beg. She glanced around the room at the piles of samples and books that had accumulated over the weeks. She'd get them tomorrow while he was gone. She stood stiffly and walked to the door. When she reached it, she turned the knob and paused briefly, fighting the urge to turn and look at him. Instead, she straightened her back and walked through the doorway, closing it with a soft click.

Chapter 10

Friday passed in a blur of pain, and on Saturday her mother reminded her Jake was invited to dinner that night to celebrate his five years at the Circle Q. Some celebration. She'd never felt less like celebrating in her life, and if he had half the feelings she had, he wouldn't be in a party mood, either.

She confided some in her mother while they weeded the garden that day, but she glossed over it, not wanting her mother to know the extent of her feelings or feel bad about the dinner she'd planned.

He was on her mind all day, and she went from anger to hurt and back again until she felt like an emotional boomerang. She wanted to call him, oh, how she wanted to call him, and convince him how wrong he was. But she knew him too well. Nothing short of a miracle would change his mind. She asked God repeatedly why He'd allowed her to fall in love with Jake when it wasn't going to work. She'd specifically asked for guidance, and she'd felt so sure it'd been right. That she and Jake had been right for each other.

You are, an inner voice whispered. She laughed derisively. *Great, tell Jake that.*

She stopped weeding, her hand frozen in midair with a dandelion. *I will. I will tell Jake that.* There'd be no holding back this time, she'd tell him how wrong he was, and he'd listen. He'd have to. Doubt wormed its way into her thoughts. *What if he rejects you again? This time it'll be worse, because you love him.*

She attacked the next weed with new vigor. *It won't be like last time. He cares for me, too, and I'll make him see we have something wonderful.*

This is awful, she thought, glancing periodically at Jake from across the linen-covered table. *It's awkward, stiff, and the tension's so thick, we could've served it for dinner.*

Her mother and Max made an admirable effort at conversation and, she had to admit, Jake was trying. But she could see right through his flat smiles and forced replies. He was hurting, too, but that was a good thing, because she planned to put an end to both their suffering. *If we can just make it through dinner. . .*

The strained evening lingered far too long to suit her. After dinner Jake sat with them in the parlor, making stilted conversation. She longed to force an end to the evening, to grab Jake by the hand and say it was time to go. How she wanted to get him alone and spill her thoughts, convince him he was wrong. Instead she waited until the talk had given out and he stood to say good night.

"I'll walk you out," she blurted, then smiled sheepishly at her eagerness.

He shot her a look of surprise. "Oh, okay. Good night, Mr. and Mrs. VanAllen, and thanks again for everything. The cottage is looking great."

After the pleasantries were exchanged, Brianna ushered him out the door. Another moment of silence filled the gap between them until she broke it. "Well, that was—"

"Awkward," he stated emphatically.

She laughed nervously. "It *was* pretty awful." His truck was parked at the bottom of the steps, and they stopped when they reached it. Suddenly her nerves clamored. This was it, her chance to change his mind.

"Did you have something to say?" he asked.

Her gaze darted to his and she wanted to drown in the depths of his eyes. "I. . .yes, I do." She took a breath and raised her chin a notch. It was now or never. "You're wrong about us, Jake." Skepticism flared in his eyes, and she spoke again before he could stop her. "This is right, I know it is, I feel it. Don't you think God is capable of working this out?"

"I think God expects us to use our common sense."

"I'm not your mother. I've been on my own for five years, I've paid my way, started my own business. How can you think I'm irresponsible and spoiled?"

He reached out as if to touch her, then dropped his hand. "I don't think you're those things, Brianna. We were raised differently. My family scraped by with the bare necessities because of my mother's spending. We got what we needed, nothing more. You grew up with everything, it's ingrained in you." He gestured wildly at her childhood home. "Look at this, it's luxury; you got everything you wanted."

She gave a choked, desperate laugh. "If I got everything I wanted, how come I'm losing what I want most?"

His eyes darkened with pain, but he issued no words of encouragement. Disappointment reverberated through her system like the deep boom of fireworks. "Rejected again." She hadn't meant to speak the words, and she dropped her lashes quickly to hide the hurt.

"No," he said emphatically, touching her cheek in a gentle caress. "It's not like that, please don't see it like that," he said in a low, tortured voice.

She wanted to believe it; but either way, he was ending it, and that hurt like nothing she'd felt before. She looked up at him, tears trembling on her lashes. Her gaze fixed on his lips. If she could just have one last kiss to remember. . . Maybe he'd even change his mind if she could make him remember what they shared. "Kiss me good-bye," she said thickly.

He shrank away, and she knew she must press her advantage. "Just a kiss, that's all; you owe me that." She clutched his shirt, pressing closer.

Misery and longing were written all over his face. She could see his inner battle. "Just a kiss," he whispered.

She closed her eyes as he drew closer and felt the soft

caress of his lips as they brushed hers. Every fiber of her body felt the touch, and she memorized every nuance of the kiss in case it was the last. But surely it wouldn't be. Couldn't he feel the promise between them?

He drew away slowly, regret in every line of his body, until they were touching no more. He opened the door of his truck and lowered the weight of his body, then turned. His flat, unspeakable eyes prolonged the moment. "Bye, Princess," he rasped.

The last spark of hope was smothered, and her throat ached with defeat. A hot tear trickled down her face, but she couldn't speak past the solid lump in her throat. As he closed the door and started the engine, she prayed he'd look at her one more time; but her prayer went unanswered, and he drove away without another glance. Another tear traced the path of the first, then another, and another, until she sank onto the brick step and sobbed.

Chapter 11

Brianna wearily kicked off her pumps and lowered herself onto a kitchen chair. She'd had a rash of business in the two weeks since her return to Los Angeles, and although she had plenty of time to complete the projects, working late helped keep the misery at bay.

She crossed the apartment to her room and changed into her nightgown. Working from dawn until late at night gave her little time to dwell on Jake, but every day that dreaded time came. The time she spent lying in bed, trying to go to sleep, while her traitorous mind replayed their moments together. No matter how late she went to bed, when the lights were out and the only sounds were the rumble of cars on the street, her memories tormented her. When would she stop missing him? Loving him? Even her friends had noticed her depression, saying she'd lost her spark.

All the wallpaper would be up by now, and some of the furniture would be arriving. Would he know where to place everything? Had she written it on the list she'd left? She'd given him a business card, but even if he didn't know what to do with the sofa and tables, he'd never call and ask.

She curled up on her bed, hugging the pillow to her chest. *Oh, God, I didn't think it was possible to miss someone so much.* To feel it as a physical ache. To find herself thinking she'd have to tell him this or that, forgetting she wouldn't see him again. Ever. *Help me, Lord, to get over him, and soon, if You please. I can't stand this much longer.*

How much longer can I stand it? Jake wondered as he stared at the pitiful arrangement in his living room. He needed her. He laughed derisively. His furniture needed her. Every time he moved it around, either the recliner wasn't facing the TV or there were pieces left over. The latest arrangement blocked the entrance to the room. How had she said it was supposed to go? He looked over the notes she'd left. Nothing. His eyes flicked up to the card.

Call her.

He quickly dismissed the thought. Four weeks of separation had only made the ache worse, and it didn't help that everything in the house reminded him of her. But he'd made the right decision, and a call would only remind him all over why he loved her.

He angled the sofa and tried the recliner at the head of the room, but sighed impatiently when the grouping left an end table with no place to go. He decided to leave it as it was for now.

❧

Later that night he hung up the phone, having just had a most enlightening conversation with his dad. He slumped on the misplaced sofa, stunned.

He'd had it wrong all along about why his mother acted the way she did. Evidently, as the only child she'd been spoiled rotten, especially by her daddy. When she'd been eighteen, she'd met his dad, who'd just gotten hired as a groundskeeper. His mother had been drawn to his father and they'd eventually fallen in love. Or so his father had thought. When Clarisse had informed her father whom she was going to marry, Jake's dad had thought it proved how deep her love was. When, in reality, she was just rebelling, wanting to prove to herself her daddy could deny her nothing. When he did, threatening to disown her, she hadn't believed him. She'd run away, marrying his father.

When she returned home, and her parents refused to see her, she was shocked. It hadn't taken his father long to figure out that she'd never loved him to begin with. Ostracized by her socialite friends, she'd been stuck with his father. Over the years, she'd threatened to leave, but with no skills and no family to return to, she'd never followed through on her threat. How sad for his father, who'd never stopped loving her.

Every conviction he'd had about rich people had been wrong. He'd been convinced he was right, but he'd been so wrong. *Oh, Lord, don't You grow weary of my bullheadedness? I ruined my relationship with Brianna over this. You tried to tell me, didn't You, but I didn't listen. And now, it may be too late.*

Did she miss him? Love him? If he called—no, if he went to her—would she take him back?

Jake pushed himself off the couch with new resolve. There was only one way to find out. He found the phone directory and flipped through the yellow pages. She'd dared to risk rejection twice for him, and he was prepared to do the same for her.

Chapter 12

"A re you sure this is it?" Jake asked the foreign cabby as they pulled to the curb. The neighborhood was a stark contrast to the VanAllen ranch, the only grass a long strip between the curb and sidewalk. He eyed the brick building with skepticism. This isn't at all where he'd pictured her living. The iron-railed balconies were stacked on the front of the building like rungs on a ladder, housing plants, toys, and grills. The only exterior embellishment was a faded green canopy jutting over the entry.

"Yes, yes."

Jake paid the man and exited the car, frowning as it pulled away. Maybe he should've had him wait. Brianna might not be home. Or, she might not want him to stay. The thought sent a rush of adrenaline through him.

This is it, Volez. He approached the door and slipped inside, catching a vague whiff of cigarette smoke. Glancing down at his scrap paper, he saw she lived in 4C, so he mounted the stairs. A wave of apprehension swept through him, gnawing at his confidence. What if she was seeing someone else? What if she didn't want him anymore?

Tension mounted with each step, and when he reached the fourth floor, his heart hammered wildly. There it was, 4C. A plain brown door, just like all the others, but behind it was the woman he loved, the woman he intended to have.

He rapped firmly on the door, then waited impatiently, his gaze glued to the peephole. What would she think when she saw him? Would she be glad to see him? Angry? Indifferent?

He knocked again. What was taking so long? How long could it take to walk to the door?

Maybe she wasn't home. He glanced at his watch, seeing that it was nearly 8:30 California time. Surely she wasn't still at work. He shifted his weight and crammed his hands in his pockets. *Maybe I should have dressed up a little instead of wearing jeans,* he thought, scanning his outfit.

He pounded on the door again, losing hope. She'd have answered by now, if she were home. His gaze darted around the landing, taking in the brown commercial carpeting and white, scuffed walls.

He sighed heavily and ran a hand through his hair in frustration. What to do? Should he sit and wait for her or catch a cab to her office? Maybe she was at the grocery or the library; she could be anywhere. Still, he wasn't in a waiting mood.

Brianna growled when she heard the knock. *Milton!* Would he ever give up? She'd told him five minutes ago she wasn't interested; did he think she'd changed her mind already? She went in the kitchen and scanned the interior of the cupboards. They were full from yesterday's trip to the grocery store, but nothing looked good anyway.

Another knock sounded and she slammed the cabinet door shut. She was in no mood for his games tonight. A person liked to have a few minutes of solitude when they got home from work, a chance to unwind.

At the third knock, she lost her resolve to ignore him and went storming to the door, flinging it open. "Milton, for the last time—" Her words died in her throat, which constricted instantly. "Jake!"

He bolted upright from his position at the railing. "Brianna. I didn't think you were home."

"I am," she said, cringing at the stupidity of the statement. Why was he here? Hope sprang up like a buoy, and she quickly squelched it. "Sorry, come in." She stepped aside to let him pass, inhaling the scent that was all Jake. Oh, how she'd missed him! Everything in her wanted to grab him and never let go. "Would you like something to drink? Coffee, tea. . ."

"No, thanks."

She gestured him to the love seat and took a seat safely across the room on the sofa.

"You're looking well," he said.

She still wore her work clothes but knew the concealer she'd applied this morning to her dark shadows was long gone. "So are you." It was no lie, an understatement, if anything. Silence engulfed the room until she thought she couldn't bear to wait another moment to hear why he'd come.

"We need to talk." His eyes bored into hers with an unreadable expression.

"About. . . ?" Her stomach churned nervously.

"I was wrong."

The words spilled from his lips, igniting hope in her heart. She was afraid to hope, afraid she was mistaken.

He leaned forward, clasping his hands between his knees. A lock of hair fell over his forehead, and she longed to brush it away. "Everything I said, about my mother, her past. I was wrong. My dad and I talked, and I've had it all wrong." He lowered his eyes until his lashes brushed his cheeks. "This isn't coming out right."

She swallowed with difficulty and found her voice. "What are you trying to say?"

Slowly, he got up and walked around the coffee table, lowering himself next to her on the sofa. She shuddered when his thigh touched hers. That look in his eyes, she knew it well. He'd come because he'd missed her. Her gaze clouded with tears, but she blinked them back, not wanting to miss anything.

His hand found hers. "You're not anything like my mother." He gave her a wavering smile. "And I'm not much like my dad, either. The point is. . ." He tilted up her chin, making sure he had eye contact. "I love you, Brianna," he whispered.

Her breath caught around the lump in her throat. "I love you, too." Her insides clamored, and she gloried briefly in the shared moment before his lips brushed hers. Her hands found his face, holding him near, reveling in the familiar feel of his whiskers.

He broke away too soon, a smile forming on his face. "I'm going to marry you, woman," he said with intensity.

She lifted her chin defiantly. "Oh, really. And do I have a choice about this, Volez?" she asked only half seriously.

His lips tipped in a cocky grin. "Nope."

"There's a lot to consider, here, you know. I have a business. I can't just pick up and leave at the drop of a hat. It takes time, planning, lots of work. And then there's the matter of marketing and contractors. I don't even know if Denver—"

He cut her off with a kiss, and she surrendered gladly, melting in the warmth of his embrace, delighting in the caress of his lips.

Then he drew away. "That's one way to quiet you." He smiled lazily.

"Do it again," she whispered.

And he did.

DENISE HUNTER

Denise lives in Indiana with her husband and three active young sons. As the only female of the household, every day is a new adventure, but Denise holds on to the belief that her most important responsibility in this life is to raise her children in such a way that they will love and fear the Lord. She began her writing career in 1996 with a manuscript for a novel that was published with **Heartsong Presents** in 1999. She hopes to give Christian readers a wholesome alternative to secular romances and to write characters that will help readers in their Christian walk. Her writing includes the message that "God needs to be the center of our lives. If He isn't, everything else is out of kilter."

Too Good
to Be True

by Janice Pohl

Dedication

To my friends and family,
who have paid me the supreme compliment
of being unsurprised at my success,
to Don Musch, who inspired this story,
and to Jim Lorentz,
who didn't believe the news of my latest sale.

Prologue

Kathryn Donaldson groped for the door handle . . .then watched her own hand fall away and curl into a little fist in the middle of her lap. The knuckles were white with tension. Could that be her hand? She never used to be afraid of anything. "I can't do it," she said hopelessly and turned to her beloved cousin, Glenn, for comfort.

Glenn made a rude noise and turned off the ignition. "Sure you can. Just pull, and the door will pop right open. Then you can get out. Piece of cake."

"I can't."

"You will."

"What if he's here?"

"We're sort of hoping he is," Glenn reminded her. "Hey, stop looking at me like Little Red Riding Hood checking out the wolf. This was your idea, remember?"

"What will I say to him?" She looked through the windshield at the small knots of people gathered around the picnic tables. The thought of seeing Daniel again filled her with equal parts dread and desire. "How can I face him?"

"Well," he said slowly, "you'll walk up to him and say, 'Hi, Dan, remember me? The gal who broke your heart?' And, *if* he remembers you. . ."

"Har, har," she said sourly.

"You'll tell him you're sorry. That you were a different person then. That you were such a control freak, you couldn't give your faith to God."

"But now I'm better," she said sarcastically.

"Yup. And that's all you can do." His blue eyes twinkled at her. Despite her anguish, she felt a spark of amusement. Even though he was a year post-op, it was still so good to see her cousin taking such joy from rejoining the human race. He derived pleasure from things most people took for granted: eating meat, staying up late, driving a car. Even standing in lines delighted him —a man who as recently as last summer needed a wheelchair to travel more than six feet. "Now, enough. Let's get out of this car. You'll make yourself sick with worry and then puke all over my upholstery."

"My upholstery," she reminded him, opening the door and climbing out. "You insisted on driving my car, remember?"

"Mine doesn't have air," he pointed out. He jingled the keys at her, then shoved them in his pocket. "Come on. You might be working yourself into a nervous frenzy, but I can't wait to see everyone again."

They walked through the grass, toward the small

group of people chatting around picnic tables loaded with food. A large white banner had been put up: "MIN-NEAPOLIS GENERAL HOSPITAL DONOR AND KIDNEY RECIPIENTS REUNION." Her cousin, whose lifesaving surgery had taken place a year ago tomorrow, practically skipped toward the sign and the people. His happiness brought an involuntary smile to her lips. If nothing else, she would love Daniel forever because he saved her cousin. She put Daniel first in her prayers every night, thanking her Father for sending hope and goodness and life in the form of Daniel Taylor.

Whom are you kidding? she asked herself. *You're doomed to love Daniel forever regardless of what he did for Glenn, and you're alone because of your fear and foolishness. Now reap what you've sown, stupid girl.*

That was a familiar litany, but now she could counter it. She reminded herself of all she had learned the past year. If God could forgive her, she could certainly forgive herself. He couldn't be too crazy about her putting herself down all the time, either.

She squared her shoulders and marched after Glenn, so keyed up with anxiety she could barely nod to the people greeting her. Glenn was embracing Erika, the head nurse from the ward where he had recovered from surgery last year. "I'm chock-full of kidney goodness," he was proclaiming when she walked up to their small group.

"Ewww, Glenn!" Kathryn wrinkled her nose then shook Erika's extended hand. "Nice to see you again."

"You too, Kathryn. What a lovely necklace."

Kathryn fingered the gold cross self-consciously. "Thank you. Have you seen—uh—do you know who else is here?"

"Well, most of the nurses made it, and all of the docs. And Jenna—the transplant coordinator—is over by the soda. She's really hoping to see you two again. Wasn't this a great idea?"

Kathryn agreed. When a patient landed in the hospital with renal failure, the family got incredibly close to the hospital staff in a very short time. They became like family. To many, they *were* family. Post-operatively, once everyone was healed and home, you never saw them again. Strange, Kathryn had thought at the time, to develop such close relationships and then turn your back on them. Strange and wrong. When the invitation to the donor reunion showed up in last month's mail, she and Glenn immediately agreed to go.

If nothing else, she thought miserably, scanning the crowd for Daniel's tall, dark-haired form, *it'll give me a chance to tell him I'm sorry. To beg his forgiveness. If I can only face him. If I can only look him in the eyes.*

"Daniel!" someone shouted, and she jumped. But it was a different Daniel, a small blond boy being shouted for by his mother. She took a last look around at the crowd and plunged among them.

If she hadn't been so nervous about her upcoming confrontation, Kathryn would have enjoyed herself immensely. The reunion was being held in a park on the edge of town, and it was a perfect spring day: sunny, with cottony white clouds and a slight cooling breeze. The grass was deep and thick and an enticing emerald green; she wanted to take off her shoes and socks and sink into it past her ankles. It was a day anyone—not just those recently on the brink of death—would appreciate.

It was a pure pleasure to see again the staff who were so instrumental in saving her cousin. It was strange to see Dr. Filkins, the woman who had performed the surgery, out of surgeon's scrubs and wearing. . .were those bib overalls? Strange to see the nurses without their stethoscopes and thermometers. Glenn bounded among them like a puppy, shaking hands and hugging and chattering nonstop.

Everyone looked healthy and happy. She recognized Sara, the mother of four teens, who had been on dialysis for six years before getting a kidney. Sara was so busy chasing her kindergartener she barely had time to look up, much less mingle. But her face was radiant. Sara's sister, Emily, who had donated the kidney, watched her family with a delighted grin.

Kathryn neatly avoided Sara's toddler and kept scanning the crowd. Her fears about seeing Daniel now seemed stupid; he wasn't here. She was about to give up the search and join Glenn when she saw him.

He was looking right at her, standing on the far fringe of the crowd. He stood with his hands in his pockets and watched her, and at the sight of his dear face, her heart contracted into a small ball of dread. The good man standing several feet away was lost to her forever. Now all that was left was her apology.

Please, God, she prayed, and for an awful moment couldn't move. She found strength from somewhere and made herself walk toward Daniel on shaky legs. *Please let me be brave just one time. Let me explain and apologize. Please don't let me run away from this. From him.*

As she walked toward him, she was reminded of their first meeting. Glenn had been right. She was a different person then. Exhausted and hurt and terrified and furious. . .at herself, at Glenn, at God. Daniel had come and tried to save her from herself. She had needed God so badly, but hadn't known what to do or how to ask. In the journey toward her Father, she had lost the man she loved.

Reunions, she thought dully, stumbling through the grass. *What a terrible idea.*

Chapter 1

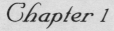

Twelve months earlier

Kathryn watched her cousin hold off death and realized she hated God. Well, no. That wasn't true at all. She didn't hate God. She didn't feel anything about God, because she didn't—never had, never would—believe in God. And if she ever had, watching Glenn fight off renal failure would have forcefully reminded her that everyone on the planet was on his own.

Abruptly she stood and crossed the small room to stare out the window. It was a mockingly beautiful day, as if everything were fine, as if someone she loved weren't battling for his life. What was it, Kathryn wondered gloomily, about hospital rooms? They all had the same smell: disinfectant and despair.

"I know that look," Glenn said, snapping her out of dark thoughts. "It's your 'there is no God and Glenn's an idiot to believe otherwise' glare."

"It is not," she automatically argued. She went back to the uncomfortable hospital chair but was unable to make herself sit down. She'd spent too much of the year in hospital chairs—as much time as Glenn had spent in hospital beds, as a matter of fact. "I was just remembering I'm out of milk, is all. It's depressing, running low on dairy products."

"Sure." Glenn smirked at her from his bed. "Hey, kiddo, I'm not dead yet. Quit mentally picking out my casket, okay?"

"Okay," she said obediently, suddenly angry at him —no, *furious* with him—but concealing it, she hoped. While part of her felt relieved Glenn didn't want to discuss funerals and the inevitable, the other part grew enraged at his steadfast refusal to see the truth: that there was no God, and if there were, He had abandoned them at the worst possible time.

Sad how, at the end, they were still having the same argument. All their lives, they had argued theology. Glenn's faith never wavered; not when Kathryn's parents died, not when he had been diagnosed with kidney failure, not as he endured dialysis. He blamed Kathryn's lack of faith on her "yucky control freak nature" and the untimely demise of her parents. Her foster families couldn't be bothered to tend to her physical and emotional well-being, never mind her spiritual side.

Kathryn, on the other hand, blamed her lack of faith on good old-fashioned common sense. Glenn was her family, the only person on this wretched globe she cared about, and now he was dying, his body swarming with toxins his belabored kidneys could no longer filter. There would be no kidney donor. Glenn had one of the rarest blood types in the world, with uncommon factors that had so far not been matched. They had been checking international databases for months, but so far a donor —live or cadaver—with compatible blood and tissue had not been found. And, of course, wouldn't be.

She felt a dull thump, stopped pacing, and whirled to see Glenn had heaved a pillow at her. "Knock it off," she said sharply, bending to retrieve the pillow. "Save your strength."

"Then quit looking like the world's coming to an end," he retorted with as much fire as he was capable of. Glenn's blue eyes, usually cloudy with pain, were wide and fairly sparking. He raked a hand through his rumpled blond hair and scowled at her. "I mean it, Kath. Bad enough to be stuck in this bed. Worse to sit here and watch you feel sorry for yourself."

She nearly fell over. "Me? Feel sorry for myself? I am *not*—"

"You *are*. It's more of your 'there is no God, everyone's out to get me, life is awful' garbage. If you're going to be like that, I'd just as soon you didn't visit anymore."

"You don't mean that," she practically whispered.

Glenn's anger vanished as quickly as it had appeared. "No, of course not. I'm sorry, Kathy."

"Kathryn," she corrected automatically.

"I've got no right to tell you what to think when you

visit. *No* right. I've got no excuse, except. . ." He trailed off as she looked away, then he continued firmly. "I have no excuse at all. I know this has been hard on you. Almost," he added, teasing, "as hard as it's been on me."

"You're a rat," she said, smiling in spite of herself.

"A thirsty rat. How about grabbing me a lemon-lime soda?"

She made a face. "Ugh. Why don't I just bring you a can of carbonated death?"

"Just because *you* never drink anything but diet colas. . ."

"Are you allowed to have one?"

"Sure." At her penetrating stare, he added meekly, "I can have half a can or so. Okay, a few swallows. Okay, one swallow. If I tell the nurse. And I *will*," he added. "Get lost, now. There's a good girl, thanks for visiting, have a nice day, and don't come back without my soda."

"Oh, you're hilarious," she said sourly, turning to leave the hospital room. Never in a hundred thousand years would she confess the gladness she felt at getting out of that wretched room, however briefly. "Back in a minute."

She left the relative quiet of his room for the hustle and bustle of the hospital hallways. Around her the business of health care went on—people living and dying (mostly dying) and fighting and failing. She would never like hospitals. Glenn had again blamed her nature. "That," he'd said last year, "and your childhood. Deep down, you know the patient and his relatives aren't in charge in a hospital. You can't stand the thought of giving control over to someone else. *Ergo,* you hate hospitals."

"The fact that they stink of death and hopelessness, and charge too much for parking," she'd said dryly, "has nothing to do with it, I'm sure."

"I just think you should—"

"Let's stop," she said gently. "We won't agree, and it's getting too hard." She had rumpled his hair affectionately, and he had backed off. That time.

In a hideous irony, given her dark thoughts of late, the soda machines were next to the chapel. Curious, Kathryn stuck her head through the doorway and observed a typical hospital chapel: so nondenominational, so determined not to offend anyone, it looked like a waiting room with pews. She waited, wondering if she'd feel some sort of spiritual urge to go in and sit down, some inner voice commanding her to pray, but nothing happened. What did she expect? It was just a room—an ordinary room that needed a good paint job.

"May I help you?"

She jumped. For a moment—a very small moment —she thought maybe it was the voice of . . never mind. It was too stupid. Especially now that she saw who had spoken. The hospital minister—priest, pastor, whatever his title—was standing behind her, holding a can of soda. He was wearing dark slacks, a white shirt, no tie, and there was a smiley face stuck to his hospital I.D.

"May I help you?" he asked again, doubtless wondering if she could talk.

"No," she said, more quickly than she intended. The last thing she needed was to pour her heart out to a stranger, someone who would pat her hand and tell her Glenn's impending demise was all part of some great big plan.

"You're welcome to sit down," he said. Kathryn felt herself warming to the friendliness in his voice and was surprised by it. It wasn't like her to immediately take to people. The man was average height, mid-thirties, with a pleasantly average face, and she was drawn to him. Maybe it was his eyes—warm, brown, and endlessly patient. "I can leave if you'd like privacy."

"For what?" she asked, honestly puzzled.

"For prayer or whatever you like," he replied, without so much as a raised eyebrow at her question.

"Thanks, but no thanks. I'd rather spend the time finding a donor for my cousin," she said, inwardly cringing at her rudeness to this man. "Not on my knees in a room by myself, not doing anything." *So take that,* she added in silent defiance.

He smiled at her. She couldn't believe it. She was rude and sarcastic, and instead of giving her the smack on the head she deserved, he acted graciously. "What makes you think," he said, "seeking a donor isn't your way of praying?"

She opened her mouth. . .and nothing came out. Still, she had to say *something*. "Oh, please," was all she managed.

The pastor—James Benedict, his name badge read —shrugged. "Just a thought. I've seen you in Glenn Donaldson's room, haven't I?"

"He's my cousin," she said stiffly.

"Do you mind if I walk back with you? I haven't had a chance to see him today."

"Sure. I don't care." Jim Benedict fell into step beside her as they walked back to Glenn's room. She noticed many of the people they passed in the hall greeted Jim warmly. The guy was a regular Mr. Congeniality. "You have to see all the patients here? It's your job?"

"No, and no," he said cheerfully. "I'm here for them. It's not the other way around. They seek me out, or their families do. I dislike showing up unannounced."

"The room," she said abruptly. "That chapel. There aren't any decorations or anything."

"It's nondenominational."

"It's just a room."

"You're right about that. The people are what make it special."

She thought that one over. "Hmph. And you pray for them?"

"Always."

"Why? It doesn't always work, does it?"

"No," he said slowly, "it doesn't."

She pounced. "Then why go through the motions?"

"Because," he said kindly, "it's an act of love."

She mulled that one over in silence. Jim Benedict seemed like an okay guy. At least he wasn't telling her she was going to hell. Not that it would have scared her. After watching Glenn's illness, she wasn't scared of anything. "Well. That's an interesting way to put it," she said at last.

"You're Kathryn, aren't you?"

She stopped so suddenly, the pharmacy tech behind her slammed the med cart into her heels. She barely felt it. "How do you know that? What, are priests or ministers or whatever telepathic, too?"

"Noooo," he said, looking at her feet with mild alarm. "Are you all right?" As she waved his question away, he added, "I guessed you were Kathryn. Glenn talks about you all the time. Unless he has two tall blond atheist cousins with green eyes." He grinned. "And a sharp way with words."

"Oh, no," she groaned.

"Now, don't panic." He paused to help the tech, who had apparently not noticed she'd nearly crippled a hospital visitor, wrestle the med cart around her. "He asked me to talk to you, is all," he said over his shoulder, giving the cart a final, helpful shove. "He's worried about you."

"He didn't," she said. Delayed reaction set in; she bent and massaged her banged heels, which were stinging fiercely. "Tell me you're not supposed to 'save' me."

"I'm only supposed to lend an ear," Jim Benedict said, smiling. He bent to look her in the eye; crouched and rubbing her heels as she was, it was difficult. "Glenn asked me to try to help you."

"Great," she griped. "Well, take a memo, Pastor

Benedict, or whatever your title—"

"My title is Jim," he said mildly, helping her stand.

She slid her shoe down over her heel, checking her sock for blood, then did the same to the other foot. Spotless! A miracle! Still hopping on one foot, she looked up at him. "I'm not going to be saved, Jim, because I can't make the leap of faith religion demands. I can't do it." She felt like a fool explaining this to a stranger in the middle of a crowded hallway, but was compelled to make him understand her. . .problem? No. Her way of looking at reality. "I need something concrete, something I can feel, smell, touch, what-have-you. I can't just blindly believe."

"Then why are you sending messages for help over the Internet? Asking for potential donors to come in and get tissue-typed? The chances that someone would see your message and come, and be the right blood type, and have a tissue match, and be willing to donate a major internal organ to a stranger—"

"Slim to none," she agreed glumly.

"Sounds a lot like blind faith to me," Jim said quietly.

Kathryn had no reply.

A stranger was waiting for them in Glenn's room, a stranger who was instantly on his feet when he saw Kathryn.

Kathryn had been trying to dispute Jim's absurd point. Using the Internet as a desperate plea for help wasn't the same as the unquestioning faith of following religion. The two were completely different. The Internet was a modern tool for modern times. Christianity was an anachronism from a time when women with beauty marks were regularly stoned as witches, a time when an eclipse was interpreted as a harbinger of the world's end. Searching for a donor through the Internet wasn't the same as putting blind faith into a creature who regularly offed babies via SIDS and gave cousins renal failure. No similarity at all. Because the alternative was—was—

"Hello," Jim said to Glenn and the stranger. "How are you feeling, Glenn?"

"Fine, Jim," Glenn lied. Kathryn knew he gave the same answer, no matter how he felt. He didn't want to burden people with his true feelings. It made her want to strangle him.

Glenn watched her hobble into the room but didn't ask the obvious question; instead, he smirked. His eyes promised an interrogation later. "Kathryn, Jim, this is Daniel Taylor."

"Pastor Benedict," he said respectfully, extending his hand.

"Jim," he corrected as he shook the proffered hand. Kathryn tried not to stare at Daniel, doing a pitiful job. The man was even more intriguing than Jim Benedict. Jim's charisma was in his warm personality. Since Daniel had said only two words, she had to assume his charisma was in his looks, which were admittedly very fine.

Daniel was tall—quite a bit taller than she—with

reddish brown hair the color of cherry cola. His eyes were blue—not faded denim, like Glenn's. More like sapphires before they were cleaned and made pretty for jewelry. His gaze was direct, and judging from Jim's wince, his handshake firm.

"This is my cousin," Glenn was saying, even though he'd already introduced her. "Kathryn Donaldson."

"Ma'am," Daniel said politely, which instantly made her feel ninety-six.

"Hello," she said. "We can come back, if you two were in the middle of—"

"Daniel's here to see if he can donate a kidney," Glenn explained.

"That's pretty nice of you." Her tone was measured, neutral. Even a month ago, her heart would have leaped with excitement, she would have hustled him down to the lab for immediate blood typing and waited breathlessly for the test results. But Daniel wasn't the first stranger the hospital had found to volunteer. She knew nothing would come of the man's gesture except a sore spot on the inside of his elbow. This wasn't a fairy tale. There would be no eleventh hour rescue for Glenn.

"The lab is at the end of the hall," she continued. "Just tell them—"

"I stopped at the lab first," he interrupted.

For the first time, she noticed his shirt sleeves were rolled up to reveal tanned forearms, and he had cotton balls taped to the inside of each elbow. "They had trouble finding a vein," he said apologetically. "Had to stick me twice."

"Ah, your selfish veins refused to yield their bloody booty. I've been there," Glenn said.

Daniel waved that away. "Ma'am," he said to Kathryn, "I noticed you're limping. Please take my chair."

"Please stop calling me ma'am," she said crossly, flushing because Daniel Taylor was seeing her at her worst: hair pulled back in a sloppy ponytail, jeans two sizes too big, a sweatshirt with the logo, "I know you are, but what am I?" *And let's not forget,* she reminded herself morbidly, *I'm limping like an orangutan with rheumatoid arthritis.* "I'm fine. Here's your pop." She tossed Glenn the can with a gentle underhand.

"I see you've met Jim," Glenn said, clumsily grabbing for the can. Just as Kathryn was scolding herself for throwing it, Daniel deftly snatched it from the air and handed it to Glenn, and he did it in such a way that, instead of coloring with embarrassment, Glenn beamed. "And, Jim, you have apologies in advance for anything my cousin might—"

"I don't want to talk about it!" Kathryn interrupted loudly. *He's gorgeous,* she lamented, *and I'm making the worst possible impression.* Worse, she was powerless to stop being a pill.

"Stubborn," Glenn said to Jim.

"A not ignoble virtue," Jim replied.

"Rotten childhood," Glenn said to Daniel.

"It's really none of my business," Daniel said mildly. He was, she noted with relief, completely unperturbed to find himself in a room with two feuding cousins and a nice minister. He sat down in the chair Kathryn refused, reached down and pulled a briefcase—presumably his—into his lap.

"Stop it!" she hollered. Daniel made a strange, smothered sound, almost like he was choking back a laugh. "Stop talking about me like I'm not here. Look, Jim, I'll give you the short version. Glenn and I have been having this fight for years. He's stubbornly faithful, I'm stubbornly faithless. I'm a scientist—"

"She's a veterinarian," Glenn added helpfully. Jim nodded sagely. "Spays cats and worms dogs. But she took personal leave until I. . .uh. . .until this kidney thing gets straightened out."

"—and I need cold, hard facts about religion, not children's Bible stories and friendly ministers. No offense, Jim."

"None taken," Jim replied dryly.

She waved her arms in agitation. "Significant things need to happen for me to reexamine my philosophy. So far, I'm not holding my breath. Thus, we are not having this discussion. Especially not now. Particularly not in front of a stranger. Two strangers."

"Don't mind me," Daniel said mildly, pulling a large, black tome out of his briefcase. "I'll just do some reading. Chat away."

"No!" she practically howled. "I need proof, something tangible, which no one in this room can give me, so we are not talking about this. The end!"

"You can't 'prove' God exists," Glenn argued, "or what would be the point of faith?"

"I guess," Jim said, "that would depend on your definition of proof."

Before Kathryn could beg them to change the subject, the door to Glenn's room whooshed open and Micki, the floor nurse, poked her head in. "Got a match!" she said gleefully. She looked at Jim and Daniel. "Which one of you two is the AB neg who just got tested?"

"I am," Daniel said, completely unsurprised.

Kathryn stared at him. "You're—you and Glenn have the same blood type? And you have all the factors that make him such a tough match?"

"It would seem so."

While normally a blood type match wouldn't be cause for much enthusiasm, it was significant because it was the first true match. Still, she cautioned herself not to get her hopes up. Then she got a look at the book on his lap. The title was stamped in gold, on the spine: Holy Bible.

"Oh, no," she said.

"I'm afraid so," he said, his dark blue eyes twinkling at her discomfort. "I'm one of 'them.' "

She sat down before she fell down.

Chapter 2

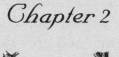

G lenn's doctor, Maura Filkins, was summoned. The semiprivate room was getting awfully crowded, what with Glenn, Kathryn, Jim, Daniel, Micki, and now Dr. Filkins scattered all over. Fortunately, Glenn was between hospital roommates at the moment.

"We'll expedite tissue testing," Dr. Filkins said, whirling her stethoscope like a lasso above her head. The floor nurses told Kathryn that Dr. Filkins did that when she was thinking hard. Kathryn couldn't begin to imagine how many eyes the woman had knocked out while she pondered. "And Mr. Taylor will remain for the rest of the day, of course."

"Of course," Daniel said.

"Do you live around here? Do you have a place to stay?" Kathryn asked, forcing herself to sound completely neutral, trying not to betray the wild excitement she felt. She took a deep, steadying breath. She did not, *did not*, want Glenn to catch her sudden, hopeful mood. "Because I could—"

"No, I don't live around here." Daniel grinned at her. Kathryn again wished she was wearing anything but a dirty sweatshirt. "And no, I don't have a place to stay. Any hotel suggestions you might—"

"Wrong, wrong, wrong!" Glenn said loudly, startling everyone except Kathryn, who had expected his outburst.

"You can stay at my apartment. I'm sure not using it. Won't cost you a cent."

"I couldn't impose. . . ," Daniel started tentatively.

"How is it imposing? I'm not there," Glenn said reasonably. "Come on, it'll make me feel better." He faked a cough and looked at Daniel with pathetic appeal. "Won't you please water my plants, kind sir?"

Daniel laughed, a deep, pleasing sound. "All right, stop looking like a starving puppy. I'll be glad to stay there. . .and grateful."

"Kathryn can give you a ride, show you around," Glenn said promptly. Kathryn glared at her cousin. Was the lout matchmaking? Again? He was wasting his time; Daniel probably thought she was a shrew. A poorly dressed shrew.

"Work it out later," Dr. Filkins said. "The lab has some free time, and I want to get the process started. Micki, grab him." The nurse, a head shorter than Daniel, promptly latched onto the man's arm and started tugging him toward the door. Daniel looked at Kathryn and set his feet. For a moment, Micki looked like she was trying to budge a redwood. Kathryn had the absurd hope that he was going to say something to her. Then he gave in and let himself be escorted out, glancing once more over his shoulder.

"Nice enough guy," Glenn said, sooooo casually.

Moving with the speed of a woman with a mission, Kathryn pulled her hair out of the ponytail and groped in her purse for a hairbrush. "Hmm? Oh, sure, a real prince." She began brushing with quick strokes, wishing she wasn't out of hair spray. Her hair *would* fly all over the place. That was why she usually wore it up, but it was her nicest feature. Glenn even said so, and they hardly ever noticed each other's looks. It was like that when two people grew up together. "Lucky break about the blood type, huh?"

"Mm-hmm. Did you see the way my nurse, Micki, was looking at him?" Glenn went on innocently. "I thought my sheets were going to catch on fire."

Kathryn glared at him. "No, I did not. I was too busy trying to explain to you and Jim why you need to leave my personal beliefs *alone*."

"Oh, here we go."

"Well, you do!" Her brush crackled with static, and her hair started flying all over the place, as usual. She glared at Glenn through the electrically charged strands. "I can't believe you. Siccing Jim on me like that. He's only got about a thousand other more important things to do than try to convert me."

"Actually, he doesn't, and see, he's a nice guy, just like me—"

289

"You're about as nice as a head cold," she said sourly.

"—so there's something to be said about religious men, after all. And, hello? Was I the only one who noticed Daniel lugs a Bible around in his briefcase? Do you know how heavy those things are?"

"Bibles or briefcases?"

"Both." He smirked at her. "Also, your head now looks like a giant cottonball. A giant, blond, ill-tempered cotton ball."

"Oh, stop it," she said, but she had to laugh.

"I wonder where Daniel lives?" Glenn went on thoughtfully. "He was planning on staying at a hotel. What's he doing here?"

"I'll ask him," she said and got up at once. "Right now. They know me around here, so they'll let me in the lab while they're running tests."

Silence. "Okay?" she added, turning, but Glenn had fallen into one of his abrupt dozes, a sign his body was too exhausted fighting the toxins in his blood to keep him awake any longer.

All at once Kathryn wanted to burst into tears. She fought it, biting her lower lip, throwing her brush back into her purse, then bending over Glenn. She brushed a stray lock of hair out of his eyes and pulled the sheet and blanket up to his chin. She did it with the impersonal efficiency of a nurse, but when one of her sudden tears splashed onto his chin, she absently wiped it away before striding out the door.

She found Daniel seated in the lab. Two techs and Dr. Filkins were standing over him, jabbering at a great rate, tossing around multisyllabic medical jargon like tennis balls. Daniel's eyes were glazing over with the effort to understand what was being said.

"Whoa!" Kathryn said, making the time-out sign with her hands. "Knock it off, you guys. He's a layman."

Daniel looked relieved. "I teach grammar school," he said, while one of the techs wrapped a blood pressure cuff around his arm and pumped it up. "The most technical I ever get is discussing how to take care of a boo-boo."

Kathryn laughed. "Too bad we can't break everything down into simple words like that. I mean, everybody knows what a boo-boo is, but how many people know what their crit count is?"

"You have a great laugh," he said admiringly.

She flushed again, she couldn't help it. She gave herself a brisk, mental shake and got back into it. "Thanks. Anyway, the gist of it is, they're going to give you a bunch of tests, but the most important is the tissue typing test."

"You have a fascinating way of brushing off compliments. Is it because you're worried about Glenn?"

She gaped at him. "I'm just trying to keep this conversation on a professional level. Now—uh—about the tissue typing. They'll—"

The tech came and asked Daniel to extend both arms onto the table.

Kathryn took the chance to slide into the seat at the table beside Daniel. The tech glanced up but, thankfully, didn't so much as raise his eyebrows. She patted Daniel's forearm. "Now, this'll be over in a sec, and it. . . um. . .won't. . ."

She could feel the spark, feel his pulse jump, even through the cloth of his shirt. Her mouth went dry and she glanced up at him, only to find his direct blue gaze on her, his mouth a thoughtful line.

"Make a fist, please," the tech interrupted, and Daniel obliged. Kathryn wasn't sure why they were taking more blood—they should have had plenty from the earlier draw. Still, it gave her a chance to talk to him, so she was grateful for whatever lab screw-up put him back here.

"Your line is, 'This won't hurt a bit,'" he prompted. Again, she chuckled. *Maybe that's why I'm so attracted to him,* she thought absently, watching the tech scrub Daniel's arm with an alcoholic wipe. *He makes me laugh.*

There had been very little laughter in her life lately.

"She's right," the technician said, "this won't hurt a bit."

"Ow," he complained.

"Want me to kiss it and make it better?" she asked sarcastically.

"Yes," he said quietly. She jerked her head up to stare at him, and pushed her chair back so fast she nearly knocked the departing tech into the Hazardous

Waste container. He added, "I'm sorry. That was inappropriate."

"Who *are* you?" she asked.

He didn't answer. Instead, he said thoughtfully, "I think we're going to remember this day for a long time."

She managed to close her mouth, which had been hanging open, and shook her head. "Inappropriate. . . *this* is inappropriate," she muttered. "My cousin is dying, and I'm making goo-goo eyes at the potential kidney donor."

"Potential, nothing," he assured her. "I will be the donor."

"Um. . .Daniel? I appreciate the thought, but the chances of that are so slim as to be—"

"Everything is going to work out all right."

"Oh, now, don't *you* start with that stuff."

He winked at her, and her heart melted into a puddle in the middle of her chest. "But it will, you know." To that, she could say nothing.

Chapter 3

And each person has six genomes in each cell. So the more of your genomes that match Glenn's, the better. Now, they can transplant with a zero to six match, and have, but it would be better with even a one to six match. Family members can sometimes manage a six/six match. So depending on how the test goes, that will determine whether or not they can proceed."

They were in the cafeteria, talking about genomes and donors and rejection numbers, and Kathryn was as content as she'd been in weeks, just for the chance to talk to Daniel, to watch his face and observe his hands, which were large and well-shaped, and seemed competent. Hands like that held chalk, gestured to children to help them better understand a lesson, beckoned a naughty boy away from his tricks, graded papers. Held a coffee cup with assurance. Hands that—that—

His lips were moving. "I'm sorry," she gulped, "what were you saying?"

"I asked about the chances of a six/six match between Glenn and me."

"Impossible," she said flatly. "You'd have to be closely related. Brothers. I'm his cousin and I'm not even the same blood type." It had been a bitter blow, that she had not been allowed to save Glenn.

"We'll hope for at least a one to six, then," he said cheerfully. "Can I get you another cocoa?"

"I shouldn't have let you buy this one," she reminded him. "I was supposed to treat you, remember?"

"You already did," he said, smiling. "Limping into the room and yelling at the pastor and your cousin, furious because they were trying to help you. It was—" He gave up and started to laugh. "It was pretty funny," he said at last.

"I'm sure," she said dryly, not liking being reminded of the wretched first impression she had made. "That's Glenn's thing, to get me to embrace Christianity—"

"The fiend!"

"—and now he's got poor Jim Benedict involved, too."

"Maybe this is Glenn's way of finishing up last-minute business," Daniel suggested.

"There's no maybe about it. It's all he thinks about, but he's wasting valuable strength—and breath, come to think of it. He knows better than anyone why I can't— why I don't believe in God."

"He mentioned a difficult childhood."

"He mentioned a lot of things, and I wish he'd keep

his mouth shut!" As soon as the words were out, she wished them back. The sentence was cruel and showed none of the depth of feeling she had for her cousin, how he was closer to her than any brother. Worse, Daniel now probably thought she was—

"I wish you weren't so frightened."

A complete jerk, a heartless shrew who— "What?"

"I don't blame you for being scared," he said, his voice rich with sympathy. "I wish I could help you."

"You—I—you—" she sputtered, groping for words, angered beyond belief. . .and scared, yes, but not of religion. Scared because this man, whom she'd known all of ninety minutes, saw too deeply. "I am *not* scared! I'm not scared of anything, Daniel Taylor!"

"Then why?"

"Why?" she repeated dumbly.

"Why not give religion a chance? Try a few church services, see what it's about. I promise, we won't drag you down the aisle, kicking and screaming, or drown you in holy water. Not on your first visit," he added thoughtfully, a credible attempt at humor, but she was in no mood.

Hardly able to believe she was about to do this crazy thing, she put down her cocoa, leaned forward, and told him how it was.

❧

Her parents, dead of an honest car accident. The other guy's brakes had failed. He had a spotless driving record, but his truck had plowed into their Saab. Her father had died instantly; her mother had lingered for nearly a week before drowning in her own blood.

Her parents had no will, so the question became, who would take Kathryn? The state would not allow Glenn's parents to take her in. Glenn was a "change of life" baby, and his parents were in their sixties before he entered high school. Worse, his mother had a heart condition. Too old and sick for more kids, said the state, so sorry.

So Kathryn went to foster homes. And homes. And homes. The state, while well-meaning, had several hundred thousand children to look after. Many fell—or jumped—through the cracks. After Kathryn's third trip to the E.R. (courtesy of foster father #4), the state got around to shuffling her into a new home. Foster father #4 sued the state for the whopping $325 a month the state paid foster families to feed the children in their care. Foster father #4 won. Back she went, until he kicked her out himself, furious when she rebuffed his constant, inappropriate advances. She had been nine.

Some years, she was in a state-funded boarding school. The worst years were when she was in one of those homes during the holidays. It was so hard to fight off people's good intentions. They tried—that was the worst part. They tried to make it nice. Cheap paper decorations in a smelly gym. Presents which were almost always secondhand clothes or toys that no longer worked. Rich families "helping," but really using her and her peers as object lessons for their children: See, these are the poor people, and we're helping them. Now we can feel good about ourselves while we shop at the upscale boutique of our choice.

Glenn's family smuggled her—sometimes out-and-out kidnapped her—into their home as often as they could—her only respite from the grind. She was terrified to love her great-aunt and uncle. . .she knew what happened when you let yourself care about anyone. Only Glenn had wriggled past her heart's walls; it had taken him six years.

Toward the end of her adolescence, the state observed she was never in trouble with the law and quit trying so hard to roust her from Glenn's house. Though Glenn's parents were older, they still enjoyed a full life and his father's health was excellent. The state allowed that there might (*might*) have been an error in judgment.

Toward the end of her adolescence, she as good as lived with Glenn's family. With day-to-day fear. . .*Is today the day Glenn gets killed? Is today the day Great-aunt Matty has another heart attack and dies? Is it tomorrow? Next week?*

This month, for certain. Glenn was done. She was the only one brave enough to admit it.

She could take all of that. Nobody ever promised anyone a free ride, or even an easy one. Bad things happened every day. She knew. She saw. But to live through so much misery and then give herself over to the Lord, to say, "Hey, I believe in You, and I guess everything bad that has ever happened was part of Your big plan. Sure.

Okay, no problem." No. And no and no. Better—saner
—to believe that the universe was a mess of random
events. Bad things happen, good things, too, sometimes,
and no Supreme Being had a thing to do with either.
Her parents had died in a senseless accident. Her childhood had been stolen through pure bad luck. Glenn was
going to die through worse luck. And there was no God.

※

"So when Glenn assures me that God loves me, you'll
excuse me if I say He's got an odd way of showing it."
She picked up her cocoa with a hand that wanted to
shake. She wouldn't let it. She sipped her cocoa instead.

Daniel was holding her other hand, which she only
now noticed. She was surprised, then pleased, then re-
signed. *Oh, boy.*

"Kathryn."

Here it comes. God loved her anyway, and everything was for the best.

"Kathryn, I'm so sorry. What a heartbreak." He
shook his head and said it again. "What a heartbreak."

"Well," she said carefully, more than a little surprised, "I always thought so." There was a pause, then
she added, "That was your cue to tell me to pray for
guidance."

He smiled a little. "And would you?"

Not *hardly*. "Would you want me to?" she asked
curiously.

He let go of her hand, leaned back, and looked at
her. Not for the first time, she felt he could see all the

way down inside her, to the bottom of her shriveled soul. "There are lots of ways to pray, you know," he said, blue eyes solemn. "Maybe you'd prefer to go to the chapel and scream at the walls."

"What?" The idea shook her, a little. She wondered why.

"God can handle your anger, Kathryn."

She was already shaking her head. "First of all, you're doing this all wrong—you're supposed to be telling me everything happened for the best, it's all God's will, blah-blah-blah, sorry about your parents but God works in mysterious ways His wonders to perform."

His eyebrows arched, dark slashes above his eyes. "Oh my. Who *have* you been talking to?"

"Second, I'm not mad at God."

"Liar."

Funny, how he made that sound like an endearment. "Well, I'm not!" she said crossly. "I don't believe in Him, so how can I be mad? Yelling inside the chapel will only get me kicked out. . .or bring Jim on the run, probably ready to sedate me."

"I think you *are* mad," he said softly. "I think you're furious. I think your heart is a secret place, and no one is allowed in."

She gaped at him. He leaned forward, put a finger on her chin, and gently closed her mouth. "Finish your cocoa," he said. She did, mostly because she couldn't think of a single thing to say. He was right, of course, but she could never dare admit it out loud. She could barely admit it to herself.

Chapter 4

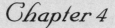

Three days later, the results of Daniel's tissue test came back. Kathryn assumed, upon hearing Dr. Filkins's announcement, that the stress of Glenn's illness had caused her hearing to fail.

"I'm sorry?" she said to the doctor.

"Three out of six," Dr. Filkins insisted, her stethoscope whirling above her head like the blades of a miniature helicopter. "Everything checks out. We've got a few more tests, but I've tentatively booked Daniel and Glenn in the transplant suite for Wednesday. Pending the result of Daniel's psych eval, of course," she added.

Six days. This wasn't happening. This was impossible. This was—

"That's wonderful," Daniel said with sincere warmth. He was seated beside Glenn's bed, reading *Life in These United States* to Glenn. He had been in the middle of a story about a crabby grocery clerk when Dr. Filkins swept in.

Kathryn had been pretending to read, while covertly

watching Daniel. He was so nice to her cousin—well, he was nice to everyone. He often read to Glenn until his voice was hoarse. He had a marvelous reading voice, deep and sonorous. Sometimes Kathryn would quit pretending to read her own book, close her eyes, and listen.

Daniel had been staying at Glenn's apartment for the last two nights. When she took him there the first night, the silence and tension between them had been so heavy, she practically ran out of the living room into the hallway. She was sure he couldn't feel the same for her, but lately, whenever she was around him, she wanted to kiss him until he had no choice but to kiss her back.

She sighed at the thought, then mentally took hold and forced her thoughts back to a less distracting track. "Even family members aren't always a three/six match," she said, leaning back in her chair as Filkins took a step toward her. She had no wish for the stethoscope bell to smack her in the side of the head. "How could two un-related people be such a close match?"

"Trust me, stranger things have happened," Dr. Filkins assured her. "Though not often. Daniel, I took the liberty of signing you up for some counseling. You've got a big decision to make, and I know you don't want to take this lightly."

"You have to have more testing and get psychologi-cally evaluated," Kathryn automatically explained to Daniel. "It's nonnegotiable, no matter how much you want to—how much you think you want to do this."

Daniel casually turned the page. "I'll do it. You have my insurance information—"

"We don't even need that," Filkins interrupted cheerfully. "Glenn's insurance will pay for everything."

He said reasonably, "I'll do it. What more is there?"

Glenn spoke for the first time. His voice was hoarse from fatigue. "No, man, you've got to think this over. The operation is a lot harder on the donor than the recipient, believe me. And you don't even know m—"

"I'll do it," Daniel said again.

"Well, we have to finish the last of the testing," Filkins said, looking at him doubtfully, "and we'll see how that goes. But I'd still like you to talk to some of our transplant team. You won't be able to work for—"

"I don't have to go back to work until September. It's June. Will I need more than three months to recover?"

"Uh. . .no."

Daniel made a "well, then, there you have it" gesture. Kathryn felt herself starting to hope. . .and ruthlessly squashed the emotion.

She wanted to say, "Oh, Daniel, thank you—thank you—thank you, you're wonderful, I love you, thank you for coming into our lives."

Instead, she said crossly, "Don't be silly, you've got to give this some thought. Dr. Filkins is right."

He just raised his eyebrows at her in that infuriating way of his. Then it occurred to her: He wasn't surprised. He wasn't remotely surprised that he was a good donor match. He had shown up out of nowhere, passed all the tests with flying colors, and now he was possibly going to save Glenn's life—and he wasn't surprised.

"Daniel," she said slowly, "where do you live? I figured you were from Rochester or something, because a four-hour round-trip drive would be kind of a pain, but—"

"I'm from Hyannis. Massachusetts," he added helpfully.

Thunderstruck silence was finally broken by Dr. Filkins. "Why didn't you stay home and get the preliminary lab work done there? Why hop a plane?"

"Why not? I knew I'd end up here anyway."

The amazing thing was, Kathryn thought, he *sounded* sane. She and Glenn stared at him in the following silence, and Dr. Filkins used the opportunity to excuse herself. Kathryn finally managed, "You–you mean you—" Kathryn felt the magazine slip from her numb fingers.

"I couldn't sleep last Friday night. So I got out of bed to surf the Web for a bit, and I found your message, asking for a donor for your cousin. I—"

"You hopped a plane and flew fifteen hundred miles because you saw an Internet message?"

"Owwww!" Glenn complained. "Quit shrieking."

She was on her feet, but she didn't remember standing. "But that's–that's—and you're a match! You're a great match! And you're not surprised. *Why aren't you surprised?*"

"Well, Kathryn," he said slowly, "I knew I was supposed to come here. As soon as I saw your message, I knew why I'd been sleepless. I—"

She clapped both hands over her ears. "Don't even say it!"

"—knew I was supposed to come here. And the only reason for me to be sent—"

"You were not sent!"

"—was to be the donor. I—"

She didn't hear the rest. She turned and ran out of the room, sprinting for the chapel. Everything was crashing together in her mind—her despair, her desperate Internet messages, Daniel showing up and being the right blood type and tissue match, Daniel saying he had been sent. . . . *Sent?*

She kicked the door to the chapel open and practically leapt through the doorway. She turned around, looking for a symbol to focus her anger on. "Knock it off," she finally shouted at the air-conditioning unit. "I don't believe in You, I *won't* believe in You, so quit messing with my life!"

She waited, but there was nothing. Only the quiet wheeze of the air conditioner slowly shutting off.

She turned to leave and nearly ran over Jim Benedict, who greeted her with a mild, "Problems?"

"It's impossible, right?" she asked, almost desperately. "It's just a bunch of craziness. It's impossible."

"Nothing's impossible," he told her flatly, in the tone someone would use if they said, "The sky is blue."

"This guy—Daniel. He flew halfway across the country to get tested for Glenn. And he's a match!" She was standing too close to Jim, and they stared at each other, eyeball-to-eyeball. "They're talking about doing an operation within the week! He says he was sent." She could feel herself talking faster and faster and was helpless to stop. "He says he knew he was supposed to come here. And he's one of your tribe."

"He's a bowler?" Jim asked.

"You know what I mean! The whole thing is just ridiculous. You know, if there is a God—and I'm not saying there is, no way—but if there is, why *now?* Why pick *now* to butt in?"

"I think the question is, why not butt in earlier?" Before she could reply, Jim's normally smiling face went solemn. "Kathryn, I don't know. That's the toughest part of faith. . .for me, anyway. We can never, ever know the why of it, not for everything. And for someone like you. . ." He trailed off tactfully.

"It's impossible," she said, but she heard the lack of conviction in her voice, felt horrible doubt start to creep through. "And I'll tell you this, Jim: This is *no* time for me to re-examine my beliefs."

"On the contrary—" was as far as he got before she flapped her hands in disgust and walked out.

Chapter 5

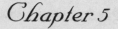

W hy now?" She asked herself that again and again, driving home as fast as she dared. Why would God—if there were a God, and there was not—why would God start messing with her head now? When she needed all her hatred—all her strength, that was—to focus on the crisis?

Daniel's seeing her Internet plea. Coincidence.

Daniel's being the right blood type. Coincidence.

Daniel's having the summer off to recover from an invasive operation. Coincidence.

Daniel's being so calmly certain, so gently positive, that he would be able to fix everything. Would be allowed by Someone to fix everything.

Even thinking about it made her head hurt. Worse, it was an awfully long string of coincidences. If she despised people who saw the hand of God in every stupid little thing (finding a good parking space, getting the last chocolate cupcake at the bakery, getting a warning instead of a speeding ticket), she could hardly see all these amazing coincidences and stubbornly insist there was nothing to them.

"I can't," she sighed and parked her car, then stumbled out onto the sidewalk. When she looked up and realized where she was, she groaned aloud. She had come to Glenn's apartment building like an agnostic homing pigeon. In times of stress he was the first one she turned to. In her dismay, her reflexes had taken over and brought her here.

". . .Here."

She whirled. Daniel was standing on the sidewalk behind her. She glanced at the curb and saw his rental car parked beside her battered little economy coupe. "What?" she practically barked.

"I said, I can't believe you're here. After you left, Glenn asked me to come by and pick up some of his things."

Sure he did. Glenn had probably known where she would end up, and the matchmaking fiend had sent Daniel after her. That, or Glenn was comforting her by proxy. The thought made her shake her head ruefully.

"I never knew," Daniel said quietly, "that someone could look so beautiful and so sad at the same time."

"Beautiful? *Me?*" She smothered a laugh.

"Ah, I forgot. No compliments, please, and certainly no religious introspection." His teasing tone took the sting from his words. "Come in with me, will you? You can help me find the stuff Glenn wants."

She obeyed, glad to prolong the contact with him,

wondering how he could be so nice to her. She was sour and rude and awkward and ugly. He was goodness and male beauty personified.

Inside, instead of telling her what Glenn wanted, Daniel moved through the small one-bedroom apartment and went to the computer in the corner of the living room. He sat down, moving the mouse to clear the screen saver. "Come here a minute," he said. "Let's try something."

"Great," she groused but pulled up a chair and sat beside him. "Another Web geek."

"It's a good teaching tool," he said absently, typing in a web page address and hitting Enter. "Now. Check this out."

She looked. The banner proclaimed, "THE ONE, THE ONLY, PROBABILITIES PAGE!" in vivid red wavering script. She glanced at the screen and instantly realized what it was.

"It figures odds for you."

"It's just for fun," he quickly assured her, "not gambling or anything. A couple of my former students thought it up. They thought it would be neat to make a site where you could figure the probabilities to silly questions. They've done all the work, figured the formulas and parameters and such."

"Former students? Who were you teaching, elementary school Einsteins?"

"We like to refer to them as gifted. Anyway," he said, patiently getting them back on track, "all a surfer does is ask the question."

"Such as?" she asked, having an idea where this was going.

"Such as, the odds of a stranger being a matching blood type to a patient dying of renal failure." Daniel typed in the question, then read aloud the answer, "One thousand, four-hundred eighty-five to one."

"Not so impossible," she said defensively.

"Uh-huh. You said you were a scientist, that you needed facts. Well." He started typing again. "Calculate the odds of that same stranger having three months off for recovery from the operation. Eleven thousand, six hundred fifty to one."

She laughed in spite of herself. "Where are you getting these numbers?"

"I told you, the web page calculates them for us. Now. Figure in everything: a stranger seeing an Internet message, flying across the country, being an approved donor, having the time off and desire to do this thing. What are the odds?" The computer hummed to itself for a moment, then came up with a number.

They stared at it for a minute, then Kathryn read aloud. "One million, eight hundred thousand, sixty-five to one." She paused. "This proves nothing. Nope. Not a thing."

There was a beat of silence, then Daniel snorted, and she started to laugh helplessly.

Chapter 6

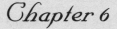

Affter practically being frisked by the floor nurse, Kathryn was able to make her way to the chapel. Their suspicion was entirely justified. Earlier in the week, she had stopped by her office and smuggled two kittens in for cat-crazy Glenn.

But no good deed ever went unpunished, as she well knew: The kittens had crawled all over her car during the short drive to the hospital, and one of them had been carsick. Repeatedly. Then, she'd stuffed them inside her coat and sauntered through the hospital, gritting her teeth to ignore the many sets of claws digging into her torso. She'd gotten a few strange looks when the occasional muffled "Meow!" escaped, too.

Glenn's pure delight in the surprise had made her pain and suffering (and investment in carpet cleaner) worth it, but now the floor staff practically patted her down when she showed up. Still, it had been fun to stop by work, even for a few minutes. Her parents had left a modest trust fund, so she could afford to take several weeks off. Still, she missed the animals and her coworkers.

Feeling like the world's biggest hypocrite, Kathryn stepped across the threshold into the hospital chapel. Sitting in the nearest pew, she closed her eyes and dug her fingers into her brow, thinking hard. Praying, maybe.

I quit asking for things for myself when I was eight, she thought. *But now I've got a favor, please. Let them live. Let them both live.*

Strange, to be as worried about Daniel as she was about Glenn. Ironically, the donor's part of the procedure was much more arduous than the recipient's. Kidney transplants were done all over the country, but still, things go wrong. Things always go wrong.

She shifted in the pew and opened her eyes. This wasn't working. This was the most ridiculous thing in the world, her being here, trying to pray when she didn't even believe in God.

Don't you?

Even if she did, she'd never speak to Him again, for taking her parents, for ensuring her horrid childhood, for letting Glenn get sick, for bringing Daniel into her life only to probably snatch him back.

Oh, Child!

Really, what was the point? What was the point of any of it? No, better to think there was no God, better to *know* it, because if there was, how could the many miseries of her life be explained?

One in one million, eight hundred thousand, sixty-five,

she thought suddenly. *Forget about life's miseries—explain that.*

She couldn't. She'd been thinking about that evening at Glenn's, about Daniel's typing in question after question, about the incredible numbers. She could not, in fact, get it out of her mind even when she tried. Because it was almost like. . .like her scientist's mind couldn't get away from the fact that. . .that Daniel might possibly have mathematically proved there was a God. To her, at least.

Which was why she was here. Because maybe, just maybe, she had been wrong, all this time. Maybe there was a God. And if so, she could forgive Him just about anything.

If Daniel and Glenn lived.

"Okay," she whispered. She rested her elbows on her knees and looked at the floor. "Okay, I haven't asked for anything in years. I know it's lame to ignore You for two decades and then come asking for favors. But if You could do this thing for me. This one thing. Then I'd—"

What? She'd what? How did one bargain with the Supreme Being? What in the world could she, Kathryn Donaldson, offer Him? Tickets to the Super Bowl? A gift certificate for Barnes & Noble?

She felt something, then. Tolerant amusement. She figured she was laughing at herself. It certainly wasn't the still, small voice Glenn had told her about. This wasn't even praying, when you got right down to it. This was. . . was talking to yourself.

As if he were standing beside her, she suddenly heard Jim's voice: "What do you think praying is, Kathryn?"

What had Glenn said? Long ago, when he'd first been diagnosed? The reason he had never prayed for his recovery? "Because you don't bargain with God," he'd said. "Ever. What will be, will be, and it's our job to suck it up, the bad with the good. It's His job to run the universe. That's it. That's all there is."

"Well," Kathryn muttered to Glenn's memory, "if you can't bargain with Him, why bother praying at all?"

Again, the memory of Jim's voice. Something he'd said about prayers. That they were an act of love.

Well, only love could get her into a chapel the night before Glenn's and Daniel's surgeries, that was for sure.

A thought popped into her head: *It was a fine first step.*

She was surprised at the comfort she took from that. Abruptly, she decided to look in on both of them. The men in her life. The men she loved. One for most of her life, one for only the last week. She rose and walked out, looking over her shoulder once at the small, still room, and wondered about bargains and running the universe.

Twelve times thirteen. . .one hundred fifty-six. Twelve times fourteen. . .one hundred sixty-eight. Twelve times fifteen. . .ah. . .one hundred eighty.

Some people counted sheep when they couldn't sleep. Daniel did the multiplication tables. He supposed he could turn the light on and do some reading, but then the floor nurse would see and pester him to get some sleep, and maybe even bully him into taking a sedative, which he was not remotely interested in.

Twelve times sixteen. . .one hundred ninety-two. Twelve times. . . .

The door opened, letting in a dim crack of light. The nurse had known he was awake, somehow. Daniel marshaled arguments against taking a sleeping pill.

Then he saw it wasn't the nurse. It was Kathryn, quietly entering the room so as not to wake him, and it was like she had brought the moon and all the stars with her. His heart seemed to swell with happiness at the sight of her.

"Kathryn," he said, and she jumped.

"Sorry," she whispered. "I was just—"

"Come here."

Shyly, she approached him and sat down in the chair beside the bed. He reached out and took her hand, careful not to squeeze, not to give any indication of how glad he was at her presence. He had known the instant he saw her that she was for him, as he was for her, and had spent the last week carefully hiding his feelings from her. She had been so hurt, and if she knew how he felt, she would back away from him at roughly the speed of sound, so terrified was she of intimacy, so certain was she that bad things happened, always, and it was best not to get hopes up.

And still, she came to him tonight.

"I'm glad to see you," he said, smiling wryly at the inadequacy of the statement.

"I was—I couldn't sleep. I came to see how you were doing."

"Better, now. I can't sleep either."

She bent her head over their clasped hands and for a heartstopping moment, he thought she was going to kiss his hand. Then she merely brushed his knuckles across her cheek, comforting herself. "Do you know what I've been doing?" she asked softly, not looking at him.

"Praying?"

She dropped his hand and jerked her head up. "Okay, that's *it*. Bad enough Glenn and Jim read my mind all the time. Don't *you* start."

He laughed. "It's not telepathy. It's knowing you. It's no secret you've been conflicted, Kathryn. Prayer is a great way to get your head together. I'm not surprised you succumbed to the allure."

She scowled at his jesting. "It was a lot easier when I knew for sure there wasn't a God, when I was positive I was on my own."

"And now?"

"Now, I'm positive I don't know. I can't make the leap. I can't go all the way, from not-knowing to complete belief. The jump is too scary." She took a deep breath. "But the thing is, I don't think I can go back to the way I was, either. Too many things have happened. It's been enough to make me question everything. That stupid calculations page!" She pounded the mattress with frustration.

"Well," he said reasonably, but he ached for her inner torment, "you knew the odds were incredibly high before you saw the page. The computer just put them in front of your face. And I think what you're feeling is a good start."

Her green eyes widened, and he was once again struck by her beauty. It would have been enough if she had been intelligent and witty and charismatic. That God had also blessed her with beauty seemed proof of His generosity, if nothing else.

"A good start?" she echoed. "I thought you'd be disappointed that I haven't thrown everything over and joined a church. I thought if I did that, it would make you happy."

"You have to come to believe on your own, Kathryn," he said patiently. "It's like a long trip that you don't know what to pack for, and you don't know how long it will take."

"A really long trip," she muttered. "I don't see an end to it."

"I'm sorry," he said. "I wish I could help you." Then, a thought struck him and he sat up. "Did you say you thought that sort of thing would make me happy? Did you pray to please me?"

"No! I don't know why I did it. I wish I *hadn't* done it, because I'm more confused now than I was before I ever started; but I know how important your religion is to you, Daniel, even if I don't understand it." Her voice dropped until it was practically inaudible. "I wanted to please you."

He reached out and clutched her hands, not trusting himself to speak for a long moment. "You do please me, Kathryn," he said at last. "In all things. You're kind and charming and beautiful and troubled and hurt. I think—" He paused, then forced it out, praying it wouldn't frighten her. "I think I've fallen in love with you."

Shocked, she looked up at him, her mouth falling open. Then her face broke into the biggest smile he had ever seen, and she flung her arms around him, nearly tumbling him off the bed with the force of her joy. "Daniel!" she almost sobbed. "It's true for me, too. I think about you all the time. I—I'd do anything to please you. Even go to church. Get baptized. Teach Sunday school. Write church bulletins. Whatever."

He gripped her shoulders and pushed her back. "You can't," he said grimly. "Not to please me, not to please anyone. You can only do it because something in you isn't complete if you *don't* do it."

She stared at him a long moment, then her shoulders slumped. "We're nuts," she said dully. "We're opposites in temperament, education, religion—everything. This will never work. You're too good and I'm so. . ." She put her hand over her face for a moment, swallowing a sob. "And if something happens to you. . .to either of you. . .I'll want to be dead."

"Hush," he said, alarmed. "Don't talk like that. Things will work out."

"You don't *know* that!" she cried, tears running down

her face. "Both you and Glenn talk like everything will be fine when neither of you knows it!"

"We've put our faith in the Lord," he said softly. "Maybe someday you will, too."

She cried, then, as he held her and tried to comfort her. Both wondered what would become of the other.

Chapter 7

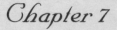

S it down or be sat down." Her uncle patted her to soften the impact of the order. "Kathryn, darling, your pacing is making me nuts."

"Sorry," she muttered and sat between Aunt Matty and Uncle Rich. Matty was knitting another potholder, never having the patience to work on a larger project like a scarf or sweater. She might have seemed unperturbed, but to Kathryn's knowing and loving eye, Matty was a wreck who was having to redo too many rows. Her uncle seemed slightly more serene, but he kept nervously stroking the cover of the family Bible.

"They'll be all right," she said aloud. She'd wanted to log onto the probability page and ask the chances of Glenn and Daniel's mutual survival, but had been too frightened. Even the smallest chance of disaster seemed too great to contemplate. "They will be *all right.*"

"We know," Matty said and dropped another stitch.

"Well, I'm just saying," she said stiffly, then groaned

inwardly. Being scared to death was no reason to be nasty to her aunt and uncle. But it was unnerving the way they pretended not to be afraid.

Of course, she reasoned, *they have their faith to sustain them. But how can they take comfort in believing, when belief is no proof against harm?* Kathryn had never understood how people didn't worry about handing their lives over to God. *How,* she mused, *could they give up control like that?*

And how could she ever want to?

Despite these dark thoughts, she wanted to pray. She despised her weakness.

"What if it's *not* weakness?" she muttered aloud.

"Kathryn?"

"What if it's just another kind of strength? The hard kind, the kind that doesn't come with a guarantee?"

"Dear, what are you—"

"Excuse me," she interrupted and got up. "I've got to—" Even now she couldn't say it. Even now she was alternately embarrassed and hopeful. "—run a quick errand," she finished, then turned on her heel and left the waiting room.

The chapel was subtly different. Instead of a cold, nondenominational room, it seemed almost welcoming. Perhaps the stress of the day was making her loopy.

Or perhaps, she thought grimly, *you're growing up a bit.*

Jim, of course, heard her the instant her toe crossed the chapel threshold. He popped out of his office at the side and was, she noted with irritation, not at all surprised to see her.

"Any word?"

"Not yet. They're both still in surgery."

"Something to drink?"

"I want to—uh—" she took a breath and coughed the words out, "I want to pray. I'm not good at it. Will you help me?"

He didn't grin in triumph, smirk knowingly, or even wink at her. If he had done any of those things (and really, she couldn't imagine Jim Benedict's being so crass) she would have instantly fled, possibly after throwing something at him. Instead he crossed the room, took her hand, and pulled her down beside him on a pew.

She cleared her throat. She said, "Should I fold my hands?"

"Not if you don't want to."

"I *won't*, then."

"As you like. Let's pray. Father," Jim began.

"No," she said quickly. At his quizzical glance, she clarified. "I don't like Father. Can we call Him something else?"

"Something else?"

"Sir, how about Sir? It's respectful, but not. . .you know. Fawning." She had, in fact, only ever called one person sir: her great-uncle. To her it was a word that summed up love and respect and honor. A syllable that, to her, spoke volumes. Fathers died on an autumn evening and left you alone.

"Sir," Jim began, "we're here to ask for Your help.

Kathryn and I are very worried about our friends."

Friends, she thought, unconsciously folding her hands. Such a mild word to express her complicated feelings for Glenn and Daniel. They were even now unconscious while scalpels flashed over them. Her friends.

She looked down and saw her fingers were clenched so tightly, the knuckles grew white.

"Please watch over them," Jim continued.

Yes, Kathryn thought. *Please, please, please. Don't let anything happen.*

"Keep them safe and help them toward a speedy recovery."

Recovery, she thought. *What a marvelous word.*

"And help us help them regain strength and health." He stopped.

"Amen," Kathryn added. She practically whispered the word, and they sat in companionable silence until she heard hurrying feet and saw her uncle poke his head into the chapel. She barely had time to wonder how he'd known where to find her when he said, "The surgeon is coming out to talk to us."

She bumped Jim aside with her hip and practically sprinted down the aisle. "Sorry," she said over her shoulder, following her uncle out the door. "And thanks!"

Jim, who had grabbed the corner of the pew to keep from being knocked sprawling, lifted a hand. "Let me know," he called after her, and she flapped a hand at him in reply.

Aunt Matty, looking small and fragile in the waiting room, smiled tentatively at Kathryn and Rich. "This is Dr. Hemze," she said. "He assisted Dr. Filkins in Glenn's surgery."

Hemze was a short, broad-shouldered man with hair the color of wheat and hands the color of flour. "Dr. Filkins will be here in a moment to tell you how it went," he began pompously. One of his strangely white hands fluttered up and he smoothed his left eyebrow with a fingertip.

"But they're all right?" Rich asked.

"Of course it's inappropriate for me to discuss anything, but when Dr. Filkins gets here, we can—are you all right?"

Kathryn knew how she must look; her hands were clasped beneath her chin as she stared hopefully at the doctor; her eyes, she imagined, probably looked enormous and full of fear. "Oh, please," she begged, "please tell us something. Anything. Don't make us wait until Dr. Filkins comes."

"Fine, it went fine," he said quickly.

"They're okay?" she asked. "They're both okay?"

"Praise God," Aunt Matty murmured, and Kathryn wholeheartedly agreed.

"They're both fine, everything's fine," Hemze was saying, but Kathryn had stopped listening. She made a mental note to come back and listen to every word the man had to say. Later. For now, she had unfinished business.

"There she goes again," Uncle Rich complained as she ran out of the room. "Girl's always been flighty."

Kathryn barely heard; she had run straight to the chapel, straight to Jim, barreling up the aisle darting into his row; he was sitting where she had left him a few minutes before.

She clutched at him. "They're both going to be fine," she said, then started to sob. "Thank You. Thank You, oh, thank You so much."

"Don't thank me," he said seriously.

"I wasn't," she replied through her tears.

Chapter 8

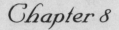

Daniel moved weakly toward the Light. Ah, so the operation had not gone well. For him, anyway. He sent a prayer for Kathryn and her family. His poor Kathryn. This development was not likely to bolster her faith.

Contrary to what he had read, the Light was not beautiful and serene. It stung his eyes and made them water. And it smelled. The light smelled like...antiseptic?

"Daniel? Can you hear me?"

It took every shred of his strength, but he managed to crack one eye open. The light was a penlight, aimed at his left eye. The angel accompanying him on his journey to the afterlife was a male nurse whose breath smelled like sausage.

"You're back." The nurse clicked off the light.

"Kathryn," Daniel croaked.

"No, Tom."

Daniel licked his lips, which felt alarmingly like sandpaper and tried again. "Where. Is. Kathryn?"

"Right here, Daniel." He tried to turn his head toward her soothing contralto and felt her hand on his cheek. "Rest," she said. "Everything went fine. You saved him. I love you."

"Piece of cake," he rasped, and the last thing he heard was the nurse telling him he couldn't have any cake.

⁂

"Your recovery will take months," Dr. Filkins lectured.

"Where is Kathryn?"

"And you certainly can't drive, not for several weeks."

"Where is she?"

"Of course, the transplant coordinator would have told you all this."

"Is she all right?"

"Except I wonder if you listened to her as well as you're listening to me." Dr. Filkins glanced once more at her chart. "Daniel, are you feeling all right?"

"Fine," he lied. In fact, he had never felt worse. His entire abdominal area felt as if someone had. . .well, cut him open and taken something out. Okay, that was to be expected; but he was also wretchedly hot, couldn't take anything by mouth without feeling violently ill, and the nurses wouldn't quit bugging him. They were fine men and women and he honored them for all the good they did, but they never let him get a full night's sleep! And making him get up—making him *get out of bed* mere hours after surgery—did they have to be quite so dedicated? "Have you seen Kathryn today? How is Glenn doing?"

327

A loud, familiar voice boomed from the hallway, and Daniel grinned in spite of himself. "Back off, blondie! I'm walking in there on my own two feet. Gotta shake the hand of the man who saved my unworthy hide."

"Unworthy is right," Kathryn said dryly. "And I think the doctors and nurses helped just a bit."

"Silence, mouthy female!" Glenn swept grandly into the room. The change in him was astonishing, and Daniel couldn't help staring. Less than forty-eight hours after surgery, Glenn had color in his cheeks and a bounce to his step. From the information the transplant coordinator had asked him to read, Daniel knew the kidney recipient often felt ready to get out of bed within an hour of waking from the anesthesia, but it was still difficult to reconcile with the "old" Glenn: wasted, pale, too weak to get out of bed.

"Ah, the dude of the hour, the minute, the nanosecond. Daniel the Great!" Glenn practically bounded toward Daniel's bed, plucked his hand from where it lay on the bedcovers, and wrung it with the fervor of a politician up for re-election. "My hero!"

"Please stop," Daniel said, embarrassed but, he had to admit, a little pleased. Behind Glenn, Kathryn beamed.

"Stop singing your praises? Never, ah say, ah say *never!*"

"You sound like Foghorn Leghorn," Daniel teased, while Dr. Filkins sat and scowled at her chart and ignored the hubbub.

"He sounds like a flaming idiot," Kathryn grumbled.

Daniel wasn't fooled; she was at her surliest when she was trying hard not to show how deeply happy or grateful she was. "Which means the operation didn't make one single improvement."

"Wrong, Scuzz-Cuzz. I've now got three, count 'em, *three* kidneys."

"It's disgusting how the kidney recipient feels better almost immediately, while poor Daniel struggles to get out of bed," Kathryn griped.

"I'm getting exhausted just listening to the two of you. Will you stop it?" Daniel felt bad for complaining —he was not a victim, he had chosen this, and would not unchoose—but Glenn's cheerful laugh and Kathryn's grin told him no offense had been taken.

"This might sound incredibly dumb," Kathryn began tentatively, coming over to sit on the edge of Daniel's bed.

"Oh, we're sure it will," Glenn said cheerfully, snagging Dr. Filkins's ubiquitous stethoscope and pretending to jump rope with it.

"But I never thought they'd just—you know—staple an extra kidney on you. In you. Whatever. I guess I was thinking. . ."

"Like when you have a flat tire, you replace the one that doesn't work? You don't just slap a fifth tire on the car?" Daniel asked then broke into a hacking cough that pained him so terribly, his vision blackened at the corners for a moment.

"Yeah, that's. . . Daniel, honey, are you okay? You don't look so good."

The love of his life was speaking to him through a tunnel. *This*, he had time to think, *could be very bad. Not for me. I've never been worried about me.* . . . "Kathryn," he managed, dimly hearing Dr. Filkins shouting instructions. "Kathryn—"

"Daniel, what's wrong with you? No, oh no, please God, God. . ."

Even as all awareness was fading, he was astonished to hear what sounded very much like a prayer from her. It made everything worth it. More than worth it. But she mustn't backslide. She mustn't. . .

He made a last effort. "This doesn't matter. . . ."

"Don't talk! Save your strength. Dr. Filkins is going to fix you right up."

It was suddenly impossible to talk. So he stopped and decided to rest.

And for a long time, he did.

❧

"Kathryn, please take a break. I'll stay with Daniel. You haven't eaten since yesterday morning. If you call half a strawberry tart eating."

"I can't leave." She shifted her weight, but the chair remained stubbornly uncomfortable. She wished Jim would go away. She wished everyone would leave her alone. Her and Daniel. "What if he wakes up and I'm not here? What if he calls for me and I don't hear?"

"He would, I'm sure, be quite annoyed at you for depriving yourself. And Kathryn, dear, it's really unnecessary," he added softly. "The doctors are sure he's going to pull out of it."

"It" was a raging post-op infection. Though uncommon, it was usually treatable. Usually. Daniel's had given the doctor cause to earn her paycheck, though.

Ignoring her "get lost" vibes, Jim took the empty chair beside her. In the bed, Daniel slept heavily. He had not moved nor spoken in three days. "Perhaps you would feel better if you were to. . ." He paused delicately.

Kathryn's head snapped up. "To what? Pray? Go into that sham of a chapel and pray?"

Jim merely looked back at her, calm as a clam. "Daniel specifically asked you not to do this, Kathryn. Not to use him as an excuse to give in to your fear."

"I'm not afraid!" She shot to her feet and would have kicked the chair over, but didn't want to be escorted out. "Of anything!"

"Oh, my dear," Jim said gently, "you're afraid of *everything.*"

"You—you are not supposed to be like this! You're supposed to pat my hand and say 'there, there' and that it's all for the best." She sputtered for a moment. "Not—not—"

"Tell you hard truths? Truths you don't want to hear, or face? You do believe, Kathryn. You've always believed, but you've spent your life pretending not to, because the alternative is terrifying to you. Now, in this worst crisis of all, you're going to leap from tentative questioner back to frightened unbeliever. And for what? Because faith is hard."

She burst into tears. "Stop it! You don't know me, you don't know *anything*."

"I told you before," he went on relentlessly. Oh, how she wished he would stop talking, faint from hunger, and hit his head so he was out of it for a week, whatever, just so he would stop saying these terrible things, things that burned her ears, her heart, and made her cringe. "God can handle your anger. Why don't you be truthful? Share your fury with Him. Better than this—this. . .hiding. It doesn't suit you."

"I hate you."

"You don't hate anybody. Except, of course, yourself."

"Enough," Daniel whispered.

They both froze, then looked at him. "Enough, Jim," he said again, then gasped. His voice steadied and he went on, "She has good reasons for her fear."

"Nice to see you back among the living," she snapped, but the way her voice cracked revealed her true feelings. "Thanks for almost dying. I'll get the nurse."

"The key word," he croaked to her retreating form, "is 'almost.' " Then he wheezed silent laughter.

Chapter 9

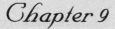

I thought," he said slowly, "we agreed we loved each other."

Kathryn wouldn't look at him. "It will never work. We're too different."

"I haven't heard you deny you love me."

"I do. Love you, I mean." Still she wouldn't look at him. "But. . .what's that line from that Cinderella movie? 'A bird may love a fish, but where would they live?' "

He feigned confusion, "Are you the fish or the bird?"

They were in the solarium. He was going to be discharged tomorrow at noon. *High noon,* he thought morbidly and wished Kathryn would smile or even snap at him.

"This is serious business, Daniel. We've both got our lives to get back to."

"Oh?"

She leaned back in her chair, squinting at the sunlight that splashed across the floor. "Yes. You have to go home and get better. I've got to help Glenn get back on his feet."

"This would be the man who won the three-legged race to the cafeteria this morning?" he asked dryly.

"It's time for you to go home," she went on inexorably.

He winced, taking the blow. "I want you to come with me. Or I want to stay here. I'm in love with you. Although," he added in a mutter, "right now I can't think why."

Her lips twitched at that, but she remained serious, "Exactly. We're opposites. You've got your faith. I don't have that, and I think I might come to despise you for it after awhile. Or you'd grow to hate me for not being able to believe. To love your God."

"Our God," he said quietly.

Her gaze skittered away again. "It would just. . .just be this splinter that would never get smaller, that would always be there, and we'd fight all the time and eventually you'd dump me because you'd know you couldn't stay with someone who didn't share your faith."

"Ah," he said. "This is about me eventually abandoning you. As, of course, your parents did. Your mother died in a hospital just like this one, I'll bet." He paused. "It's much easier to run the other way first, isn't it?"

She flinched, took the blow. "Yeah, I deserved that. I deserve every bad thing you could ever say about me. And you still have to go."

"Kathryn." He heard the desperation in his voice

but was helpless to stop. "Sweetheart, I don't want to say bad things. I want to help you."

"I—don't need—your help."

"But what about us?"

She stood, and he watched a lone tear trickle down her cheek. She wiped it away furiously. "There is no us," she choked out.

She passed Glenn in the hall and burst into fresh tears when he shook his head at her. "Kath, you poor idiot," he said softly as she went by. She kept going until she was outside, away from the hospital, the stench of sickness and death and despair. Glenn's room, her mother's room, had smelled exactly like that. She didn't notice it when she was at work, before taking indefinite leave. . .perhaps the smell of the animals or the animals, themselves, distracted her. Whatever the reason, she couldn't breathe it another second.

Well, that's done, she thought in despair, stumbling toward the sidewalk. *Glenn's better, you got rid of Daniel, and everything's going to be just dandy. Except you've got the rest of your life to figure out how to live without Daniel's love. You poor idiot.*

Epilogue

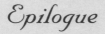

Present day—at the reunion

She had stopped walking toward Daniel; she needed another moment to gather herself. She could hear the happy chaos of the reunion going on around her, but couldn't tear her gaze from him. What could she say to him? How could she even dare approach him?

"Steady, Cuzz," Glenn said from behind her.

Without turning to look, she said, "Finished hobnobbing already? Or did you want to give out autographs?"

He laughed at her. "Ah, taking out your nervousness on those you love. It's just so *you*."

"Sorry. You're right, I'm a wreck, and you're right, I took it out on you. Glenn, I don't think I can do this."

"Sure you can." He dropped a comradely hand to her shoulder. "Just repeat after me: 'Daniel, I love you.'"

"Daniel," she parroted obediently, "I love you." Fortunately, the focus of their discussion was still at least thirty feet away, looking at the two of them but not approaching. She wondered if he was as nervous as she.

"I did some cruddy things, and I'm sorry."

" 'I did some cruddy things, and I'm sorry.' "

"The biggest idiot who ever lived, that would be me. Also, I look like a rhinoceros and I smell like one—"

"You are not helping me. Go away."

"Fine, I'm going." He rubbed his arm where she'd pinched him. "But don't underestimate the guy, or your effect on him. You think it's so easy to fall out of love? He still cares."

Ha, she thought, resuming her walk toward him. Not after the way she had treated him. Sending him away without even a word of gratitude. The real miracle of faith was that God was able to forgive morons like her.

"Hello, Kathryn," he said as he approached. "I see you got the necklace."

She had been clutching it like a good luck charm and now dropped her hand. The small gold cross had shown up in her mailbox a week after Daniel returned home. No card, just his return address.

"Yes, I did." She tried to smile at him; her lips felt huge and rubbery and the expression felt about as real as fool's gold. "I've treasured it ever since. Thank you."

At first she had worn it because it was something from him. She certainly hadn't attached any significance to it. But then came a day when she felt undressed if the cross wasn't around her neck. By then Jim had been tutoring her in Bible studies and her world was opening up.

"I wanted to tell you," she said rapidly. "I believe now. I mean, Jim was right, I always did, but I'm not afraid anymore. I mean, I am, sometimes, but not about. . ." *Yuck, you sound like an idiot,* she groaned inwardly. If only he wouldn't look at her so intently. If only he weren't so handsome, and if only her heart weren't beating almost loud enough to drown out the reunion.

"Glenn seems to be feeling well," he said, and she silently groaned again. He was being so polite, so distant. *Well, what did you expect?* she asked herself savagely. *Roses and a marriage proposal? After the way you behaved? Be serious.*

"He hasn't felt this good in ten years. Since he was a kid. All because of you. I can't thank you enough. But I wanted to explain. . . ."

"Yes?"

She plunged. "I took no joy in leaving you. I haven't—hadn't—taken joy in anything in a long time. I said that was what I wanted, but of course what I really wanted was to stop being such a fool. After you and Glenn were discharged I started volunteering at the hospital."

He showed interest for the first time. "But you hate hospitals. They remind you. . ."

"Well, I decided I was sick of being afraid, so I wanted to kind of jump into it. And I saw a lot of Jim while I was there, and we got to talking. Then you sent me that cross, and I had so much to think about, and it was all mixed up. I was so *stupid* about everything, so I asked Jim to be my mentor."

"Oh, to be a fly on the wall of a few of your Bible sessions," he murmured, and Kathryn laughed.

"Teaching me religion is his just deserts after those things he said while you were unconscious." She stopped smiling, serious once more. "But after a few months I realized just how strong a hold fear had on me, for—all my life, really. Eventually I came to realize that whether you lived or died—whether anyone lives or dies—it's God's will. And that's it. So all a good Christian can do—or a mediocre Christian, like me—is accept it. And Him. It sounds so simple, but for a long time I couldn't make myself believe it."

He was looking at her curiously. "Do you really believe that?"

She nodded. "Jim came up with a great way for me to put it into perspective. He said you couldn't explain college to first-graders. It's beyond their grasp, they can't get it; but just because they don't understand, doesn't mean it's not out there. And that was like me and God."

"I see."

She waited, but that was his only comment. "Yes, well. I came today hoping to see you, to explain that I'm a little different now. Oh, not an incredibly perfect, wonderful person, but perhaps a somewhat nicer one. Last year I. . .I was beyond awful. I was too afraid, I loved you too desperately and worried that loving you made me vulnerable, like loving Glenn made me vulnerable." She was talking faster and faster, almost babbling, but couldn't slow down and certainly couldn't stop. "And those things I said. . .I'm sorry, so sorry. I don't expect forgiveness, but I just wanted to see you to tell you how badly I felt about last year—how much I hope you're all right, and that you're well and happy."

"But if you felt this way, why didn't you try to get in touch with me earlier?"

Shocked, she said, "I couldn't. I chased you away, I *made* you leave! I knew I had hurt you too badly to dare to ask for another chance. I knew I had to let you go." She paused, gulped for breath, and went on. "I'm not here to try to win you back. I just wanted to look you in the face and apologize."

"That's too bad," he said, and her heart froze. He took his hands out of his pockets, held out his closed fists like a child playing Pick One, then turned one over and opened it. A diamond ring nestled in his palm. "Because the *only* reason I came was to try to win you back." He paused. "And, of course, the free food."

She stared at the ring. All the saliva in her mouth had dried up and she couldn't speak, just made a "Gaaak, ga-haaak!" sound. It was probably, she realized wryly, the lamest response to a marriage proposal in the history of human events.

"Kathryn, I love you. I never stopped, and I thought about you all year. I thought keeping away from you was what you wanted, but after awhile I couldn't take it. And Glenn—"

"Glenn?"

"Don't be mad," he said quickly. "He just. . .we've kind of been in touch. For the last year."

She glanced over her shoulder, looking for Glenn. Daniel didn't want her to be mad? Mad was the last thing she was feeling. She should have known her darling cousin wouldn't have given up. On either of them.

"He told me about how you've been studying with Jim. He told me about your journey, your—your 'baby steps,' is how he put it. Knowing that didn't change my mind, of course. I always knew I'd come for you. Glenn just made it easier."

Daniel was bending slowly, getting down on one knee, still holding the ring up to her. "I contacted Dr. Filkins last month. The reunion was my idea, and Glenn helped. I prayed you would come."

"But you—you've been so cool and distant—"

"Because I was afraid I'd grab you and kiss you and kidnap you until you loved me back. I probably wouldn't have let you go even if you never loved me back."

"Are you sure about this?" she choked out. Not crying, but only just. "Are you really sure you want to be with me forever? Because I'm not going to get rid of you this time. You'll be stuck with me."

"I was always sure," he said gently, reaching up and slipping the ring onto her finger.

She sank to her knees in front of him and flung her arms around his neck. This was probably some sort of fever dream or perhaps the early symptoms of food poisoning. No, that was the old Kathryn talking, the one who viewed good things with suspicion, waiting for someone to take them away.

"God is good," he whispered then kissed her deliciously and thoroughly, in front of the world.

She tightened her grip; she never wanted to let him go, and she happened to agree wholeheartedly. She reached up, clasped the cross around her neck. "Thank You," she whispered when Daniel broke the kiss. "Oh, thank You."

"Don't thank me," he said.

"I wasn't," she assured him.

From behind them: "Ewwwww, gross! They're touching!" Glenn strolled over. Kathryn knew at a glance that he had overheard everything, the shameless eavesdropper.

"Last chance," she said. They were still on their knees in the grass, and she should have felt silly, but she didn't. She felt wonderful. "I come with baggage. And I'm not talking about childhood traumas. Well," she added under her breath, glancing at Glenn, "one childhood trauma, anyway. . ."

"The Lord will give me strength," Daniel assured her gravely, and they both burst out laughing.

"What's up with you two? You'd better not be making fun of me. Hey, Daniel, get your hands off my cousin. You're not married yet. I know you saved my life and all, but what have you done for me lately? Kathryn, stop laughing like a hyena and get off the grass. Dr. Filkins! Daniel and Kathryn are making out in the grass!

Come here and give them detention, or something. Hit 'em with your stethoscope. Is anybody listening to me?"

Later, after the reunion, after the hot dogs had been consumed, after sodas had been poured and spilled and poured again, after Glenn had worn everyone out with his exhausting charm, after a chorus of promises to get together for the reunion next spring, Kathryn and Daniel made their way to the hospital chapel.

It wasn't far—only a five-minute drive—and the strange, bare little room had become one of the places Kathryn liked best.

"I used to think this place was ridiculous," she confessed as they sat in the pew, drinking in the calm, drinking in each other. "I thought it was a waiting room with pews."

Daniel snorted at that but didn't comment.

"Then, the more I studied with Jim, the more comfortable I got examining my faith, the more I liked it. I don't even go to a regular church," she added. "I come here on Sundays. Isn't that silly? There's no stained glass, no hymnals, the air conditioner works too hard so it's usually freezing in here, and the place has stunk of new carpet for three weeks."

"Want to get married in here?" he asked quietly.

In response, she covered her eyes with one hand, her other gripping Daniel's with desperate strength. "You keep doing that," she said thickly, while he gently tugged her hand away from her face so he could look at her. "Reading my mind. That's why I brought you here. To ask. . ."

"Yes," he interrupted and kissed her softly on the mouth. "Yes, wherever you want. Whenever you want. Only make it soon." He grinned crookedly at her. "I waited for you a year, the longest of my life. I don't want to wait any longer."

"Oh. I was thinking we could get married at next year's reunion. It's only another twelve months."

He groaned, and she giggled at his long-suffering expression. In the chapel, which had once seemed so distant and was now a second home, they laughed together. Like a family.

JANICE POHL

Janice lives in Hastings, Minnesota, with her husband, two children, and dog. . .and all are adept at keeping her from her writing at any moment! She has been writing since age twelve and is an avid reader, devouring any written material she can get her hands on. She writes for one reason only: because she must. *Too Good to Be True* is her first inspirational romance, and she is currently working on her next book. You can write to Janice at alongi@usinternet.com. She loves getting E-mail!

A Letter to Our Readers

Dear Readers:

In order that we might better contribute to your reading enjoyment, we would appreciate your taking a few minutes to respond to the following questions. When completed, please return to the following: Fiction Editor, Barbour Publishing, Inc., P.O. Box 719, Uhrichsville, OH 44683.

1. Did you enjoy reading *Reunions?*
   - ❑ Very much. I would like to see more books like this.
   - ❑ Moderately—I would have enjoyed it more if _____
   _____
   _____

2. What influenced your decision to purchase this book? (Check those that apply.)
   - ❑ Cover
   - ❑ Back cover copy
   - ❑ Title
   - ❑ Price
   - ❑ Friends
   - ❑ Publicity
   - ❑ Other

3. Which story was your favorite?
   - ❑ *That Special Something*
   - ❑ *Too Good to Be True*
   - ❑ *Storm Warning*
   - ❑ *Truth or Dare*

4. Please check your age range:
   - ❑ Under 18
   - ❑ 18–24
   - ❑ 25–34
   - ❑ 35–45
   - ❑ 46–55
   - ❑ Over 55

5. How many hours per week do you read? _____

Name _____

Occupation _____

Address _____

City _____ State _____ Zip _____

If you enjoyed

Reunions

then read:

❧

Resolutions

Four Inspiring Novellas Show a Loving Way to Make a Fresh Start

Remaking Meridith

Beginnings

Never Say Never

Letters to Timothy

$\mathcal{H}$EARTSONG ❤ PRESENTS

Love Stories Are Rated G!

That's for godly, gratifying, and of course, great! If you love a thrilling love story, but don't appreciate the sordidness of some popular paperback romances, **Heartsong Presents** is for you. In fact, **Heartsong Presents** is the only inspirational romance book club, the only one featuring love stories where Christian faith is the primary ingredient in a marriage relationship.

Sign up today to receive your first set of four, never-before-published Christian romances. Send no money now; you will receive a bill with the first shipment. You may cancel at any time without obligation, and if you aren't completely satisfied with any selection, you may return the books for an immediate refund!

Imagine. . .four new romances every four weeks—two historical, two contemporary—with men and women like you who long to meet the one God has chosen as the love of their lives. . .all for the low price of $9.97 postpaid.

To join, simply complete the coupon below and mail to the address provided. **Heartsong Presents** romances are rated G for another reason: They'll arrive Godspeed!

YES! <u>Sign me up for Hearts❤ng!</u>

NEW MEMBERSHIPS WILL BE SHIPPED IMMEDIATELY!
Send no money now. We'll bill you only $9.97 postpaid with your first shipment of four books. Or for faster action, call toll free 1-800-847-8270.

NAME _____

ADDRESS _____

CITY _____ STATE _____ ZIP _____

MAIL TO: HEARTSONG PRESENTS, P.O. Box 719, Uhrichsville, Ohio 44683

YES1-99